The TENDER MERCY *of* ROSES

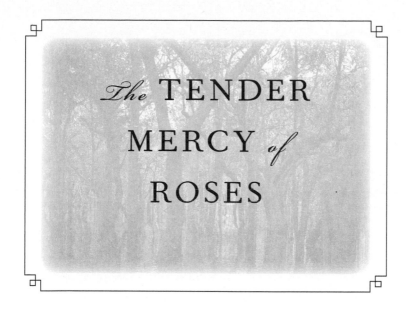

The TENDER MERCY *of* ROSES

ANNA MICHAELS

GALLERY BOOKS

New York   London   Toronto   Sydney

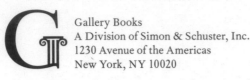

Gallery Books
A Division of Simon & Schuster, Inc.
1230 Avenue of the Americas
New York, NY 10020

First Gallery Books hardcover edition May 2011

GALLERY BOOKS and colophon are trademarks of Simon & Schuster, Inc.

For information about special discounts for bulk purchases, please contact Simon & Schuster Special Sales at 1-866-506-1949 or business@simonandschuster.com.

The Simon & Schuster Speakers Bureau can bring authors to your live event. For more information or to book an event contact the Simon & Schuster Speakers Bureau at 1-866-248-3049 or visit our website at www.simonspeakers.com.

Designed by Leah Carlson-Stanisic

Manufactured in the United States of America

10   9   8   7   6   5   4   3   2   1

Library of Congress Cataloging-in-Publication Data
Michaels, Anna.
    The tender mercy of roses / Anna Michaels.—1st Gallery Books hardcover ed.
        p. cm.
    1. Fathers and daughters—Fiction. 2. Children—Death—Fiction. 3. Mississippi—Fiction. I. Title.
PS3573.E1985T46 2011
813'.6—dc22

2010033602

ISBN 978-1-4391-8099-0
ISBN 978-1-4391-8101-0 (ebook)

In memory of

Mama (Marie Westmoreland Hussey),

who taught me the music of words, and

Daddy (Clarence T. Hussey),

who taught me the magic of nature.

And always to my magnificent

Unicorn.

Acknowledgments

I couldn't have written this book without two powerful angels at my side: my amazing agent, Christina Hogrebe, and my remarkable editor, Abby Zidle. They were the gentle wind at my back when I was running with my muse and the safety net when I stumbled and fell. Both of them are hereby instructed to stay put (in other words, at my beck and call) and furthermore to enjoy a long, healthy, happy life (in other words, don't go running off to the Great Beyond before I do).

I owe a huge debt of gratitude to the awesome team at Gallery Books: Louise Burke, Jen Bergstrom, Lauren McKenna, Jean Anne Rose, Danielle Poiesz, Anne Cherry, and so many more I haven't met. (But you can bet your britches I plan to!) They loved Pony, fought for her, and then gave her wings to fly. Endless thanks!

In addition to my own guardian agent, Christina, there are so many extraordinary people at the Jane Rotrosen Agency who gave Pony their support. Among them are Meg Ruley, who opened the door and took me in, and Kelly Harms Wimmer, who first gave me a thumbs-up on my rodeo cowgirl.

Dearest of the dear friends, Johnie Sue Long Street, has been my sounding board for so long I automatically call her when I write myself into a corner. The best reader and cheerleader ever, she listens patiently while I blabber my way toward a solution. She is hereby ordered to always keep her cell phone handy and to always put up with me, no matter what.

And how could I do without Debra Webb, my twisted "sister" (that means we're not kin but we ought to be)! Though her dark thrillers are miles from my magical realism, she can pinpoint holes in a plot from across state lines.

Many other wonderful friends have been my cheering squad forever, and my beloved family is my anchor—Misty, Trey, Anita, Dodd, Cecilia, Susan, David, and William. As long as I have you, I am truly blessed.

I believe much trouble and blood would be
saved if we opened our hearts more.

—Chief Joseph, 1840–1904
WALLOWA BAND, NEZ PERCE

NEAR THE TENNESSEE-ALABAMA LINE

It don't take no high school education to figure out I'm in a pickle.

First off, there's cow shit on my boots. Dirty boots is a sign of a shoddy upbringing. Since I mostly brought up myself, I can guarantee you I ain't no low class woman.

I ain't no fool, neither. The good Lord give me plenty of brains, then shoved me out of the womb a buckin' and a-rarin'. I come into this world with my eyes wide open and I ain't shut 'em in twenty-six years. I aim to see what's coming my way, and if I don't like what I see I'll dodge or run or dig in my spurs and beat the living shit out of it.

But I sure didn't see this coming. How did this happen? Did I blink? Is that how I ended up flat on my back in a bunch of piney woods not being able to feel a thing, not even my own skin and bones? I'm laying here with my eyes wide open under one of them cloudless skies the good Lord strews through Alabama in the summertime and I ain't got a single urge in my brain. Not even to get up and saddle my horse.

Since I can't figure out no reason for all that, I might as well lay here till the good Lord gives me a clue.

Now, I ain't no religious nut, but me and God come to a understanding thirteen years ago.

I was setting in Doe Valley Baptist Church listening to the preacher shout, "The road to redemption is straight and narrow," after which he passed around the collection plate. Dollar bills began dropping like faintin' goats. Then Brother Lollar commenced hollering about tithing, which is just a fancy way of asking poor folks to part with their butter and egg money. Twenties began drifting into the plate, and it looked to me like the road to redemption was paved with greenbacks.

I just about resigned myself on the spot to eternal damnation. Then lo and behold the preacher waxed eloquent about a option called endowments.

Now, I had two of them suckers setting on my chest. I knew on account of my science teacher. The week before he'd invited me to his house to look at the stars through his telescope. While I was on his back porch trying to find the man in the moon, he sneaked up behind me, told me I was "well-endowed," then proceeded to try to feel both of 'em. I run back into the kitchen, grabbed the nearest weapon and whacked him over the head with his own corn bread skillet. He's the one ended up seeing stars.

Be that as it may, setting in the Baptist church with sweat rolling into my endowments, I figured that finally me and redemption might make a nodding acquaintance.

As soon as the shouting was over, I asked the preacher how I could use the gifts nature bestowed on me for the Lord. After he got his jaw back in the right place, he laid his hands on my head and prayed for "the soul of this pitiful, unfortunate orphan."

I ain't no orphan—I got a daddy—and I sure as hell ain't

pitiful. I walked out and marched myself back up Doe Mountain and never looked back.

Daddy found me sulking in the hayloft. "Pony," he said to me, which is my name on account of being so little everybody said I reminded them of a Shetland pony, "ain't no use fumin' at God. He didn't see fit to give you no riches, but He give you a brain and plenty of grit. What you do with it ain't up to that preacher, it's up to you."

Me and God had us a understanding that day. I promised if He'd understand why church was gonna be nature from here on out, where ain't no bird nor tree ever looked down on me, I wouldn't never let Him down about using what He give me. I reckon God was okay with that bargain, because I done proved my daddy right a million times over.

Now, I ain't what you'd call a woman of the world, but I done traveled a good bit and seen how things is north of the Mason-Dixon line. And let me tell you, I ain't seen nothin' I can't handle if I set my mind to it.

I try wrapping my mind around laying here stiff as a poker, but don't nothing come to me except the scent of Cherokee roses—seven star-white petals, seven tribes of displaced Cherokee, the tears of a grieving nation turned to flower. I feel a rushing across my skin like the flow of cool blue water, the kiss of greening spring winds, the brush of a starling's wing. Right before my eyes a wall of roses springs up in the piney woods, blankets the trees, swings from the branches and covers the ground.

This ain't happened but once in my life—the day I kicked free of my mother's womb, the day she died. His heart split in two, my daddy took his chain saw and cut down my mother's climbing

Cherokee roses. She was Morning Star and she'd planted them roses as a reminder that half the blood running through her veins was Cherokee. Daddy raved through the woods like a madman till there wasn't nothing left standing but him and the trees stripped of scented vines.

Satisfied there wasn't a single rose left to remind 'em of his loss, he marched out of them woods with tears streaming down his face. The midwife laid me in his arms, a screeching bundle of kicking wildfire. When he turned back around to show me that we was starting over—just me and him—ever' one of them Cherokee roses had sprung back to life.

As I watch now, the Cherokee roses start dancing, a-swinging and a-swaying like a wild wind's shaking 'em. But the air is so still you can't see nothing move except them roses, not even the wind over a eagle's wing.

My heart strains upward, trying to rise, and rose petals drift down and cover me like snow, like stars, like the tears of my ancestors.

I figure I must be dead.

If that's the truth, there ain't nothing I can do about it. I might as well hang around and see what happens next.

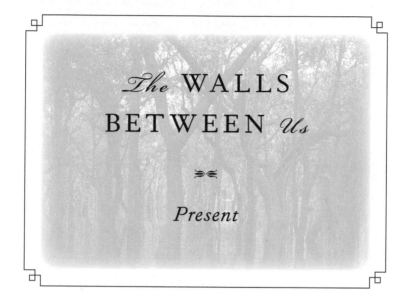

The WALLS BETWEEN *Us*

⊰⊱

Present

The walls between us are as high
as the mountain ranges.

—*Chief Dan George, 1899–1981*
GESWANOUTH SLAHOOT
COAST SALISH, BAND OF THE
TAKIL-WAUTUTH NATION

One

DOE MOUNTAIN, TENNESSEE

Titus Jones stood in the middle of his tobacco patch, lifted his hoe from the hardscrabble earth and listened. What he was listening for, he didn't know. Pulling a blue bandana out of the left back pocket of his faded overalls, he took off his straw hat and wiped the sweat from his face.

Nothing stirred, not even a crow's wing. He glanced toward the flock of pesky birds that had landed earlier in the blackjack oak high up on the ridge above his fence line, and that's when he knew what he was listening for.

Five minutes earlier the mountain had bustled with sound—the soft hum of sweat bees seeking a place to light, the skittering of field mice along the edges of the fence line, the mocking call of the blue jay. Now there was nothing. Just Titus and the mountain and the silence and the ever-present scent of Cherokee roses.

Pulled by forces he didn't understand but had learned not to question, Titus left his hoe in the middle of a tobacco row and walked toward the split-rail fence that separated his farm from the deep woods that belonged to the mountain. All of it did, really. He'd learned that from Morning Star. The land belonged to the universe. He was just a caretaker, that's all.

He'd learned other things from his beloved wife, as well—
the magic of roses and totems and signs that would tell you
everything you needed to know if you practiced the art of
stillness and listening with your heart.

He was listening now, and he was listening hard. As he
approached the fence, the roses came to life. He couldn't have
told you how or why, but the flowers started glowing, sending
beams of light so powerful the white petals looked like deep
snow under a blazing sun. Scorched by memories, blinded by
pain, it was all Titus could do to remain upright.

What fresh hell did the roses have in store for him? He knew
it would be useless to cut them down. He'd tried that when
Morning Star died, but roses with a message refused to be
destroyed.

Undefeated, Titus shook his fist at the roses. "You ain't beat
me yet." His voice cracked apart like heirloom china smashed
with a hammer. In his heart, he knew. He *knew*. Still, he defied
the roses. "Bring it on. I can take whatever you got."

Transfixed, he saw a wolf emerge from the roses. Pure white,
the kind not found on this mountain or any other save for the
frozen confines of the Arctic Circle.

Pony's totem.

The wolf stared at him with beaming yellow eyes, his message
so clear Titus could see a new pathway opening beyond the wolf
and the trees, even beyond the sky, a path that spoke of harmony
and bravery and freedom. But it also spoke of loss and death, the
passing of a remarkable soul from the earth.

Titus understood the wolf's message as few men could,
understood because he had loved and learned from a Cherokee
woman, because he lived with a mind wide open. Staring into

the eyes of the wolf, Titus would have given his life to be like the rest of the world, dismissive of events that couldn't be explained, blind and deaf to miracles.

But he understood how you could be transformed in a twinkling from joy over the birth of your child to despair over the death of your wife, and how the roses you'd cut down only a moment earlier could spring back to life when your red-faced, squalling daughter was placed in your arms. And when she wrapped a tiny fist around your finger and hung on, you knew: it would be just the two of you from that moment till the end.

A story foretold by all the signs. If only you knew how to look.

From the direction of the stables, the Appaloosa whinnied. With a stillness born of living in harmony with nature, Titus watched as the wolf turned his majestic head toward Pony's horse then vanished. As the Arctic wolf slipped through the ominous jungle of roses, the petals flew loose and covered the ground—an elegy in white.

The wind picked up, then, crying and howling his daughter's name, lifting Titus's thinning gray hair and chilling his bones, though it was summer and already hotter than any northeast Tennessee summer in his memory. The weight and sorrow of the signs broke Titus, drove him to his knees. He joined his voice to the wind, pleading for God to strike him dead.

Under a sky so hot and cloudless it felt like a burning blue bowl turned over your head, there was a tiny sound, like the cracking of a nutshell. But it was not a black walnut or a Southern pecan that made the sound. It was Titus Jones's heart.

Pony was dead and there was no mercy left anywhere in the world.

·　　·　　·

HOT COFFEE, MISSISSIPPI

In Hot Coffee, where blueberries grow when folks said it wasn't possible—they'd never survive the Mississippi heat—there's a feeling along the twelve-mile stretch of Highway 532 that anything can take root and blossom. Even hope.

The feeling is so pervasive, it attaches itself to blueberries, seeps into coffee, dives deep underground to permeate the aquifer that supplies drinking water. In farmhouses and businesses loosely connected by the legend of an 1800s inn that was the last stop for travelers going to Mobile, Alabama, it's possible to dream with your eyes wide open.

Possible for everybody except Jo Beth Dawson.

On a blue and gold summer morning, while fairies sipped dew from the cups of wood violets and sleepy-eyed citizens ate blueberry muffins with their morning cup of coffee, never knowing the dark java was the source of hope taking root in their bones, Jo Beth lay in her narrow bed under the covers, hating the sun. Soon the intense light would make it impossible for her to hide in the deep caverns of sleep.

She pulled the sheet over her head but the insidious sunlight crept under the ill-fitting trailer door, slid through cracks in the Venetian blinds, and pierced the percale.

There was only one place left to hide. Holding a head already pounding from last night's encounter with Jack Daniel's, Jo Beth stumbled into the kitchen and searched her cupboard. Scotch, vodka, Kentucky straight bourbon whiskey, Baileys Irish Cream. All her old friends were there, all of them empty.

Dragging out the garbage can, she stood in her bare feet smashing bottles. Bits of colored glass flew over the rim of the can and rained over the floor like heartache. Jo Beth didn't even flinch when the shards pierced her skin. What were a few drops of blood on her feet compared to the river of blood that drenched her soul?

Glancing at the clock on her kitchen wall, she tried to judge whether the liquor store would be open, but the edges of her vision blurred. Did that signal a need for glasses? A hangover? At forty-eight, it could be either. More than likely both.

She thought about throwing on a trench coat and driving to Bob's Package Store to wait for the door to open, but she didn't want to add to the talk. *Hot Coffee's newest resident sighted on the hottest morning in June wearing nothing but a full-length coat and her underwear.* Only six weeks in a podunky town you'd miss if you blinked, and already she had the reputation of being eccentric, unsociable and stark raving mad.

Which was fine by Jo Beth. She didn't put down roots. She was a turtle, traveling with her home on her back, a 1968 Silver Streak camper-trailer bought dirt cheap after her divorce and held together with baling wire and determination. A pity you couldn't do the same thing with a life. Or maybe a blessing. She hardly knew the difference anymore.

Jo Beth shrugged into a T-shirt then grabbed a pair of denim shorts and tried to get into them standing up. She ended up perched on the edge of her mattress, a skinny-legged migratory bird ready to take flight at the least change in climate. When her cell phone rang, she almost fell off the bed.

If she continued fooling around with Jack Daniel and Tom Collins every night, she was going to have to turn the ringer off. Fumbling among the empty potato chip bags and candy wrappers on the end table—last night's supper—she plucked the phone and checked the caller ID. Maggie. The only friend she had left in Huntsville, Alabama. Maybe in the whole world.

"Jo Beth, in case you've forgotten, the rodeo starts day after tomorrow." Maggie never said hello. "When are you coming?"

"I can't come."

"You promised."

Maggie had known her for twenty years. She should know better than to trust Jo Beth. People who made that mistake ended up dead.

"Jo Beth? Are you still there?"

"I'm here."

"You can't avoid Huntsville forever."

She had for ten years, and she saw no good reason to go back.

Except one. Maggie was the only person who had stood up for her when everything she had was stripped away—her gun, her badge, her honor, her pride.

"I'll be there, Maggie."

Jo Beth's promise sucked all the air out of the trailer.

Huntsville—the city of her disgrace, a city of accusations, ghosts, and severed ties.

The rodeo—her history, her love, her long-lost safe harbor, full of forgotten dreams.

When she was a child the rodeo had been home to Jo Beth. Her grandfather, Clint Dawson, had organized a vanishing breed—the American cowboy—into the first professional rodeo. It symbolized the father she'd barely known (a rodeo cowboy), the grandfather she loved, and all the sawdust stories of her childhood turned to stardust because Clint Dawson made her believe in miracles. If a bowlegged, one-eyed cowboy could wrestle to the ground a steer so mean daffodils forgot to bloom the year it was born, Somebody in Charge could bring her daddy home so she'd have a regular family. If a rodeo clown in baggy britches and floppy shoes could outrun a bull as big as the four-bedroom house on Madison Street where her mother sang in a kitchen smelling of gingerbread and Maxwell House coffee, then Whoever Was Up There could put a baby sister in her mother's belly so Jo Beth would have a little girl to play with, someone better than her phantom friend, Grace, who rarely suggested games and vanished so completely in chairs, people tended to sit on her.

Sometimes her mother cried in that house, though. Once when she'd been eight, Jo Beth had asked her why. And Cynthia Wainwright Dawson, displaced Boston blue blood who'd left dreams of Juilliard for a rodeo Romeo named Rafe Dawson, had looked at her with eyes as sad as faded pansies, eyes that held the story of a man who'd promised her the moon then given her a child to raise by herself.

"Because that's what adults do, Jo Beth."

Rejecting her mother's sorrowful viewpoint, Jo Beth grabbed two cookies and went back into the yard to resume her game of cowboys and Indians with Bob Houston. He was her best and only friend, partly because he lived next door, but mainly because Jo Beth was such a tomboy the neighborhood girls didn't want to play with her.

A few Madison Street mothers tried to push their daughters into playing with her till Jo Beth overhead Mrs. Claude Upton refer to her as "poor little rich girl with a no-good daddy." Though she had been only six at the time and hadn't seen her daddy in two years, Jo Beth lit into Mrs. Upton like one of the wild bulls Rafe Dawson used to ride at the rodeo.

"You take that back! If you don't I'll have my granddaddy hogtie you behind a mean bull and drag you all over Tupelo."

Then she'd spat on Mrs. Upton's Etienne Aigner shoes. Jo Beth didn't cry till she got home.

The truth was she didn't have a clue about her daddy. He was mostly absent with the rodeo the first four years of her life. And then he took off for good.

The only true thing Rafe Dawson had left her was the Legend of the Wisdom Keepers. Sitting on the edge of her bed, he'd explained the magic of trees and rivers, stars and flowers, birds and animals who were more than they seemed, who appeared in unexpected times and places, who knew things ordinary mortals could not, who would tell you their secrets if you invited them in.

"The Wisdom Keepers will watch over you, Jo Beth."

Her daddy had told her good night, kissed her on the cheek, then walked out the door. That was the last she'd heard of him, except for an occasional card, until his death at fifty.

Still, she'd pushed pity aside in pursuit of the so-called normal life—college and a career. When she joined the police academy, her mother got a great deal of satisfaction out of telling the neighbors that her tomboy daughter had matured into a tough woman who could handle anything with a gun.

Her mother had been wrong. Jo Beth's facade hid a tender heart burdened by the need to keep everybody around her safe. After she started police work, the souls of the accusing dead started to collect over in Huntsville, falling like pollen she couldn't get rid of no matter how hard she scrubbed herself. They were the hard cases, the ones where she arrived too late to a distress call or couldn't put together a strong enough case to convict. For a while, she'd clung to a life raft made of memories of her grandfather.

"Jo Beth, your daddy's got a bit of wanderlust," he used to

say. "But I'm here and your mama's here and we've got the rodeo. A girl who has all that and a red cowboy hat, to boot . . . why, the world's your oyster, just waiting for you to find the pearl."

Hope in a red hat. Clint Dawson had given both to her on her tenth birthday.

On her eleventh while she ate hot dogs and drank Pepsi, while Cherokee girls with bells on their skirts danced at the head of a rodeo parade, Clint Dawson dropped dead.

The newspapers said he died with his boots on. They said he was a legend, one of the last true American cowboys.

They said nothing about the scared child who had to be rescued by a cop with red hair and freckles on his hands. They made no mention of the little girl who had sat in the police cruiser while strangers paged Uncle Mark, her loss turning to a river of silver tears.

But while her mother had made an art of holing up in dark rooms waiting to drown, Jo Beth learned that if you pretended everything was okay, you could swim in tears. You could float on their aching surface and hardly notice that underneath, deep in the shadows, lurked unspeakable things. Horrors whose names you'd discover one by one after you were grown, after it had all vanished—the grandfather with candy and optimism in his pockets, the father with his wild ways and big dreams, the mother who couldn't drown in tears but found a lake near a place called Witch Dance on the Natchez Trace Parkway to do the job.

Her mother's death had shocked Jo Beth at the time, though when she thought about it later, she knew it shouldn't have. The Dawsons lived in extremes—Rafe in Never Land, Cynthia on the edge of a precipice, and Clint in the clouds. Even the way they died was extreme—her father in the middle of a river, her grandfather in the middle of a rodeo parade, and her mother without witness at a place where no grass grew because legend said witches had once danced there.

There was no middle ground for the Dawsons. Jo Beth was living proof.

Faced now with the choice of returning to the ghosts of Huntsville or letting down the only person who could look at Jo Beth and still see something worth saving, she couldn't breathe.

Jo Beth plunged through the front door, leaned against the silvery shell of her movable home and sucked in air. But it wasn't a fresh breeze that swept through her hair and coated her skin, twined around her feet, wound up her legs and buried itself in her heart. It was the scent of roses.

There were no flowers in this godforsaken trailer park. Why bother? The people who ended up here were not looking for beauty and permanence. They were looking for a rock to crawl under.

Shading her eyes against a sun so bright it bleached everything in its path except souls, Jo Beth scanned the uneven pavement, the scrawny pines that pushed through the cracks, the overgrown banks of the creek that rarely had water because of recent drought. High on the creek bank a rose bloomed, white with golden center, a single blossom so fragrant the scent brought Jo Beth to her knees.

The only thing she still believed in besides the oblivion of vodka was the omens of the Wisdom Keepers. Bad ones.

That was not just any rose, but a symbol of the Trail of Tears—the legend of the Cherokee Nation forced to leave their rich green lands in the Southeast and embark on a killing journey across the Mississippi Valley, the tears they'd shed for their fallen touching the ground and turning to roses.

Kneeling in the trailer park with her face pressed into the dusty pavement, Jo Beth tried to pray. There was only one hitch: she didn't remember how.

Two

Titus left his fields at dusk and walked toward the split-log cabin he'd built with his own hands, built with love and hope and the timber from the high mountain ridge. Built for Morning Star.

His wife had been a beautiful, educated Cherokee woman so full of spirit she'd shunned a job in the sciences to follow in her mother's footsteps and embrace the joy of being a rodeo dancer with bells on her skirt. That Morning Star had taken a chance on a broken-down cowboy who could no longer ride the bulls was a testament to her courage. That she had loved him was an outright miracle.

When Titus stepped onto his front porch, the Redbone hound lifted his head and wagged his tail.

"Hello, Dog." Titus always returned the hound's greeting. Loyalty should be honored.

Inside the cabin, the scent of honeysuckle and roses greeted him. Morning Star had loved flowers and always kept the cabin filled with whatever was growing in the fields and woods. Gifts from the mountain, she'd called them.

After she died, Titus kept it up. Not one day passed that he didn't kneel in the dirt, give thanks for Morning Star, then bring the beauty she treasured inside.

Some folks called him foolish. He guessed he was.

Titus hung his straw hat on the peg inside the door then walked down the hall to wash up. As he passed Pony's room he was not surprised to see the door standing open, though it had been shut tight for three days, ever since she'd left for Alabama wearing her boots and her spurs, her Stetson hat and her courage.

She was sitting on her bed on a Cherokee diamond patchwork quilt—a shadow, a vision, an unexpected and tender mercy.

"Pony?"

She turned her face toward him, her long black braid swinging down her back, her blue eyes alight with the fierceness that had always been inside her. Around her, the air pulsed like a beating heart.

Ain't no use cryin', Daddy.

He put his hands to his face, amazed to touch tears. When he looked at the bed again, Pony was gone.

Titus walked on down the hall, his bones heavy with truth.

When you leave home, even if it's just to go to the Piggly Wiggly for a loaf of bread, it's possible to become somebody else. It's possible for regret to fly out the window like a blackbird and something wonderful to fly back inside and perch on your shoulder. Something with yellow wings that sings a song you heard in childhood but thought you'd forgotten.

As Jo Beth drove east, the song grew faint, and when she crossed the Alabama state line it stopped altogether.

She didn't dare pick up the phone and tell Maggie she couldn't come after all, that she couldn't face what lay behind her and was afraid of what lay ahead. When she'd still believed in marriage and answered prayer and her own ability as a police detective to keep crime from taking root in Huntsville as fast as shopping malls and McDonald's drive-throughs, she'd told Maggie every thought that entered her mind.

But that was before her thoughts turned so dark they grew claws and teeth. That was before they got so fierce they would eat you alive if you brought them out in the open.

Gripping the wheel of her Dodge Ram pickup, Jo Beth hurtled doggedly toward her destination, pulling her house behind her. You never knew when you'd need to turn tail and run. Besides, she was staying in a trailer park twenty miles north of the city.

The city was the last place she wanted to be, even if she wasn't going to the police station where ghosts of people who died under her watch would be hiding behind doors and floating on the ceiling and perching under the rims of toilets.

Was it possible a few hours of good barrel racing and bull riding would take her mind off the wrongfully dead? Was the rodeo still a nexus for silver dreams you could stick in your pocket and hope that burst in your mouth like cinnamon candy?

After Clint Dawson died, Jo Beth's mother had refused to take her to the rodeo.

"The rodeo will only break your heart," Cynthia had said.

After Jo Beth was grown, she'd gone anyway, sneaked off to Jackson, Mississippi, with a group of friends from the police academy. She'd gone with the fragile faith she could recapture all she'd lost—magic and the grandfather whose boots were so big they could straddle a river and never get wet.

When she found out about it, Cynthia had cried so long and hard, Jo Beth had never gone back to the rodeo. Not until long after her mother's suicide. Until long after the souls set up housekeeping with her. Until she was desperate.

She'd gone alone. At the time, she'd been holed up somewhere on the Mississippi Gulf Coast. Where, she didn't remember, nor did it matter. All that mattered was finding out if the little shiver she still got in the fall was true, the shiver that came when the first frost turned everything in its path shining and silver— mailboxes, trees, front porch steps, even dogs that stood still too long. Everything looked whitewashed then. Clean. A world temporarily frozen before it took a deep breath and started over.

As the road had flattened out, she'd stopped at a cowboy store outside San Antonio to buy boots and a red hat. At the rodeo, sitting in the third-row seat of a packed arena while sawdust turned incandescent and cowgirls turned to stars, a girl no bigger than a sliver of soap had turned rodeo rules upside down.

Jo Beth could almost believe in redemption. Was it possible the tragedy collecting on her like green scum on dead water was not her fault?

Now she barely remembered the details of that long-ago rodeo. She'd pushed it far back in her mind, deep into a corner where bones lay scattered and demons prowled under waxing summer moons.

What she did remember was this: just when she'd rediscovered the magic, she'd seen Lucky Lou Lewis topple from his bucking bronco and be dragged from the saddle horn until there was nothing left of him to identify.

She'd never been to another rodeo.

Until now.

Still, she wouldn't call Maggie to say, "I'm turning around, going back home." Maggie was the one human connection Jo Beth hadn't severed, the one real thing that kept her from falling off the edge of the world.

So she pressed forward on the two-lane roads, keeping a careful watch on the speedometer and a lid on her feelings. She was in Alabama, where anything could happen.

Snuggled in the foothills of the Appalachian Mountains, the state is a land of deep caves and steep ravines and red clay colored by the blood of fathers and brothers and sons too young to bear arms fighting for a lost cause. Hope can get buried so deep in Alabama, it can take three generations to dig it back out.

But it's also a land rampant with beauty and promise where the great American bald eagle keeps watch over the rivers, wild canaries turn treetops gold during migratory flights, and redbirds decorate cedars at Christmas then in summer fly under your front porch to share a sip of your sweet iced tea. It's a land where the scent of gardenias and lilies of the valley and Confederate jasmine overflowing gardens in wide-spot-in-the-road towns like Red Bay and Hamilton and Russellville can get under your skin, take root between your shoulder blades and sprout into wings.

Today it was not wings Jo Beth found as she drove through the scattered towns of north Alabama, but dread.

She navigated the hairpin curves with caution. Accidents meant written reports by the highway patrol. And reports meant her name being sniffed out by newshounds who still remembered her.

She'd been in her mid-thirties when the fourteen-year-old boy had plunged over the railing at the mall and smashed to pieces for no reason at all. She'd been the one sent to save him, then watched, horrified, as his blood bloomed at the feet of unsuspecting shoppers. Huntsville newspaper banners had screamed *Detective Jo Beth Dawson Under Investigation*. A vicious whispering campaign had hammered at her conscience. She hadn't needed newspapers and gossips to tell her she was at fault. Just as she'd been when Bob Houston had barreled down an ice-covered hill on a metal garbage can lid, skidded across Highway 45 and plowed into the path of a Peterbilt rig.

She was the one who'd said, "Let's go sledding." She was the one who stole two large metal garbage can lids and talked her best friend into sneaking off to the steep hill near St. James Catholic Church.

"Come on, Bob. We only get ice once in a blue moon."

There'd been headlines then, too. *Tupelo Teen Dies in Freak Accident*. Nobody had blamed Jo Beth. And she'd been too young then to think of ways to punish herself.

The difference between fourteen and thirty-three is that you know how to drown yourself in a bottle.

By the time she was thirty-eight, Jo Beth had lost everything—job, husband, friends, even the remnants of her family. Her disgrace had been splashed across every newspaper and TV screen in the South.

That's when the unquiet souls had started roaming at will. As she hurtled closer to the city of her disgrace, Jo Beth hunched her shoulders against impending doom.

Just outside Russellville, she stopped at an Exxon station to stretch her legs. After she'd filled up with gas and paid with a credit card at the pump—blessed anonymity—she dialed Maggie's number.

"Mags, I'm here. I made it to Alabama."

"I knew you could. When will I see you?"

"Tomorrow morning. Early."

"I'll be waiting with blueberry muffins and a big grin."

Easy for Maggie, who had lots to smile about. An adoring husband, two teenage boys who chose sports and academics over nose piercings and punk hairdos, a roomful of third graders who thought she walked on water.

Jo Beth had met Maggie when she was a rookie cop, assigned to talk to Maggie's elementary students about law and order. Before Jo Beth and idealism had parted company. Back when she was somebody else.

The person she had become, exposed on the hot asphalt of the gas station parking lot, climbed into the cocoon of her Dodge Ram. Her stomach rumbled but she didn't even consider going inside for a bag of potato chips, an Almond Joy, a cool strawberry ICEE. She was too close to Huntsville. Somebody might remember.

Reaching into the cooler on the floorboard, she pulled out a bottle of water and headed east.

Fifty miles from Huntsville the first soul landed between her shoulder blades with the plop of an overripe plum. She hunched forward, trying to shake it free, but it sat there growing heavier with every mile. The second soul attached itself at the city limits. The third struck with the force of the Saturn V rocket rising over the city's skyline.

It was dusk when she pulled into Sleepy Pines Campground. The internet called it "a bucolic setting where whispering pines and a clear, running brook guarantee a haven of peace." Jo Beth didn't care about printed hype. She'd selected the site based on the allure of nature and the fact that it was on the Tennessee line, where the souls of the Alabama dead shouldn't have found her.

She drove through the campground entrance and reconnoitered the area, a habit she hadn't been able to shake since her academy days. Selecting a spot with plenty of shade, she started backing her Silver Streak. And that's when she heard it, a small thumping sound no louder than the whisper of angel wings.

Across the fence, a wall of Cherokee roses swooned, like somebody dying, like somebody trying to tell Jo Beth to turn around and run.

She eased her trailer forward then sat in the cab of her pickup, sweating, dreading to see what she'd backed over.

It didn't make any sense to be terrified of lost souls prowling in the purple shadows between sunset and sunrise. The dead can't put a bullet through your heart or slit your throat. What did make sense was being terrified of unseen things that could pounce on you, even if you were in a bucolic setting, peace guaranteed.

She reached for a flashlight and her gun—no longer police issue—then stepped into the dusk and a nightmare of roses. Behind her camper, white petals were piled high as snowdrifts.

And underneath was the shape of a body, nothing showing but tiny boots, silver spurs, a glimpse of red cloth. A small arm?

Automatically Jo Beth pointed her weapon and swept her flashlight into the darkness.

"Who's there?" Nothing answered her but silence and the scent of roses. "I've got a gun and I know how to use it." She pulled back the hammer.

A white wolf appeared through the wall of roses. Transfixed, Jo Beth listened to his chilling ululation. As it echoed through the campground, every star fell from the sky till nothing showed in the deep black night except the thin light of a cold blue moon.

The wolf watched her with eyes that knew secrets, and she stared back with eyes that had seen too much.

She didn't want to be sucked into legends that reminded her of the past—her grandfather filled with Native American lore from a beloved Oglala Sioux nanny, her father with his Wisdom Keepers. She didn't want to know what the wolf could tell her about a body covered with roses.

The pull of the wolf's eyes was strong, but she refused to invite him in. Instead, she stared him down until he vanished.

Dropping to her knees, she carefully raked at the rose petals. A young woman's pale face emerged, blue eyes staring at nothing, lovely features twisted by the cold hand of death.

"My God." That face. Those blue eyes, staring at her. Begging. Pleading.

Jo Beth jerked backward, landed among rose petals. Sweat poured down her face and she couldn't stop shaking.

She knew her. She knew the victim.

Or did she?

She'd felt the same way about every victim on every case she'd worked. In her heart, she knew them all, knew the fifteen-year-old teenager who had wanted to be a ballet dancer, knew the old man at the shoe shine stand who had wanted to retire to Florida and live with his grandson, knew the young housewife who had wanted to have children, even if it meant getting artificially inseminated behind her husband's back.

Jo Beth's first instinct was to run. Then long-buried detective instincts pushed to the surface and she focused on the victim.

So young. So very young.

Who could have killed this girl? Why? What mysterious forces had covered the body with roses? Except for souls of the dead who wouldn't stay put, Jo Beth refused to believe in mysterious forces. She refused to believe in magic and second chances and Arctic wolves in Alabama.

The only way to stay safe was to believe in nothing except what you could see, touch, smell and hear. To avoid attachments. To invite no one in.

But the pull of this young woman sucked Jo Beth in. She put her fingers on the slender neck where the pulse should have been. The flesh was cold and stiff. She'd been dead awhile, probably several hours.

Jo Beth jerked her hand away. After all these years, what right did she have to be thinking like a cop? She'd left Huntsville under a cloud of suspicion so cold and dense it had blocked the sun and caused birds to migrate out of season.

She knew what she should do, what she *had* to do. Just report the body, then leave.

But something was calling to her from the moon-cold earth, singing to her in a voice like a river, chanting in tongues as ancient as the hills.

Placing her hand over the victim's eyes, Jo Beth closed the lids. And as she did, the prayer passed to Clint Dawson from his nanny rose to her lips, spilling into the death-still night.

"'Grandfather, Great Spirit, once more behold me on earth and lean to hear my feeble voice. You are older than all need, older than all prayer. All things belong to you—the two-legged, the four-legged, the wings of the air, and all green things that live.'

"'You have made me cross the good road, and the road of difficulties, and where they cross, the place is holy. Day in, day out, forevermore, you are the life of things.'"

The words of her grandfather, originating with Black Elk of the Oglala Sioux, then passed from generation to generation, echoed through the deep woods and whispered through the roses. Prayers for the innocent. Winds before the storm.

Dreading the storm to come, Jo Beth pulled out her cell phone and dialed the number that was as familiar to her as her own.

"Huntsville Police Department."

The perky female who answered probably believed in the goodness of justice. She'd probably never know that if you stripped off the blindfold and looked justice in the eye, it could send you straight to hell.

"I've found a body."

It was too late now. The minute she'd spoken, Jo Beth had become involved. Connected.

She strode back to her trailer, jerked open her cabinet and grabbed a bottle of whiskey. Her glass was already half full when Jo Beth stopped. Soon cops would be swarming the campground. Her appointment with Jack Daniel would have to wait.

I never expected to be declared dead by a little bitty woman who smells like regret.

I didn't expect to be dead, period. And I sure didn't expect to be laying on the ground with a stranger staring down at me. Though there's something about her that's not so strange, something that reminds me of the picture I had in my head of the person I used to ask God to please send me—sister, cousin, aunt, grandmother. Anybody would do as long as she was female and sassy and smart and had a heart as big as a moon.

Maybe I actually have female kinfolk; I don't know. And now I ain't likely to find out.

Me and Daddy lived like we'd sprung from wolves, the only two people on the planet. The only time I asked him about my mother's people, he said, "Hush, now, Pony. It's just me and you."

This scrawny little dark-haired woman looks like she could whip wildcats in a heartbeat and would be what you'd call a knockout if her eyes wasn't so dead. She walks all around me, her thoughts so dark I can feel 'em crawling over me like spiders. She stops at my Justin boots and stares down at them a while before she kneels on the cold earth and brushes the roses from my face.

The way she says, "*Dear God,*" I can tell she ain't praying. Matter of fact, I'd say this little closed-up woman ain't had no truck with God in a long while.

She puts her hand on the side of my neck where my life's blood used to flow so strong and swift it felt like my insides was a wild river. I told Daddy that once, and he said, "Pony, that's your restless nature tellin' you, you goin' places."

He for durned sure wasn't talking about these dark piney woods. I want out of here.

I try to send my thoughts to the woman bending over me, but telepathy don't work when one mind is shut so tight can't nothing get in, not even your own reflection.

"My God." This woman likes to repeat herself. "You're nothing but a child. Who would murder you?"

Her question would chill me to the bone if I wasn't already dead. You can't get no colder than dead. Unless it's murdered. Now who'd want to go and do a thing like that? I ain't got no enemies, except them that's in the rodeo ring, and they ain't really enemies, just critters I gotta get on speaking terms with.

The splintered-apart woman touches my face, and though her eyes are dry, I feel tears dripping all over me, every one of them shaped like a heart.

"You look like a teenager," she whispers. "Your parents must be worried sick."

Daddy ain't never been one to worry. When I got old enough to make up my own mind about what I wanted to do, he said, "Pony, use the sense the good Lord give you and stay out of trouble, that's all."

And that's what I done.

Up until now.

Sirens scream in the distance and I know they coming for me. Suddenly I'm jerked out of my body. Weighing no more than a canary's wing, I follow my heart, fly through the trees and beyond, all the way to Doe Mountain where my Daddy waits, already feeling my absence like a severed limb.

My room's exactly the way I left it, bed made up neat and nice, my books on horses and dogs and snakes and every kind of critter the good Lord made all lined up in the shelves Daddy built, my diary and a picture of my mother in a field of Queen Anne's lace on the bedside table, the Mason jar setting beside it filled with the honeysuckle I know my daddy picked fresh and put there.

This is home to me. No matter how far my travels take me, I always end up back here on this mountaintop in Tennessee. Safe. So far above wars and pestilence and hatred, it seems like they don't even exist. So high in the sky it feels like you can just reach up and take ahold of God's hand.

The first thing I used to do when I'd get home was take off my boots and polish them. I ain't what you'd call poor no more, but I ain't never been one to condone waste. And neither has my daddy. I take care of what the good Lord give me—trees and critters and boots and kitchen floors.

I set down on my bed but I reckon I'm just kind of floating above it because I can't feel my butt on the quilt. And I sure as hell can't take off my boots. Looks like I'm doomed to be wearing shitty boots forever. The only good thing I can say about that is I didn't leave no tracks on the clean floor.

My daddy's over there in the door with loss showing all over his face. That don't mean nobody else is gonna notice me, though. Ain't everybody got the kind of seeing heart my daddy has.

I try to speak but don't nothing come out. Then I feel my thoughts flying toward him, a reassuring whisper that settles in his soul like burning stars.

Suddenly I feel like somebody besides my daddy is tugging my heartstrings, and I take off in the direction of my yearning. The next thing I know I'm at the back of the cabin in the garden Daddy made after my mother died. Standing in the sacred circle with my feet not touching the ground, I hear her spirit call to me. Long ago my daddy scattered her ashes in the four quadrants—north, south, east, west, each defined by river rocks and planted with swamp sunflowers and four o'clocks and daisies and the herbs I used in our kitchen, basil of all kinds, rosemary, oregano, thyme and sweet marjoram.

"Pony, my beloved child." Her voice is sweet as the music of songbirds.

"Mother? Is that you?"

"Yes. I'm here."

I strain to see her face, but all I see are herbs and flowers swaying as if a light breeze is passing through. "Can I see you? Please? I ain't never seen nothin' but a picture."

"Oh, Pony . . ." My mother's silence falls on me like a hug. "When you know me, you'll see me. But first you have a mission to complete."

"What mission?"

"When the time is right, you'll know. You'll know everything."

The next thing I know I'm arguing with a mother I ain't never even seen, telling her, "I ain't no shirker, but I don't see how I can do a job I don't know nothing about. Especially since I don't seem to have a body."

I guess she'll leave me for good now. Impatient daughter that I am, I'll be the only spirit in history never to be reunited with her dearly departeds.

To my great surprise, I hear laughter. Not one woman, but two. "Is somebody with you?"

"Your grandmother. We have much to tell you."

"Tell me who done this to me, and after I skin him alive, I got a lot of other questions. Me and my daddy had a good life, but he didn't tell me nothing about your side of the family."

When my mother don't answer me, I figure I've done run her off for sure. And my grandmother, too. No wonder the good Lord didn't see fit to let me grow up with female relatives. The shock of raising me woulda killed 'em.

"I'm sorry. I'll give up my bad habits if you'll come on back." I don't hear nothing. Not even that old mockingbird that scolds everybody who invades his territory. "Mother?"

"Don't be afraid, Pony. Each soul must meet the morning sun alone."

I feel a great big void, and I know she ain't there no more. Before she left, I wish I'd a told her I loved her. I wish I'd a told her I wasn't afraid. Ain't no use in her worrying over me.

If spirits worry. I don't know. There's a lot I don't know, but I aim to find out.

While I'm floating around the garden wondering what comes next, I feel them strange yearnings again, like somebody's done latched onto me and won't let go. Or else I've latched onto them. It's hard to tell which.

Pulled by forces I don't understand but can't ignore, I fly through the air again then land with a thump on the sunless, brutal ground in the piney woods on the Alabama-Tennessee line.

Them sirens come a-squalling through the gates and cops start crawling everywhere, talking about me like I was a piece of meat.

"Trauma to the back of the head . . . blunt object, looks like . . . no ID. Luther, get this area cordoned off. Sam, get over there and question the woman who found her. Mike, search the area for a weapon, footprints, anything you can find." The man speaking is a big, no-bullshit kind of guy. He spits and I can smell Bull Durham.

All of a sudden I have a vision of my daddy standing on the front porch looking off to the west, admiring the fading sunset, knowing in his bones that soon he'll be listening to somebody from the valley tell him his only child has done been knocked in the back of the head.

If I'd a known I had enemies, I might a looked over my shoulder more. Of course, if I'd spent my time looking over my shoulder, I might never have got where I was going. And there's something to be said for that. Twenty-six, and I always ended up where I was aiming to go.

Present circumstances being the notable exception. I sure didn't aim to be tagged, bagged and hauled off to no morgue.

And I for doggoned sure didn't aim to die and find myself still earth-bound, flying all over Doe Mountain one minute, then the next, drawn back to a stranger for no reason I can think of.

I guess the good thing about being dead is there ain't nowhere else left to go. You got all the time in the world to just lay around and figure out how come somebody bashed your head in and how come your soul landed square in the middle of that scrawny little shattered woman's chest.

❧ *Three* ❧

You don't forget nearly thirteen years of police work. Jo Beth stood deep in the shadows, knowing they hadn't recognized her yet, watching while they puzzled over a corpse in the middle of nowhere covered with roses.

What she ought to do was go inside and lock her door, but she couldn't make herself leave while that poor, defenseless girl was out there, lying so still and cold on the ground.

Snatches of cop conversation drifted to her through the dark.

"It's not natural."

"The petals are fresh, like they've just been picked."

"Who in the hell would kill somebody, then hang around long enough to cover the body with roses? Look over there at the split-rail fence. There's no visible trail of any kind."

"If one word of these damned roses leaks to the press, I'll have somebody's head on a platter."

The air glowed orange with superstition. Then the wind picked up, shaking the pine branches, bringing the threat of rain, and once again the night turned as blue as the mystery of death.

The detective in charge, somebody Jo Beth didn't know, yelled, "Sam, get over there and find out what that woman knows."

Even then, Jo Beth didn't bolt, couldn't move. It was as if her bones were connected to the dead girl.

Sam Donovan spat on the ground for good luck and strolled her way. His nonchalant manner didn't fool Jo Beth. He was a pent-up ball of fury, turned that way by murder and by a prissy, shallow wife who packed her bag eleven years ago and left him for a Sears home appliance salesman with a boat and higher social aspirations.

"Hello, Jo Beth."

Donovan and Dawson, the best detective team on the force. If folks still remembered, chances were they pretended they didn't.

The last time she'd seen her former partner, he'd been standing in a severe blue line of uniforms witnessing her humiliation.

She acknowledged him with a nod, unable to speak past a clogged throat. Unshed tears? Unspoken rage at what she considered his betrayal? It could have been either, and both reactions surprised her. She'd thought she was beyond tears, beyond caring about anybody or anything, past or present.

"It's been awhile, Jo. What brings you to town?"

Awhile didn't begin to cover the years of living under a rock. She wanted to strangle him.

"Cut the small talk, Sam. The only reason I'm talking to you is that I found the victim."

Sam swatted at a mosquito buzzing his head and trained his flashlight behind her, onto her Silver Streak, before he pointed the beam directly at her face. Jo Beth didn't flinch. Instead she turned her head away and watched the coroner load the victim and head toward the gate. That meant they were treating this case like an Alabama murder when technically it could be turned over to Tennessee.

Jo Beth should have known not to stop in a campground that straddled two state lines. She should have known better than to come to Alabama in the first place.

"All right, Jo Beth." Sam moved his flashlight, and Jo Beth felt the blessed relief of shadow. "We'll play it your way. What happened here?"

"I found her like that, alone, no signs of anybody else near the campground. I brushed enough rose petals away to see her face and check her pulse, but I didn't disturb the scene." She fired the facts at Sam like Colt .45 bullets, then lifted her chin and dared him to prod for more.

"Do you know the victim?"

She'd expected that question. "No."

"You sure you've never seen her before?"

"Positive." Jo Beth refused to ponder why she had prayed over a dead girl she didn't even know. She refused to be seduced by that beautiful, innocent-looking face and those pleading blue eyes. And she certainly had no intention of hanging around Sam Donovan the rest of the evening. "Can I go now?"

"What can you tell me about the roses?"

Everything. Nothing.

Once, long ago, she'd shared with Sam the legend her father had told her. Chances were, he no longer remembered. If he did, he was covering it up.

"The roses were here when I found her."

Sam jotted notes, took her phone number, then turned the light back on her face. "Don't leave town." Her curt nod said she already knew this routine. "We may want to bring you into the station for further questions." She nodded again, then marched into her movable home and slammed the door hard enough to make sure Sam knew it was no accident.

Jo Beth didn't bother to turn on the lights. In the dark and waist-deep in hell, she lit a cigarette. She'd promised Maggie she was quitting. But that was before the corpse of a young girl she didn't even know had shaken her to the core. That was before she'd found herself breaking all her own rules. No involvement. No connection. And definitely no police.

Tomorrow reporters would be all over Sleepy Pines Campground. Murder was news. Especially when the body was found by tainted former police detective Jo Beth Dawson.

Maybe she'd get a horse. Go to Texas. She didn't know a damned soul in Texas, which was reason enough to go.

Sam stood outside the Silver Streak staring at Jo Beth's closed door like a man gut-shot. He'd never expected to see her again. Not after what had happened. Not after she'd left Huntsville.

Sure, he'd tried to see her before she left. But not very hard. Sam was lots of things—a slob, a stubborn cuss, a junk-food addict even after his doctor swore he wouldn't live past fifty-five if he didn't start eating right. In his profession, he'd be one lucky son of a gun if he even made it to fifty-five.

What Sam was *not* was the kind of man who thought better of himself than he was. But he'd be damned if he could see how he was to blame for her getting kicked off the force.

He was a good detective, some even said great, with an unblemished record, saddled with a female partner who was hanging onto control by a thread. So he covered for her.

And Jo Beth blamed him, called him an enabler, said the department would have dried her out and straightened her up if they'd seen what was happening while the problem was still manageable.

It had been ten years since Jo Beth had left the force, and not a day had gone by that he didn't wake up tasting regret; didn't wonder if he could have saved her.

What would he have done all those years ago if she'd opened the door after he'd pounded on it for fifteen minutes, calling her name? Say, *I'm sorry?* He was, but what the hell good would that have done her. Say, *I wish I'd let you take the fall?* That would have been a lie. He was the kind of man who protected women, even if they did carry a badge and a gun.

Though he still wrestled with his conscience, not a day went by that he wasn't thankful for what he had—his badge and gun, a sober partner, his chance to make the city of his birth, the city he loved, just a little bit cleaner, a little bit safer for the people who mattered. Mailmen and garbage collectors, farmers and engineers, ditch diggers and doctors, schoolteachers and priests, mothers and fathers and children. Especially children.

And now Jo Beth was back, like an unruly puppy you'd given away. A puppy you loved but knew you couldn't keep because it was tearing your house apart.

He didn't have to rack his brain to know why she was here. Back in the good days Jo Beth had talked about rodeo in the same reverent voice some people used when they mentioned God.

Those were the days when she still believed the jerk she'd married was a good guy and Sam had been under the illusion he could fix anything—refrigerators, stoves, marriages.

Swatting at a mosquito buzzing for blood, Sam walked to the door of Jo Beth's Silver Streak, lifted his hand to knock. Then just stood there. What was left to say?

"Sam?" The captain was calling him.

"Yo?"

"You finished over there?"

"I'm finished."

Leaving the trailer and his damned inconvenient introspection behind, Sam headed toward the pile of rose petals surrounded by yellow crime tape.

He had a job to do.

Deep in his dream, John Running Wolf moaned and tossed.

"Get off my mountain." Titus Jones held a 12-gauge shotgun pointed at him, and Running Wolf knew he would use it. The eyes always told the truth.

"I've come to take the child."

"I'll see you in hell first."

"She belongs with her people."

"I'm her daddy. That's all the people she needs." Titus leveled the shotgun toward Running Wolf's chest. "Get. I ain't countin' to three."

Running Wolf had faced down wild cougars. He'd killed in Korea bare-handed. He'd even tried to prevent this wild mountain bull rider from marrying his niece. Titus Jones didn't scare him.

"There are things you don't know. Things I came to tell you."

"She's mine. That's all I need to know." Titus cocked the gun. "If you ever so much as look sideways at my daughter, I'll hunt you down and gut you like a boar hog."

John Running Wolf jerked awake. Every night for the past two weeks it had been the same, first the dream-travel back to Doe Mountain then the call of the owl. When the Wisdom Keepers and the Spirit Guides joined forces, the message was too powerful to ignore. The Great Spirit used dreams to teach you, to guide you.

He'd shut his ears against their lessons long enough. Running Wolf sat up and threw back the covers. Beside him, Martha didn't stir. With her hands folded over the gentle rise and fall of her breasts, his wife of sixty-five years lay in dreamless sleep.

He slipped from the room to stand on his screened-in back porch. As bent and gnarled as the corkscrew willows Martha had planted behind the patio home she cherished and he despised, Running Wolf tilted his head toward the sound that had awakened him. An owl. Deep in the woods beyond the ninth green that stretched behind his house.

It was time. Even before the owl called his name, John Running Wolf had known this day was coming. A few more moons, and he would go the way of his ancestors.

He'd turned to go back inside when a strong fragrance stopped him. The Cherokee rose, its stout thorny vines a symbol of strength, its delicate petals the scent of death.

Lifting his face to the moon, John said a prayer. Then he left his porch and lay down on the ninth green, lay there cradled by the earth and the wide arms of heaven. Once this land had belonged to his family. Deer had walked here. Foxes and rabbits and quail. It had been a land of winding water and sacred soil, a land where a man could pull off his moccasins and feel the heartbeat of his ancestors.

"Sell it," Martha had said. "It will provide for our old age."

Before his sister died, even she had urged him to barter the land for financial security. "Our ancestors live in your blood and bone, John, not the land. I look at this acreage and see independence."

They had both been right, but selling the ridge had been like selling his mother. While Martha waited for her zero-lot-line home in the high-dollar complex on the green to develop, she'd watched every tree fall, every inch of earth gouged. John couldn't. His only part in this travesty was to put in the contract that the developers had to keep the name, Cherokee Ridge, a reminder of what the land had once been.

With the scent of sweet, damp grass clinging to his nightclothes, John rose from the ground and went back inside. There was much to do and little time. The money he'd sent back two weeks ago was not enough. It was time to make amends.

Taking the key from his desk, he opened an ancient steamer trunk. The diary lay underneath his sister's skirt of white fringed leather, its yellowed pages held together with faded red ribbon.

John picked it up, feeling his sister's spirit watching. It was time to break his stubborn, prideful silence.

He and Martha had no children of their own. If he could leave her with someone to fill his absence when he was gone, then it was worth returning to the arena that had been the catalyst for every bad thing that had happened to his family—the rodeo.

Full of remorse and determination, John went to his closet and tucked the diary into the inside pocket of his blue denim jacket. Then he crept back into bed and lay down beside Martha. But his eyes remained wide open.

There would be no dreams for John Running Wolf that night, only memories—the years of watching and waiting as hope gradually faded from the Wolf household.

And all because of the bargain he'd made with the white devil.

Whispers of his ancestors came to him in the wind outside his window. "As a child I learned how to give. I have forgotten that grace."

John pulled the covers over his head to shut out the voices. He was unworthy to ask the Great Spirit for a return of mercy and grace.

 *Four*

Jo Beth unhitched her camper-trailer from her pickup and left early the next morning without turning on the TV.

She drove on winding roads through thick forests that housed songbirds and squirrels, bobcats and white-tailed deer, wild turkeys and coveys of quail. Twenty minutes south of the state line, the forests gave way to a city rich with Native American history and built by technology. Huntsville—home to Redstone Arsenal, NASA's Marshall Space Flight Center, and the remnants of Cherokee whose ancestors had hidden in the mountains to avoid President Andrew Jackson's removal order.

But it wasn't history Jo Beth thought of as she drove: it was the murder at Sleepy Pines. When indigestion forced her to stop at a 7-Eleven in search of Pepto-Bismol, she didn't buy a paper. She didn't want to know the victim's name, she didn't want to know her age or where she went to school or that she loved basketball and ponytails and boys in tight black T-shirts.

What she wanted was to go back to the blessed anonymity of the trailer park in Hot Coffee.

Now she was trapped. Jo Beth would like to make that Sam Donovan's fault, but the one shred of decency she had left wouldn't let her.

She needed a drink. But you couldn't drive and drink in this town without getting caught. If Jo Beth were a woman who cared about bettering herself, she'd join AA, learn the twelve steps. But she didn't give a whippoorwill's ass about herself, and she sure as sin was no joiner. Never had been. Even in the days when she'd fooled herself into thinking she was normal.

She'd *looked* normal in those days, a slim, dark-haired woman who'd come whistling into the Huntsville PD every morning, swap her jeans and cowboy boots for gun and badge, then go home every evening to a husband who had understood when she'd wanted to keep her own name.

Maggie had introduced them.

"Here he is, Jo," she'd said. "The man I've been telling you about." Roger Blake. Handsome. Successful lawyer. Salt of the earth. Those were the things Mags had told her. "The great thing about Roger is that when he's *out with the boys,* you'll know it's only James." Mags's husband. He and Roger were not only best friends, but both were lawyers in the DA's office.

It had been a three-week courtship, long-stemmed roses and candlelight and good sex obscuring the underlying truth: she and Roger had nothing in common except a desire to mete out justice. Young and idealistic, they hadn't known that justice cast dark shadows, that if you weren't careful they'd collect on you, hunt you down, swallow you up.

For ten years Jo Beth had kept on the move so the shadows couldn't catch her. But now she was stuck, stitched to this city by murder.

As she approached the city limits, she made sure all her windows were up, her locks on. But the shadows crawled in the pickup with her anyway, took a seat and sat there staring at her with accusing eyes.

After she'd left Huntsville ten years earlier, she'd launched a careful campaign to erase the entire city. She'd started with Roger, which turned out to be easier than she'd thought and led her to wonder if she'd ever loved him in the first place, if she were even capable of love.

Next was the police department on Weatherly. It was already so shadowed with restless souls you could hardly see it. But erasing it had been like peeling away pieces of herself until finally there was nothing left but skin stretched over bones.

Driving along now, the city materialized in sharp bits and pieces — Dunkin' Donuts, a favorite haunt where the night-shift waitress always saved the corner booth for Donovan and Dawson, the La Quinta Inn where Jo Beth started holing up to keep from going home to Roger and his endless logic.

When Madison Square came into view, Jo Beth began to shake. If she hadn't been driving she'd have shut her eyes. But she had to drive with eyes wide open, and there was the mall, agonizing and unavoidable.

That fateful day had started like any other for Dawson and Donovan. They'd been at Barnes & Noble on University Drive having a latte and discussing what Sam could get Lana for Christmas.

"She wants a diamond necklace. Hell, she knows I can't even afford cubic zirconium."

"Then don't get jewelry, Sam. Get two tickets to Cancún. Take her on a vacation."

"I don't have time for a vacation."

"It would be good for you. For both of you."

Then the call came from the mall across the street and they took it, got there first. And there was the kid, red hair, freckles, high-top tennis shoes untied, jeans hung so low you wondered what was keeping them up. No hip bones. This kid was bony as a wet alley cat.

And he was poised to jump.

They'd tried to talk him down, first Sam, then Jo Beth. As she'd pleaded with the kid, Christmas in Madison Square Mall had metamorphosed to a snowy day in Tupelo twenty years earlier. The kid with red hair became Bob Houston, spinning down an icy hill toward twenty tons of death on wheels.

"Please don't do this," Jo Beth had told the red-haired kid. "You can't undo it."

For a moment he'd stared at her, uncertain, and then his emotions shut down. He reached into the pocket of his baggy jeans and whipped out a weapon.

"He's got a gun, Sam!" Jo Beth slapped her hand over her holster, went down on one knee.

The kid was looking straight at her when he sailed off the railing. He never even screamed. Lying in a pool of his own blood, his body twisted in impossible angles, he'd looked like a pile of broken Tinkertoys. In his hand was a cell phone.

Shaking so hard her teeth chattered, Jo Beth stared straight ahead and focused on getting past the mall. She found a liquor store and pulled into the parking lot. Maggie would kill her.

Jo Beth went inside, grabbed the first bottle of cheap whiskey with a screw-on top she could find and paid cash.

One drink. That was all. She kept Juicy Fruit gum in her purse to cover the smell. Maggie would never know.

As Jo Beth headed back across the blistering parking lot, she glanced around to make sure no one would witness her quick nip, no cops lurking in nearby doorways, no early-morning oblivion seekers headed toward the liquor store.

Who was that sitting in the cab of her truck? A small person. Probably a teenager looking for trouble.

Jo Beth sprinted that way, silently cursing her out-of-shape body. Gasping for breath, she flung open her door. The cab was empty.

"Where are you, dammit?"

She leaned down to look under her truck, then circled behind to see if the culprit had jumped out the opposite door and hidden in the truck bed.

No one was there. A small blessing. Her only weapon was the liquor bottle. It would be a shame to waste it over the head of an aspiring thug.

Still heaving for breath, Jo Beth climbed into her truck, locked the doors and pulled the cool bottle from the bag. She held it briefly against her hot face before unscrewing the cap.

But it wasn't the smell of mashed corn whiskey that swirled up from the open bottle; it was the scent of roses. The fragrance seeped into the upholstery and crawled under the floor mats. It clung to the dashboard and drifted across the windshield. It cocooned Jo Beth so that she was temporarily paralyzed, bound by the weight of roses.

But there was someone else in that cab, too, a presence she could feel but not see. The soul hovered over her, and her skin tingled as if it had been brushed by the wings of singing canaries.

"Leave me alone." Wrapping her arms around herself, Jo Beth wondered if liquor and neglect had finally stolen her mind.

In the distance she heard a ringing. Somebody's phone. The roses held her tight. The ringing became persistent, important.

Jo Beth closed her eyes, almost overcome with the need to

drift off and let the scent of roses and the touch of canary wings take her where they would.

The jangling phone wouldn't be ignored. It pushed the rose vision aside and took over the cab. Jo Beth fumbled in her purse for her cell phone.

"Jo Beth?" It was Sam. She almost hung up. "Are you there?"

"How did you get this number?"

"It was in my notes. From the campground. Remember?"

Jo Beth didn't want to remember anything about that evening.

"I've told you all I know, Sam. I found the girl. Period. Leave me alone."

"This is not about the case. It's personal. Can you meet me at Denny's on University Drive?"

"Where the man who hated meat loaf shot five senior citizens enjoying the Thursday special? I think not, Sam."

"Wait. Don't hang up. We need to talk."

"We have nothing to talk about."

The only good thing Jo Beth could say about Sam's call was that anger had replaced her need for liquor. Putting blessed distance between her and the mall, she drove to Devon Street.

Jo Beth hadn't seen Maggie since her friend's visit two years ago. She'd been living in Biloxi then. Or had it been Ocean Springs?

Names didn't matter. Jo Beth never stayed in one place long enough to get attached. Never stayed long enough for Uncle Mark's obligatory Christmas cards to catch up with her. Unlike Maggie, who had lived in the same city all her life and turned the Carter family Christmas into tradition.

Maggie and her husband, James, lived in an upscale

neighborhood of well-kept houses, clipped lawns and flower beds that wouldn't dare overflow their borders. On Devon Sreet dogs never marked the trees, stray cats found other porches to howl on, and stars always found a way to shine, even on overcast nights.

Yet the taint of murder followed Jo Beth into Maggie's house and refused to leave, even when Maggie served blueberry muffins and coffee, even when Maggie's husband kissed her as he left for his office and said, "You girls have a good time today." As if they were sixteen, as if they could wrap innocence around their shoulders like a shawl and pretend they'd never tasted Kentucky straight bourbon whiskey and that nobody in his right mind would leave them.

Of course, nobody would dream of leaving Maggie, who drank only on social occasions and then no more than half a glass.

"Have another muffin, Jo Beth."

"I don't want another muffin."

Maggie put it on her plate anyhow. "You're still having Snickers and potato chips for supper, aren't you?"

"No. Sometimes I have a Baby Ruth."

"I'm serious, Jo. You could use some nutritious meals."

"Don't try to save me, Mother Teresa." Didn't Maggie know? Mercy was easier to grant than to receive.

"One more thing and then I'll shut up."

"Your track record won't back that up."

"Probably not." Maggie topped off their coffee. "You shouldn't be staying in that ratty old trailer, either. You should stay here. The boys want to see you."

Jo Beth no longer belonged in a pink damask wing-back chair next to a marble-topped table where Maggie had arranged a crystal vase of freshly picked yellow roses that smelled like citrus.

This was a room of polished surfaces and gleaming mirrors, Oriental rugs and slick magazines neatly stacked, expensive earth-toned sofas and chairs with just the right number of pillows in yellow and hot pink and burnt orange and amber.

Except for new rugs and sofa, the room hadn't changed in all the years since Jo Beth had last seen it. Yet she felt as if she were in a foreign land, a place she'd once visited and had known by heart. The names of all the streets, the best café for croissants and coffee, the best shops for jeans that fit and dresses that didn't look as if they were all made for anorexic fifteen-year-olds.

Sweat collected along Jo Beth's upper lip and rolled down her cheeks. The only safe topic would be Maggie's sons, whom Jo Beth adored.

"How are the boys?"

"Great. Joel's hoping for a football scholarship to Auburn, and Bill wants to go into law enforcement."

Jo Beth anchored herself to her teacup to keep from saying *Don't let him strap on a badge and gun.*

"More coffee?" Maggie refilled the cup from the silver pot on the table between them. "All Bill's talked about since the ten-o'clock news is that poor dead girl they found up near the Tennessee line. Possible homicide, they said."

Jo Beth's teacup rattled against the saucer.

Maggie leaned forward, her body a question mark of concern. "What's wrong?"

Everything. Everything about Jo Beth's life was wrong and backward. Mothers and grandfathers don't leave little children; careers don't end when you're in your prime; dead girls don't land on your chest after you've turned tail and run. And they certainly don't die in June, which was the month of her daddy's death.

"I found her, Mags."

"Who?"

"The victim. In Sleepy Pines Campground. I'm the one who found her."

Maggie's hopes toppled like baby birds in the path of a hungry cat. She'd hoped this visit with Jo Beth would be different, that coming to Huntsville was a signal Jo Beth was finally willing to face her past and move forward.

And now this. Murder. Wide awake and dragging you under. Like some sleeping mad dog you'd tiptoed around for fear he'd rouse and chew off your leg, tear out your liver, swallow your heart whole.

Jo Beth had been a rookie cop when Maggie saw the first murder start gnawing at her. It had been a domestic disturbance call. The wife, who had assured Jo Beth her husband had not laid a hand on her, was beaten to death later that night.

Maggie had helped Jo Beth get through the tragedy with a six-pack of Hershey bars and a monster movie marathon. Then there had been a death at the Botanical Gardens, a shooting spree at Denny's, the tragedy of the kid at the mall—so many murders Maggie couldn't remember them all, so many she could no longer shore up Jo Beth's spirits with chocolate.

"You can't make everything and everybody turn out right," Maggie had told Jo Beth after the restaurant shooting.

"I'm a cop."

"Still, you can't save an entire city. Nobody can."

"I can try."

Helpless. Maggie had watched her friend attempt the

impossible, and then drown her failures in the bottle. When that wasn't enough, Jo Beth had run.

Over the years during the course of visits Maggie had made to little towns with names you could hardly find on the map, Peppertown, Mantachie, Frankstown, Blue Springs—wherever Jo Beth had flown—she'd tried different tactics. *James and I want you to move in with us.* Jo Beth had laughed at that one. *I'll go to AA meetings with you.* Jo Beth had changed the subject. *I found a wonderful clinic outside Nashville. Nobody will know you. James and I will pay.* Jo Beth's gracious *thanks but no* had been a small mercy for Maggie.

Even if she couldn't fix what was broken in Jo Beth, at least she had evidence that her friend had one little piece of herself to remind her of who she was. Daughter of a blue blood and granddaughter of a legend. Magnolias in her manners. But where was the steel in her backbone?

Sitting in her Victorian-style house in her pink and yellow living room that smelled of roses and the blueberry muffins she'd baked fresh that morning, Maggie thoughts veered to her reasons for never giving up on Jo Beth. When she'd been a successful detective, she was a good friend to Maggie, a second mother to Maggie's boys, a hero they could look up to.

But truth is not always noble, and the plain truth was that Maggie was afraid of losing her own hero. If Jo Beth went under, Maggie would have to give up her mantra. *Someday when I get up enough nerve, I'm going to be like Jo Beth—a gutsy, strong-willed woman who knows exactly who she is.*

Maggie wished she'd never mentioned the dead girl. She couldn't afford to be careless around a woman holding herself together in a net as thin and vulnerable as a cobweb.

She couldn't afford to knock another prop from under her hero.

She studied Jo Beth, the pale skin, the blue jeans hanging on her bones where rounded flesh used to be, the dark hair turning brittle from lack of proper nutrition, the face so thin her cheekbones looked like knives. Who would have believed she would come to this?

Still, Maggie refused to be daunted. After all, she was holding the ace. If anything could stitch the jagged pieces of Jo Beth back together, it was the rodeo.

"Let's not talk about it, Jo. Let's go to the rodeo."

Even to her own ears, Maggie sounded so perky she could brew coffee. She used to be a cheerleader. It wasn't rocket science, but it was a darned sight more useful to Maggie Carter. It had come in handy more than once when she'd needed to cajole a miffed husband, motivate reluctant sons, talk a stubborn third grader into doing his homework.

Jo Beth was not the kind of woman you could cajole, but thank goodness, she seemed relieved.

"I have my pickup truck."

"We'll go in my car." Maggie didn't smell alcohol, but the way Jo Beth looked, dazed and vulnerable, she wouldn't put it past her to find a way to get some.

When Jo Beth started to protest, Maggie said, "I insist."

Thank God she won. Thank God she didn't have to say, *Listen, I wouldn't get in the truck with you if my coattail was on fire and you knew the whereabouts of the only bucket of water.*

She had a husband to live for, children, students, even a hundred-pound chocolate Lab so dumb he still thought he was a lap dog.

Maggie needed to throw off the sense of doom and gloom. She needed revitalization. She needed speed. James said driving too fast was her only fault. She didn't consider it a failing, merely a way of finding her inner daredevil, a way of being just a bit like the Jo Beth she'd so admired when she'd first walked into Maggie's classroom. A cowgirl in the blue uniform, smart, witty and confident, lit from inside with her passion for being a cop.

And now, Maggie couldn't see a single ember.

She got behind the wheel of her black Lexus and proceeded to treat Memorial Parkway like it was her own personal Talladega Superspeedway, defying death at every turn, oblivious to the blistering stares and vulgar gestures of irate motorists. When she swung down the exit ramp and barreled toward the open-air arena where the rodeo was set up, Jo Beth stirred like somebody waking from a ten-year sleep. She smoothed the front of her chambray shirt, flicked a piece of dust from her boots and straightened her cowboy hat.

Was Jo Beth remembering the stories of rodeo daring and magic she'd told at the house on Devon Street, sitting at the dining room table eating rosemary chicken with new potatoes? Was she thinking of her grandfather, her rodeo history?

Before Jo Beth's life went so wrong, Maggie would have asked her. Now she watched her covertly, pleased to see her perking up, taking some pride in her appearance. It wasn't much, but it seemed like a start.

James had cautioned her not to get her hopes up. "You're expecting too much, too soon, Maggie," he'd told her. But what was the use of expecting too little? Or nothing at all?

"The first thing I want is a great big ole hot dog with all the trimmings." She grinned at Jo Beth. "How about you?"

"Are you trying to put some meat on my bones again?"

"No. Mine. James says my butt's getting too bony."

Jo Beth actually laughed. If you looked close enough, you could find all kinds of hope in laughter.

They could smell the rodeo from the parking lot, the earthy scent of high-strung horses and rough stock mingled with the excitement and fear of cowboys awaiting their turn in the ring with a plaited rope, a bit of rosin on their hands and two thousand pounds of bucking bull.

It was the last place you'd expect to be abuzz with news of murder.

I never expected to be entering the rodeo through the spectators' gate, hanging around with a woman called Jo Beth Dawson. I always entered through the chutes, alive and kicking, attached to the top of a snorting, bucking, wild-eyed bull. The only thing familiar is my name on the lips of everybody in the bleachers—but last time they was shouting it.

My name is flashing in lights on the scoreboard—In Memory of Pony Jones—while the whispers of it wash over the crowd in waves.

"Rodeo cowgirls will come and go, but there'll never be another Pony Jones."

I've always knew I was a crowd favorite, but I never knew they held me in such awe. Maybe some things are worth dying over. I just wish Daddy was here to see.

Jo Beth perks up considerable when we get in the middle of the rowdy rodeo crowd. I give the rebel yell, but don't nobody hear me except the good Lord and I can see him a-grinning. I guess He's done seen I've about reached my limit with this woman who ain't learned nothing from rodeo. Hell, if a bull throws you, you don't waller around in the dirt. You get up, dust off your britches and ride him again.

If I didn't know better, I'd argue with God about being some kind of spirit that can't leave this earth on account of some durned mysterious mission. But the thing is, I ain't sure whether it's God keeping me here or my own stubborn heart.

So we mosey on up the bleachers, Jo Beth's shoes making big sounds and mine nary a peep. We set down right next to the big-bosomed lady in a cheap cowboy hat who said there'd never be another me. Now she's calling me a "true American hero." Wiping her eyes with a lace-edged handkerchief, the yellow-haired lady is telling her beer-bellied, balding companion, "Can you imagine the courage it took for a little bitty thing like her to ride a bull?"

"Other women do, Louise."

Louise ruffles like a turkey in strut. "How many, Clarence? You tell me how many."

"Two dozen, maybe."

"Twelve, you old fool. And that's in the women's rodeos. On small bulls and riding with both hands. Plus, a helmet. She took on the entire testosterone-driven Professional Rodeo Cowboys Association. Challenged the men in their own territory then beat their socks off."

"If she'd stayed in the women's ring, she might not have been found murdered in the Sleepy Pines Campground."

"Shut up, Clarence. You don't have the sense God gave a billy goat."

Maggie leans around Jo Beth and tugs Louise's sleeve. "Pardon me. Did you say the girl who was found dead at Sleepy Pines is a rodeo cowgirl?"

"Not just any rodeo cowgirl, ma'am. Pony Jones. She's the first and only woman in the world to ride the big bulls against the men

on the professional circuits. Cops and reporters have been swarming all over this rodeo since eight o'clock. It'll be all over the news by noon."

Jo Beth shrinks into her seat till she's no bigger than a thimble. Now, I ain't never been no shrinking violet, but since it looks like I'm gonna be stuck here awhile, I try to find something me and Jo Beth can agree on. I can sorta see why she wouldn't want no word leaking about her part in my murder. Reporters are poking and prodding, interviewing folks who don't know nothing about me except my name. They'd drop the unreliable witnesses in a second if they knew who was setting on the third row trying to act invisible.

If I was in her shoes, I'd get up and beat the tar out of 'em, but that's just me.

The cop with shaggy brown hair and the innocent grin that don't fool me for a second, Sam Donovan they call him, spots Jo Beth and looks like he's fixing to head this way. Even across hundreds of people, she feels his intentions. Before I can get used to the feeling of being stuck up here in the bleachers instead of being in the pens putting on my chaps and sizing up the bulls, Jo Beth jumps up and hightails it to the bathroom with me running alongside her.

She don't care how many toes she steps on. I apologize, but don't nobody hear me.

Crowds waiting for public toilets is a surly lot, resentful they had to go off and pee while the fun is fixing to start up in the ring. Today Jo Beth pushes right past them and don't nary a one say a word.

She goes into the first available contraption and shuts the door then sets down on the pot without even pulling down her britches.

She can hide out here and brood all she wants to. I ain't fixing to *set here and miss the rodeo. Hell, I'd ruther be stuck to my body in the morgue than setting here in the toilet.*

The rodeo cowgirl in me tries to leave, but the motherless child in me holds fast to Jo Beth. Is it because she said that prayer when she found me in the woods? Ain't nobody ever said a prayer that beautiful over me, not even my daddy.

Is it because of her eyes? It's like some wounded animal is peering out.

And there's not a durned thing I can do about it. Hell, I can't even open a toilet door.

"God, how come I'm in this fix?"

I don't hear nothing except a big fat Heavenly Silence.

Though giving up ain't in my nature, I resign myself to the sound of exploding bowel movements in the potty next to ours instead of the roar of a rodeo crowd.

If I ever find a way to break the spell this wrecked woman holds over me, me and God is gonna have us a serious talk.

Five

Titus shaded his eyes and watched Jim "Buck" Buckley struggle up the mountain, mopping sweat and cussing every breath. Under different circumstances, Titus would have smiled. Now he sat in his rocking chair drinking ice water from a Mason jar, feeling nothing but the cool liquid going down his parched throat.

When Buck came even with the front porch, he pulled off his hat and mopped sweat. "Titus, when are you gonna get a telephone?"

"I ain't got no need for them modern contraptions. There's enough trouble in the world without bringin' it into your home."

"I hate to be the one bearing this news. I most surely do."

Titus showed no surprise. He'd read the signs. Still, he just wasn't ready to hear the Johnson County sheriff confirm what the mountain and the roses and the wolf had already told him.

Even Pony, herself.

"Come on the porch and set a spell while I get you some water. It's a long way up the mountain."

A man could get a pickup truck about three-quarters of the way before the road played out, turned to a dirt trail the fainthearted wouldn't dare navigate with a vehicle. Titus had meant to haul gravel in and finish the road, but after Morning Star died, he'd wanted nothing more to do with the outside world. The mountain was all he needed, the mountain and Pony and the memories.

He took his time fixing Buck's drink. The ice started to melt the minute it touched the sides of the Mason jar. Titus filled the jar to the rim with water from his artesian well, water already cooled by the mountain.

Then he stood there, caught in a net of time by the vision of Pony at six, her overalls rolled up to her knees, laughing as she stomped through the water, challenging him.

"You can't catch me, Daddy. I got wings."

Did Pony have wings now or was she a star? The good Lord might never see fit to let him know.

Titus walked back to the porch being careful not to spill a drop of water. Heartache was no cause to make a mess.

Buck took the Mason jar from him and held it to his hot face before he drank. Then he wiped his mouth with his sleeve.

"Titus, they found Pony. Up near the Tennessee line in Sleepy Pines Campground. She's dead."

"How?"

"You don't want to know."

"She's mine. I got a right."

"Somebody knocked the back of her head in. It was instant, Titus. She didn't suffer none."

Paralyzed by the evil that could kill a girl so full of life the sun didn't shine till she got out of bed, Titus sat very still. What was the use of talk now?

"You'll want to go to Huntsville. I'll take you, Titus."

Titus had a truck. It wasn't much, but it would still run if he took a notion to leave. But boulders didn't take notions. That's what he was, a lump of granite sitting in a rocking chair.

Buck drained his Mason jar and set it on the porch steps.

"I'll be going now, Titus. If you need me, give a holler."

Titus thought he nodded. But he might not have. He was dead, himself. He couldn't even feel his own unbloodied head.

He couldn't have told you how long he sat in his rocking chair. Dog came over and laid his big paws across Titus's work boots. God's creatures knew. They didn't need words. They didn't need funerals with fancy caskets and flowers that wilted on the grave. They didn't need engraved tombstones. They knew the stones were already there. In your heart.

After a while Titus got up and went into his house. He selected the .44 Magnum from the gun rack over his stone fireplace and walked straight to the pasture. Ole Rocky Top saw him coming. The two-thousand-pound bull lumbered up from his dust wallow and headed Titus's way, taking his time at first then picking up speed, coming full tilt, snorting and bucking like a yearling instead of a shaggy, mean-assed old critter past his prime.

Titus had rescued him when Pony was thirteen.

Now he was going to kill him.

The bull stopped three feet from Titus, kicking up clumps of sod and sweet summer grass then standing there with his nostrils flared, nothing but a split-rail fence separating them.

Titus raised his rifle, caught the bull in his sights, felt the cold metal against his trigger finger.

His vision blurred. When he blinked he saw Pony racing across the pasture on Rocky Top's back, riding a bull yearling so mean his owner was going to take him behind the barn and shoot him, till Titus heard about it and went down the mountain with an offer.

"I'll give you ten bucks for the yearlin'."

"Hell, he ain't fit for nothin' except dog meat."

"Fifteen."

"What you want with 'em?"

"Twenty."

"Take the damned yearlin'. But don't say I didn't warn you."

Some warnings were worth paying attention to. Some warnings settled in your heart like tea leaves, steeping for years till they finally spewed forth, staining everything in their path.

It was Titus who had romanticized the rodeo to a little girl who thought her daddy was God's right-hand man. It was Titus who plaited her first rope and showed her how to hold on tight. It was Titus who taught her that riding the bulls was not about strength and stamina but about balance and heart.

His heart cracked in two then, like an ice floe breaking apart in a cold river.

Through his sights, he saw the bull get down on one knee and lower his head. He saw the teardrop roll down the bull's face. Or was it his own tears? Was it his own agony he saw reflected in the mean-assed old critter Pony had conquered, then tamed?

Titus and the bull stared at each other, their tumultuous energy rising upward till the air became electric. Songs died in the throats of mockingbirds, tree trunks turned the color of old bones, and summer leaves loosed their hold to drift toward the forest floor.

On the ridge beyond the pasture, the Arctic wolf howled. The air shimmered, crackled, then became so brilliant it nearly blinded Titus.

High on the hills he saw a shadow, a hint of a form. Then the charged air turned the vision solid. It was Pony, flying toward Titus and the bull. Her braid streamed out behind her, and everywhere her red boots touched, she left footprints of sorrow.

The bull lifted his head toward the slip of a girl who had held onto his back no matter how he spun and bucked and twisted. He lowered his head once more, his tears flowing blood red. And where they drenched the pawed-up earth, a Cherokee rose sprang to life.

Titus didn't question whether he was being blessed or cursed. He simply waited.

Bit by bit it all dissolved—the wolf, the rose, the bull's tears and Pony herself, vanished in a twinkling as if she'd been made up of stars, fireflies, regret.

Titus lowered his rifle. If old Rocky Top had killed Pony, then so had he.

He walked back to the house under a sun so unforgiving it was fire and brimstone pouring down on his head.

Jo Beth had never considered herself a coward until she finally emerged from flight mode and discovered herself holed up in a toilet at the rodeo. She was vaguely aware that she'd been there for some time, probably ten minutes or more, while irate bathroom desperados took turns pounding on the potty door.

She was glad Clint Dawson couldn't see her now. She was glad he hadn't been around to watch her turn into the kind of woman who ran so hard and so fast she left pieces of her history scattered in the dust like unwanted confetti after a Mardi Gras parade. She'd been running so long there was not much left now except faint outlines of where she'd come from and who she'd been.

"Bathroom hog! Get out of there!" A woman wearing yellow boots the size of river barges rattled the door hard enough to pop the lock and push open the door. "You've been on the toilet long enough."

Jo Beth kicked the door shut again and nearly lost her balance. Flailing her arms to keep from falling, she heard the voice of her grandfather echoing around the curves and ricocheting off the ceiling.

They said the spirit of the American cowboy was dying, but by George I showed them. I rounded up every ragtag bunch of them who loved roping and riding so much they were pitting their skills against each other in whatever corral or pasture they could find.

Clint Dawson's voice was so real, Jo Beth halfway expected to open the toilet door and see him standing outside.

They first called us The Cowboy Turtle Association because we'd been so slow seeing our own potential. But the point is, we saw it. That was in 1936, and look at us now. Nine thousand cowboy members riding in more than six hundred fifty sanctioned rodeos every year with more than twenty-three million folks watching.

Don't you ever let anybody tell you you're not good enough or smart enough or strong enough. You've got winning in your blood, Jo Beth.

The woman in yellow boots battered the door again. "Are you coming out, or do I have to break in there and drag you out?"

Jo Beth flung back the toilet door with the force of a level 5 hurricane. "Diarrhea!" she roared, then marched out of the toilet ignoring the accusing stares. Somewhere, Clint Dawson was applauding.

Maybe even a young hero named Pony Jones.

Full of adrenaline-fueled anger and rodeo moxie, she slammed into a wall of unrelenting sun and unmovable cop.

Sam Donovan smelled faintly of the Old Spice he used to cover his more distinctive scents—the sharp sweat from an Alabama summer sun, his perpetual wad of Juicy Fruit, the underlying hint of Irish Spring soap. A scent as familiar to her as her own skin.

Before she became a pariah and he the enemy, she'd spend hours with him on stakeout or driving the city searching for clues. Or sometimes even in her own living room in the middle of the night, listening to Sam talk about his shaky marriage, his falling-apart dreams, his impossibly complex wife. Jo Beth would never notice her own marriage crumbling around her.

Or maybe she didn't have the energy. Bent crooked under the weight of Sam's problems, the whispers about her drinking and the souls collecting on her like wolves around the bones of the dead, she hadn't uttered a word in her defense when Roger walked out the door with his three-piece suits and his briefcase, flinging accusations. *Jo Beth, I can't compete with Jack Daniel's and Sam Donovan.*

It was not until she'd been put on permanent suspension that Jo Beth realized the partner she'd thought would take a bullet for her wouldn't even try to save her from the bottle.

The police force created partnerships like no other, two people who laid their lives on the line for each other every day. He was the only one she'd have allowed to hustle her off to Alcoholics Anonymous. Why hadn't he?

Planted in front of her, shifting his gum from one side of his mouth to the other, he was little changed from the partner who was once her only chance for salvation. Hometown boy made good, local football hero turned cop trying to impress a town he would never leave and a wife he thought he could convince to stay, Sam still had the shine of idealism in his eyes.

He was the kind of man who put a woman on a pedestal, then stood with sword drawn against anybody who dared hint she was flawed. Sam couldn't afford to drag her to AA. Heroes had to have perfect partners.

If she had half the spunk of her youth, she'd bulldoze right past him.

"Hiding, Jo Beth?"

"Loss of bladder control." She started around him but he sidestepped, an avalanche of wide chest, muscled arms and linebacker's legs.

"What brings you to the rodeo?"

"I'm just another spectator, Sam."

Jo Beth figured if she held onto her tough side, Sam wouldn't notice how close she was to snapping. She almost had once, right after she'd been drummed out of the police department. The only thing that stopped her was the awful thought that nobody was there to care if she killed herself.

"Right after finding a dead rodeo cowgirl this is the first place you come? I don't buy it."

"I'm not selling anything, Sam. I've already told you everything I know."

He unwrapped another stick of Juicy Fruit and stuck it in his mouth. "A little piece of advice, Jo Beth. Don't try to prove a point by messing around in this case."

"Screw you, Sam. You can take this case and stick it where it never snows."

"You sure about that, Jo Beth?"

Sam looked at her the way he used to when she'd stumble to her door after he'd pounded his knuckles raw. "I called in sick," she'd tell him, and he'd usher her into the kitchen and put on a pot of coffee.

Once she'd mistaken that look for compassion. Not anymore. Hindsight is a hard teacher. The look held an edge of *poor slob, ought to know better* and *thank God it's you and not me.* It was a double-edged look that would slice you to pieces if you got too close.

Jo Beth didn't plan to ever get too close again. Not with Sam. Not with Maggie. Not with a man who promised *till death do us part* when he really meant *till the going gets rough.* And sure as hell not with a dead rodeo cowgirl named Pony Jones.

Furthermore, Jo Beth was going to throw away the Juicy Fruit gum in her purse and replace it with Dentine or Wrigley's spearmint. Anything that didn't remind her of Sam.

He had her by a good three-quarters of a foot, but Jo Beth stuck out her chin and glared at him, giving the impression she was looking straight into his eyes.

Still, she was paralyzed by his question. *You sure about that, Jo Beth?*

In a world where rodeo heroes were felled by blunt objects, teenage boys were driven by despair to jump over mall railings, and Arctic wolves were sighted in Alabama, how could you be sure of anything?

"Sure enough that I'm going to walk away and dare you to stop me, Sam."

He wouldn't even try. Short of physical violence, he couldn't. He didn't have anything on her.

She barreled forward and he stepped aside, but only at the last possible minute, only after she wondered if she'd have to snap her knee into his groin.

As he watched Jo Beth storm off, Sam studied her. She'd once been a striking woman, not beautiful in the classic sense, but the kind of woman you couldn't help but notice. And once you did, it was hard to look away. Maybe it was her cheekbones, sharp and arresting, giving her the kind of face that would have looked good on magazine covers. Maybe it was her eyes, always alive, shooting sparks of some kind, rage, joy, passion. Jo Beth's eyes were her soul.

The cheekbones were still there. The face too, though it had lost its softness, its lovely *you-can-come-close* appeal. But it was the eyes that bothered Sam most. The fire was gone and in its place the resignation of somebody who had just been told cancer was eating her alive and she had six days to live.

Sam tried to remember the precise moment everything had started falling apart for Jo Beth. He wouldn't get on a witness stand and swear to it, but he thought it was when that fourteen-year-old kid had nosedived over the railing at the mall.

Jo Beth told Sam it was her fault. But she hadn't cried, hadn't fallen to pieces.

And that's what had fooled Sam, fooled them all. They'd thought she was a tough cop, tough enough to wade through blood and gore then go home at night, wash it off and go to bed. Sure, she'd have a nightmare or two. That's what you did. Then you got up, hit the streets and forgot about it till the next case got to you.

Sam covered for her, wrote in the report that he thought the kid had a gun too. *Anybody can make a mistake.* That's what he told her, what he believed.

For a while he thought she believed it too. Then he'd noticed something so small it almost escaped him. Jo Beth stopped wearing her cowboy boots.

Before the kid tried to fly, she'd stood out from the rest of them. It was the boots, but something else, too, something he couldn't quite put his finger on. Like something vital was glowing inside her, something necessary to her survival.

Sam wasn't much at description. He could tell you the color of a perp's hair, his height, weight, even the color of his eyes. But he didn't fling around words like *borderline personality, angst-driven, psychopath.* He didn't go digging around in psyches. There were too many sickos out there. He figured if you dug too deep in the muck, you could get stuck and never find your way out.

Sam's Juicy Fruit tasted like straw. He threw it in the garbage can, then peeled a fresh stick and started over.

He didn't have time to stand in front of the toilets all day and speculate about Jo Beth Dawson's psyche. Somewhere in this bunch of cowboys was somebody who knew why Pony Jones was murdered. Maybe even somebody who had hated that little girl enough to kill her. A little slip of a girl who'd ridden the bulls.

That took guts.

Sam headed toward the bull pens, weaving his way through the painted ponies, the Cherokee dancers, the city slicker cowboys in their polished boots and new Stetsons, the real McCoy in their well-worn Justins and their battered hats. There was even a group of teenage girls, all dressed in red cowboy shirts and Justin boots, their hair dyed jet-black, waving signs reading *Get Pony's Killer*, while they chanted, "Pony Jones! Pon-ee Jones! Pooon-eee Jones!"

Death had immortalized if not sanctified Pony Jones. Already the dead cowgirl hero had a cult following.

The opening parade was over and Mark Dawson was standing outside the rodeo ring, his Western suit and hand-tooled boots reeking of money. Obviously he was waiting to be announced.

It was big doings when the son of the legendary father of rodeo showed up to bestow his blessing. Too bad his well-publicized appearance would be overshadowed by murder.

Dawson looked too frail to bear the weight of his daddy's big reputation. Too much show and not enough substance. Or maybe that was just Sam being prejudiced. After Dawson's well-publicized shunning of his niece when Jo Beth got booted off the force, Sam had never had any use for the man. Let the press and the public fawn over Dawson. Sam would not be among his admirers. Not that he was without blame. But he liked to think his reasons were more admirable.

He was not the only one who had seen Dawson. A Native American man as old as God was standing on the fringes of the crowd watching Dawson in a way that put all Sam's senses on alert. There was something personal in the old man's unflinching stare, something worth looking into.

Heading his way, Sam reached into his pocket for a fresh stick of Juicy Fruit. When he looked up again, all he saw was a young cowboy—twenty or so, Sam would guess—dusty boots, frayed bandana and big attitude.

Sam strode in his direction. "An old man was here a minute ago. Native American. Silver hair. Denim jacket. A watch with a big turquoise band. Did you see him?"

"Didn't see him. Don't know him. Don't want to know him."

Sam reached for another stick of Juicy Fruit. Murder made everybody suspicious and cranky. Sometimes he wished he drove a school bus. Had a postal route. Sliced sirloin at a meat market. Anything except digging information out of smart-mouthed jackasses and working on a murder case where Jo Beth Dawson had popped up from the bowels of hell.

Six

Jo Beth scanned the crowd, looking for reporters, looking for cameras and microphones, looking for a reason to run. But the TV cameras and press corps had turned toward the commanding presence in the center of the rodeo ring. In spite of his white hair and deeply lined face, the aging cowboy was still fit. Uncle Mark, heir to the Dawson legend, chronicler of the family history and keeper of the family pride.

She hadn't seen him in years, but she wasn't holding her breath for a family reunion. After her grandfather died, Uncle Mark had made a token effort to fill the void. He'd send her birthday gifts, include her and her mother in his annual Fourth of July barbecue blowouts, and invite her to the ranch to ride horses, but never for more than a three-day visit.

As soon as Jo Beth was drummed out of the Hunstville PD, he'd cut his contact down to Christmas cards. For Mark Dawson, public disgrace was an unforgivable offense.

When her uncle stepped to the center of the ring, Jo Beth felt a vague sense of nostalgia and a burning thirst for strong drink. She clenched her fists till nails bit flesh. She wasn't about to let herself believe in the possibility of Thanksgiving dinner with family. And she certainly wasn't going to ruin her reunion with Maggie.

"The rodeo world is saddened by the tragic loss of one of our own." Mark Dawson's voice was amplified by a wireless microphone. "Before the competition begins, let's observe a moment of silent prayer for Pony Jones."

Jo Beth was probably the only person in the audience who knew his grief-stricken sincerity was carefully orchestrated. Everything he did was for Dawson image.

Her instincts told Jo Beth to leave, to call Maggie on her cell phone then hightail it from this place of swirling dust and faded dreams. The last thing she wanted was for Uncle Mark to see her looking like something the cat had dragged in and left on his doorstep.

Still, she was unable to move as her uncle left the ring, spellbound as he spotted her. Mark Dawson headed her way and Jo Beth felt the tug of history, a longing for Fourth of July picnics with her daddy and Uncle Mark and her granddaddy at the grill, her mother in the kitchen frying green tomatoes.

When he waved the reporters off, Jo Beth pulled the hard shell of reality around herself and waited. He stopped a good three feet from her and nodded.

"Jo Beth."

"Uncle Mark." Her politeness, thin as an eggshell, cracked under his dark scrutiny. "I'm surprised you know me. Especially with the press hanging around."

"I sent them away to spare you."

"And I'm the purple Easter bunny."

"I see age has not improved your manners. I don't know why I even bother with you."

"Did I miss something? Were you at the hospital last year when I had pneumonia? How about two years ago when I threw myself a surprise birthday party?" She felt no wicked glee at his obvious discomfort, only an expansion of the void where her soul used to be. "If I recall, nobody came except Johnny Walker and Jack Daniel."

"Drag yourself into the gutter, Jo Beth. Just don't try to drag me with you."

She watched her uncle walk off stiff-backed, her eyes smarting and her throat parched. If she had her truck, she'd head straight to the nearest liquor store. Fighting tears and demons, Jo Beth caught the tiny hope of rodeo and held on. Maggie was waiting for her. She found herself drawn back toward the bleachers, pulled by nostalgia and history, goaded by murder and the memory of a young cowgirl covered with roses.

As Jo Beth made her way up to where Maggie sat enthralled, another soul wound around her so tightly it might be her own skin. Her face flushing, she could feel the weight of the soul on her chest. And yet she felt strangely buoyant too, as if this particular soul were trying to pull her out of herself.

Jo Beth.

A person who hadn't grown up with a grandfather steeped in legend might have said the wind was picking up, sighing her name. But she knew better. Jo Beth was not alone.

"What took you so long?" Maggie handed Jo Beth a bag of popcorn, tough from too much salt and not enough butter. "I was getting worried."

"I was hiding." Jo Beth sat down, careful to leave room for her invisible guest.

"From what?"

"Uncle Mark. And Sam." Jo Beth nodded toward her former partner, sitting on the opposite side of the ring, front and center, his boots propped on the fence railing, his eyes scanning the crowd. She had the eerie sense her tagalong spirit also turned in that direction.

"If Sam's harassing you, I'll have James call the chief of police. Shoot, I'll call him myself." Maggie's mouth tightened. "After what he did to you, he ought to be shot."

"He's good at his job, Mags. The right one left and the right one stayed behind."

"Bullshit, Jo. I'd like to slap his face. And your uncle too."

The idea of pretty little Maggie Carter, tenderhearted wife, mother, and friend, slapping anybody's face was enough to make Jo Beth smile.

"When's the last time he called you?"

"Who?"

"Your uncle."

Jo Beth shrugged. "We don't have anything to talk about."

When Kay Eagle entered the ring, Maggie dropped her questions to jump up, whistling and stomping. Relieved, Jo Beth consulted her program. Bull riding was up next.

Kay was the last of the contenders in saddle bronc riding and a huge threat to current champion Brick Farraday. She was the first woman ever to compete against the men in saddle bronc riding, a sport considered too dangerous because of the possibility of getting caught in the stirrups and dragged to death. Society tended to make rules in the vain belief they were protecting women from brutal death.

After Kay broke the men's sacred hold on saddle bronc riding in 2000, the stage was set for Pony Jones to turn men's professional rodeo upside down a few years later in a dusty ring in San Antonio, Texas.

When Kay Eagle left the ring and the first bull stormed into the chute, Jo Beth flashed back to the arena in Texas. Suddenly she understood why she'd thought she knew the victim in Sleepy Pines Campground. On a day so hot mockingbirds refused to sing and dogs wouldn't bark, even if burglars were in the kitchen stealing the silver, Jo Beth had witnessed Pony's historic ride. Six years ago, standing in that rowdy Texas crowd, stomping and yelling and clapping till her palms were blistered, she'd watched Pony Jones turn courage into a kite. And every spectator there had soared briefly in its tailwinds.

Pony had covered her bull for the full eight seconds. During those adrenaline-pumping, heart-thumping seconds, Jo Beth believed in miracles. She believed if she ran fast enough and traveled far enough, she could leave pieces of herself behind and emerge somewhere on the other side of her sordid history, free.

Afterward, she'd thought about writing a letter to Pony, had even composed it in her mind. *Thank you for making me see life's possibilities.* Like many good intentions, it had fallen prey to reality even before she left the rodeo arena.

Now, while she sat beside Maggie in the stands, a memory of Pony's cold, young face under the roses, devoid of all animation, hit Jo Beth hard. Pony was Bob and the red-haired kid multiplied a thousandfold by a mystical connection Jo Beth couldn't explain. Loss struck without warning, bent her double, and she lowered her head to her hands.

"Jo?" Maggie put a hand on her shoulder. "What's wrong? Are you sick?"

"I'm okay."

"You want to leave?"

"No. I'm fine."

"You're sure?"

"Let it go, Mags."

A little line of concern appeared between Maggie's eyes. Still, she turned her attention back to the chute where a massive black bull pawed and snorted.

The air shimmered then turned misty, and on the mists came the scent of roses. Jo Beth felt a rushing like the beat of a thousand wings, and Pony Jones burst from the chute, her smile as wide as the Mississippi. Slight and sassy, she stormed into the ring on a bull so mean high school bullies hid in their mama's closets and songbirds fell from trees.

The moment was surreal, a double exposure of Pony as she'd spun magic in Austin, Texas, and the spirit of Pony, stealing the crowd's heart in Huntsville—a petite cowgirl with a long black braid and tiny red boots whirling around the ring on a two-thousand-pound bull, one hand on the plaited rope, one hand waving the air.

Visions of blood and gore and crushed small bones pulled the crowd to its feet. And there they stayed. Counting down the seconds. Eight, seven, six. *Impossible. She was still aloft.* Five, four. *Would she fall?* Three, two. *Would she die?*

One.

And Pony still rode while the thunder of approval rolled through the crowd and the sky wept roses.

Three rows below Jo Beth, a group of young girls wearing red cowboy boots stood up, their shout of *Pony, Pon-y, we want Pon-eee* rising above the crowd.

In the rodeo ring, Pony looked up at Jo Beth and winked. And then she was swallowed up by mists, leaving behind an empty feeling in Jo Beth and the lingering scent of roses.

"Good grief!" Maggie turned a flushed face to Jo Beth. "I thought I'd pee in my pants. The way that cowboy stayed on the bull was nothing short of a miracle."

For Jo Beth, the miracle was not that a seasoned bull rider kept his seat at a rodeo in Huntsville, Alabama. It was that a young girl named Pony Jones had a spirit so fierce she could ride the bulls even after she was dead.

The minute Jo Beth sets back down by her friend I fly off like a canary shot from a cannon, boots over butt, as out of control as a two-second bucking bull being chased by a rodeo clown, wondering what in the world's going on.

If I can't figure out where I'm headed, I'm fixing to be skewered by the flagpole. Right before I'm flying up there with Old Glory, I see what's below me and it all becomes clear.

Sometimes the heart's longing is so strong you simply take flight.

Grinning, I set myself down in the rough stock holding area. So light I don't even leave footprints.

"Buckin' Billy" Rakestraw is leaning against the railing with a wad of Garrett snuff poking out his lower lip. That ain't his real name. It's Hubert, which don't sound too good if you're a bull rider and a big crowd is shouting your name. He changed it to Billy. When I come along and he found out I was trying to overturn the notion that a cowgirl couldn't do nothing much but barrel racing in the men's professional rodeos, he started calling hisself Buckin' Billy and doing everything in his power to keep me from riding the bulls. Held press conferences and rallies and I don't know what all. Even tried to bribe a few folks, I'm told.

Not that it made a whit of difference. I busted the rules wide open and beat his pants off.

Course, that ain't nothing new. He's from Johnson City, Tennessee, and every time I come down Doe Mountain I'd stomp him into a dishrag. Not because I'm mean and enjoy fighting. Shoot, I'm a girl, no matter what some folks might say. I didn't want to whip no boy's ass. I could tolerate him calling me "baggy britches" and "ignert red neck dropout," but when he called me and my daddy "pore white trash," I lit into him. Hit 'em so hard I chipped his front tooth.

He ain't never had it fixed. When he spits, the tobacco squirts through the gap with a little pop that's earned him the nickname "Old Fizzle Spit."

Buckin' Billy ain't had no use for me since. It got worse when I took the bull riding championship away from him.

Still, there's a unspoken code of courtesy among us bull riders. I sashay over to speak to him.

When I walk around a rodeo, I like to stomp so the sound of my boots makes me seem bigger. I try stomping over to Billy but my feet don't even touch the ground.

I stop just short of ramming right into him, so close I can see his beard stubble. Another tactic of mine. I like to show the cowboys I ain't afraid of their macho posturing and bloated self-esteem. I ain't afraid of nothing.

"How you doin', Billy?"

He looks right through me and spits. A big wad of tobacco sails outta his mouth and lands on my boots. I'm fixing to slap him into next Sunday over that when I notice the glob hadn't even left a stain. Nary a sign.

"*I reckon that's one way of sayin' hello,*" *I tell him, but he ain't paying me no more attention then if I was a ghost.*

Which I reckon I am. It's beginning to have its advantages, though. Seems like I can go about anywhere my heart desires in the blink of a eye. The thing I ain't figured out yet is what is this job that's keeping me from being in the Great Beyond with my mother?

Another thing I ain't figured out is how come I ain't got no clue what happened to me? But I ain't never been one to fret over God's mysteries. That's how come they're called mysteries. If we knew everything what'd be the use of a Higher Power? Of miracles?

Instead of fretting, I'm rejoicing that I'm at the rodeo. Seems like in my present form I can do 'bout anything I please, and ain't nobody gonna stop me. At the moment, that just so happens to be riding a bull. That's what I come to Huntsville for in the first place, and I don't aim to be deprived of the pleasure.

I pick me out the meanest one in the pen, Devil at the Crossroads, a bull so ornery ain't nobody ever stayed on his back more than two seconds, a big ole black monster so dangerous his tail has shaped itself into a pitchfork.

I step right through the fence, plant my boots in the dirt and look him straight in the eye. "I been waiting to make your acquaintance," I tell him, and he gives me this look that says he's been waiting to make mine, too.

"Me and you's got lot'a entertainin' to do today."

He bows down and I leap onto his back. Now, I guess you're thinking ain't no bucking bull fixing to do such a thing, but what most folks don't know is that God's critters ain't here for us to conquer and tame. They're here to teach us. We all live in this universe together, and if we can't get along with God's lower critters, how do we expect to get along with each other?

I bust into the ring astraddle the snortin'est, buckin'est bull at the rodeo.

But I'm also standing by the holding pen watching Sam Donovan approach Buckin' Billy. I'm on Doe Mountain watching my daddy fill the automatic dog feeder then load his .44 Magnum and his 12 gauge shotgun into the Chevy pickup he calls Ole Blue Eyes after his favorite singer, though there ain't more than a few patches of blue paint left on it. I'm on the winding road that leads off the mountain, standing in the shroud of mist and the glare of headlights, tears running into my mouth as I open it to tell my daddy I love him but I'm done here. I want to leave this earth so I can be with my mama.

That's what I want him to hear, but I can tell by the set of his jaw he ain't hearing that a'tall. He's hearing the sound of his child weeping in the rain.

Seven

Maggie loved watching her husband put on his tie. Any other morning she'd have been content to simply lie against the pillows admiring the skillful, efficient movements of his hands, the way his forehead puckered in concentration, the lock of sandy-colored hair that fell across his forehead.

Not today, though. Not since the tumultuous wind that was Jo Beth had blown into Huntsville rearranging everything in its path. Instead of throwing back the covers, putting her arms around James and leaning her head against his strong back as she usually did in the still hours when the morning was fresh and the day uncluttered, she sat on her bed feeling upside down. Like she was caught on the whirling blades of a windmill and couldn't get off.

"Roger needs to see her."

"He's seeing somebody else, Maggie. That's not going to happen."

"You don't forget eight years of marriage. For Pete's sake, James. Just ask him."

"Then what, Maggie? You think Jo Beth is going to listen to him any more than she listens to you?"

James was right. She knew he was. But a stubborn heart has

no logic, and if there was one true thing Maggie Carter knew about herself, it's that she had a stubborn heart.

"Please. Just ask, that's all."

When James sighed, she knew she'd won. "All right. But if he says no, that's it." He got his wallet and cell phone off the chest of drawers, then walked over and kissed her. "Promise me, Mags. Roger says no and you'll back off."

She nodded, but it wasn't the same as a promise, so she wasn't going to feel guilty about it.

When Sam Donovan walked through the double front doors of the station, he saw the man sitting on the hard chair in what the cops referred to as the "cesspool." Ordinarily, he'd have paid no particular attention. He'd have dismissed him as just another poor slob waiting to post bail for a wayward son or to plead for a daughter who "isn't like that," never mind that she was nabbed on the streets in her come-hither clothes trying to solicit a police officer.

But there was something about the man that made it impossible not to stare. Maybe it was his face, sharp angles and craggy lines that reminded you of a mountain. Maybe it was the eyes, blue and deep and cold as chunks of glittering, glacial ice.

On closer inspection, Sam didn't have to speculate on the magnetic aura that surrounded this stranger. Something unspeakable clung to him like a shroud, fitted his muscled shoulders and lean, rangy frame like he'd been measured for it. Grief? Danger? Vengeance?

Sam couldn't tell, and he didn't have the time to find out. He sensed that this man would show you nothing, reveal no emotion that would give you a clue to his inner workings.

Sam hurried past the man, winked at Barb, the receptionist with the great legs and the overbite, grabbed a cup of coffee so strong it could jog to Louisiana and back, then made his way to his piled-to-the-ceiling desk.

This Pony Jones case was killing him. No suspects, no leads, no inside tips floating around on the street. The longer she was dead, the colder the trail would get.

And the more time he'd have to spend wrestling with his conscience because Jo Beth Dawson was still in town.

Picking up his notes from yesterday's rodeo, Sam leaned back in his chair and began to read. Buckin' Billy had been forthcoming, if you believed everything he said. Sam didn't. Still, he had nothing on him except possible motive. Pony Jones had stolen his championship title. It made him a suspect, but was not even close to cause for arrest.

Same with Steve Carlson and Jimbo Mabens. Both bull riders. Both fallen in the national ratings because of a woman who had the audacity to ride the bulls against the men.

You couldn't pin murder on a man because of rodeo ratings.

"You the one found Pony Jones?"

Sam spilled coffee on his notes and nearly tipped over his chair. The stranger from the reception room was standing over him, and Sam hadn't even heard him coming. How did he get past that line of tight-assed dragons whose job it was to keep order out front?

"Who wants to know?"

"Her daddy."

That's all Sam needed. A grieving father falling apart in his office. A mountain man demanding answers.

Up close, Sam noticed the large callused hands, the longish graying hair, thinning on top, showing a glimpse of scalp parched by the sun, the weathered face etched like a map of what men in wagon trains had called the Northwest Territories.

Sam's now-defected wife used to describe her movie heroes as having "sun-bronzed skin," which had sounded romantic to Lana. He wished she could see this man. She'd change her tune. Sun-bronzed was not the way you'd describe him. Leather, maybe. A wadded-up piece of rawhide.

And there sure as hell was nothing romantic about him. If he was Pony's father, he must have sired her by Immaculate Conception.

"Mr. Jones . . ."

"Titus."

"Won't you sit down?"

"I ain't got time. I come to get Pony."

Sam considered himself an astute judge of character. The man looming over him wouldn't be bothered with rules and regulations. He probably wouldn't even bother with the finer points of law.

"Her body hasn't been released yet."

"Pony belongs on the mountain."

"I understand your need for closure. But I'm sure you understand we can't release her till the forensic team has had sufficient time to do their job. Every shred of evidence is crucial in catching her killer."

Titus Jones bowed his head like a man taking a heavy blow, like a man seeking strength in the scuff-marked tiles at his feet.

"Can I get you some coffee?"

"I want to see 'er."

"Titus . . ."

"Lieutenant Donovan, I *aim* to see 'er."

The man's chipped-ice eyes told Sam arguing would be no

use. Titus Jones was fully capable of standing in that same spot for hours, days, weeks if necessary, till he could see for himself what one moment of blind, careless rage had done to his daughter.

Wouldn't Sam do the same if he had a daughter? Probably. Lana had always thought too much of her figure to risk a sagging after-birth belly. And Sam hadn't argued. He didn't have enough paternal urges to make arguing worth the price, to risk her wrath or worse.

The worst had happened anyway.

It made Sam tired just to think about it, so he seldom did. Except on days like today. Days when he was called upon to lead a grieving father to the morgue then stand beside him while the sheet was pulled back from his daughter's cold face.

Sam didn't know what he'd expected, but not this, not a man who didn't reveal by one ticking jaw muscle, one flicker of his hard blue eyes what he was thinking.

They stood that way for a long time, side by side in front of the gurney that held the remains of Pony Jones, Sam beginning to sweat and uncertain what to say, Titus not saying a word.

What was he thinking? What was he feeling?

They stood there so long the clock on the wall sounded like a ticking time bomb. Sam wiped his face with his sleeve and Titus didn't move.

Was he silently cursing his daughter's killer? Was he weeping inside? Was he praying?

Finally Titus Jones nodded then turned around and left the room before they re-covered his daughter's face, walking fast, his large boots sounding like gunshot on the hard tiles.

Sam was glad to see him go. He was headed toward the door himself before he realized Titus Jones had not asked who killed his daughter. He hadn't asked about suspects or arrests. He hadn't even asked if they were close to solving the case.

"Wait," Sam called after him.

But he was too late. Titus Jones had already climbed into an old rattletrap pickup truck and was pulling out of the parking lot.

Sam knew then, understood with the same clarity he'd had when he'd gone home from work and found Lana's closet empty. Titus Jones had no interest in how the cops were trying to solve the crime: he was going to hunt down the man who had murdered his daughter.

God help the killer.

Eight

Titus had driven all night in the rain—four hundred miles from the top of his isolated mountain in Tennessee to Huntsville, Alabama, without stopping. Not even to pee. Though the rodeo circuit had carried Pony as far west as Arizona and as far north as Boston, he'd seen fit to leave the haven of Doe Mountain only twice after Morning Star died. The first time to see his daughter ride her first big bull in the men's professional rodeo, and now to see what it had done to her.

Pony's white face and small, still body on that cold slab in the morgue haunted him as he drove away from the Huntsville Police Department, would have blinded him if he'd let it. But grief would have to wait. Somewhere out there was the coward who'd knocked a hole in the back of his daughter's head. He aimed to find him and kill him. Period.

How he'd do that, Titus didn't want to think on. He was not a violent man. He honored all living things. Though he owned weapons, he didn't hunt for sport, didn't hunt out of season. He only killed what he needed to put meat on the table.

And now he was planning to kill for another reason. Anybody who would snuff out the life of a shining star like Pony didn't deserve to be on this earth.

Titus knew the law. Up to now, he'd always abided by it. If what he planned to do broke the law, so be it. Some folks would call it murder. He called it justice.

But justice would have to wait. He was no longer a young whippersnapper who could ride bulls all day then court the most beautiful dancer at the rodeo all night. He had to rest. He had to plan.

Spotting the La Quinta Inn just past the mall, Titus pulled his truck under the portico and shook himself to clear his head, then walked into the lobby and asked for a room.

A small TV attached to the wall was turned on low behind an attractive middle-aged woman with patent-leather skin and a friendly smile.

"And which credit card will you be using?"

"I'm usin' cash."

Her smile wavered a bit and Titus almost smiled. He knew he didn't look like the kind of man with enough cash in his pocket to pay for a sixty-dollar-a-night motel room. He didn't even look like the kind of man with enough cash in his pocket to pay for a Coca-Cola and a Tootsie Roll.

Still, she scribbled in her books and rummaged around till she found a piece of plastic that passed for a key.

"Are you here for the rodeo?" She passed the key to him.

"You might say that."

On the TV screen behind her a commercial for Dial soap faded and a young red-haired woman with a painted-on face stood in front of an old silver camper-trailer talking into her microphone. But it was not the woman who captured Titus's attention: it was the sign in the background. Sleepy Pines Campground.

A female reporter was saying, "We're here today where the

body of Pony Jones, a young cowgirl who made rodeo history, was found."

Titus studied the scene behind the reporter. Rustic fence, tall trees, mostly pines, and thick undergrowth gave way to a patch of earth surrounded by yellow crime tape.

"Whether she was murdered here or brought here later by her killer, we don't know. But sources say her body was discovered by the woman in this Silver Streak Sabre."

Urgency exploded in Titus like a shattered glass picture window. The camera panned across the camper-trailer, the windows shut tight, the blinds drawn. He had to talk to that woman.

"A woman who, ironically, was once a partner to Lieutenant Sam Donovan, one of the team of detectives assigned to this case." The reporter leaned toward the camera, and dropped her voice to an intimate level.

"We've been camped here all morning and have yet to get a word with her . . . Wait a minute. I hear movement inside. Apparently she's coming out."

The camera panned to the trailer. "So far, she has refused to talk to the press." A close-up of the door showed no movement, no handle turning. "And . . . it looks like she's still not budging."

The camera panned back to the reporter. "She once solved murders on a regular basis, but left the Huntsville Police Department with a sullied record and dropped out of sight. She didn't resurface until she made the 911 call that led police to this spot."

Titus's insides quivered like a grapevine in a bad wind.

"She is Jo Beth Dawson. And we'll be right here until she talks. This is Sonja Livingstone for WHUN signing off."

Titus's bones turned to stone. The only part of him that

moved was his hands, fists clenching and unclenching. The silly plastic key slid to the Mexican tile floor.

"Sir?" The motel clerk leaned over her desk and touched his sleeve. "Are you all right?"

He nodded, then bent over, picked up his key and walked out.

Jo Beth Dawson. A woman he knew only by name.

But it was a name he'd despised for nearly half his life.

Jo Beth's phone jarred her awake. Unable to see the caller ID through sleep-blurred eyes, she answered.

"Hello?"

"Jo Beth, what do you know about an old Indian called John Running Wolf?" It was Sam. The arrogant ass.

"Would this be the same detective who warned me not to mess around in his case?" She made her voice sweeter than molasses dripping through magnolias.

"Come on, Jo. Help me out here. You've got all that Native American junk in your background."

"I'm taking your good advice, Sam. Dig up your own *junk.*"

Outraged, she shot from the bed. Her urge to defy Sam surpassed her urge to drink till she passed out. All she had to do was walk outside her door, and she'd be right in the middle of *his* crime scene.

"Fool. Imbecile." She didn't know whether her habit of talking to herself came from years of living alone or signaled a mind finally coming unhinged, and she didn't much care. Introspection was for people who had real lives.

Go. A whisper no louder than a single raindrop seemed to be coming from the ceiling and inside Jo Beth's head at the same time. *Go.*

She turned on the TV to drown out the racket in her head and then poured a bowl of frosted shredded wheat. After the last of her milk drizzled into the bowl, she sat at her pop-up table waiting for her insane investigative urge to go away.

"It's the rodeo." She couldn't get the image of Pony riding the bull out of her mind. "It's this damned town." It brought to life things she'd thought dead—curiosity, protective instincts, the desire for justice. Involvement, for God's sake. As if she had anything left inside her worth giving.

"Pony Jones, who was born right here on Doe Mountain, was found murdered near the rodeo that made her famous. Cut down on June thirteenth . . ."

Jo Beth dropped her spoon. A male reporter in a yellow rain slicker grinned from her fourteen-inch, wall-mounted TV. She slapped her hand against the off button, and the image faded. But it wasn't that easy to black out the reporter's words.

June 13th. The day Rafe Dawson had died.

"I'll take care of you," Uncle Mark had said when he delivered the news. "Anything you need, just ask." *Lies.*

"No such thing as coincidence," Sam always said. *Truth.*

Jo Beth threw on shorts and a T-shirt, then fitted plastic bags around her shoes and hands with rubber bands. She had no intention of destroying evidence, and she certainly intended to leave none.

Her Silver Streak was the only trailer in the campground, not surprising considering the remote location, the horde of blood-sucking mosquitoes and the heat so intense it stole your breath.

Not to mention the taint of murder and the possibility of a killer lurking in the forest.

Thank God yesterday's deluge had run off the reporters.

Jo Beth stood just outside her door surveying the area.

Nothing moved in the deep woods. At least, nothing she could see. The campground stretched around her, peaceful with early-morning stillness. The earth, dripping with yesterday's rain, smelled rich and secretive, while winds riding on the coattails of the thunderstorm swayed the branches of trees, scattering the fragrance of pines and innocence.

But there was nothing innocent about the bright yellow tape.

She moved in that direction then stood on the periphery, searching the crime scene. Nothing presented itself except a pile of rose petals, their edges curled and turning brown.

Turning away would be the smart thing to do. But Jo Beth was irrevocably drawn to the spot, pulled by mystical forces and a connection to the victim she did not understand.

She knelt and put her hand on the ground. Sometimes the dead left behind an energy that pulsed with rage at being cut down. Turbulent thoughts as their spirits were jerked brutally from their bodies. Unfinished stories.

The earth jolted under her touch, and Jo Beth rocked back, amazed at the strength of Pony's energy. But what amazed her more was the emotion attached to that energy. Pony Jones was not angry, not shocked, not sad. She was laughing, striding around the campground in her little red Justin boots laughing.

"There she is!"

The yell startled Jo Beth and swung her around so fast she sprawled in the dirt. Parked beside her camper-trailer was a van from WHUN, and barreling toward her was a thirtyish woman with careful makeup and determined stride.

Jo Beth scrambled to get up, cursing the plastic on her shoes that kept slapping her back down.

"Jo Beth Dawson?"

If she said yes, Sam Donovan would be here in twenty minutes asking why she'd been at the crime scene, her shoes protected with plastic. And he wouldn't budge until he had answers.

"No." Jo Beth finally found her footing. "Don't know her." Thank God she could still run. Thank God she'd had cereal for breakfast instead of Kentucky straight bourbon whiskey.

She got through her door before the TV team could get the camera set up, shove the microphone in her face, and drag her back into the glare of a spotlight that would expose bones she'd kept buried for ten years.

Inside, she sagged against her walls and recovered her breath. Outside, somebody banged on her door.

"Jo Beth? We know you're in there."

Not for sure, you don't. Jo Beth didn't look anything like her younger self. She hardly resembled the picture she knew would be plastered all over tomorrow's papers.

Going to the cabinet, she took out a bottle. Then selected two more. If she was going to be a hostage in her own home, she needed a few old friends.

Nine

When Titus woke up he was not surprised to see a thorny Cherokee rose vine in full bloom climbing up his motel wall and the Arctic wolf standing underneath.

"Get."

The wolf stood his ground. His glaring yellow eyes and glowing white coat would have blinded fearful men. Titus wasn't scared of the devil.

"Go back where you come from, wolf. I done seen what I gotta do."

Titus shoved back the covers and stood up naked, a tall, knobby-kneed man who didn't give a rat's ass how he looked.

The wolf and the vine vanished, leaving behind the fragrance of roses. Titus shut his mind against the scent. He didn't need roses to tell him he'd lost Pony.

He didn't need clocks, either. It was early afternoon. He could tell by the shadows outside his window. They were already deep across the parking lot between his room and the Denny's restaurant on the west side. He'd slept four hours.

It was enough. He pulled on his overalls then laid out his guns and Pony's diary. Seeing them side by side in a motel room far from Doe Mountain—and knowing why—could not be much different from hell.

Titus didn't have time for hell. He turned his back and made his bed.

Pony didn't have a bed. She was laid out on a cold slab.

Titus shut his mind to the morgue and completed his task. He saw no reason to drop good habits just because the motel was paying somebody to come in and do his tidying for him.

His stomach rumbled when he got in his truck, but he wasn't about to spend six dollars on food at a sit-down restaurant.

Ten minutes out of the city he stopped for gas at a 7-Eleven and went inside to pay cash. They had two bologna and cheese biscuits left. He got both of them for three dollars.

He'd meant to get a map, too, but Titus didn't aim to spend five dollars just so he wouldn't have to ask somebody the whereabouts of Sleepy Pines Campground.

Though he wasn't the kind of man you'd catch standing at a magazine rack reading for free, he knew there was a time for everything, "a time to weep and a time to laugh; a time to mourn and a time to dance; a time to be born and a time to die."

Today was somebody's time to die.

The sorry, no-account bastard hadn't even had the decency to look in his daughter's eyes when he killed her.

Titus was no churchgoing man, but he knew his Bible. There were times when the Good Book got it just right.

He took a map off the rack, unfolded it and traced his finger along a northward path from Huntsville to the Tennessee state line. If Titus could follow the scent of any of God's critters on Doe Mountain, he could track a bunch of campers who threw their trash everywhere but the garbage can.

Satisfied, he folded the map like he'd found it, then stuck it back in the rack. No call to ruin it for paying customers.

In the truck he tore into his food, then closed his eyes to say grace. Decent people held to rituals. Titus prided himself on being a decent man.

"Thank you for the food, Lord. Amen."

He ate quickly, threw his wrappers in the garbage can, then cranked up and hit the road. When the city gave way to deep woods, he spotted yellow eyes in the forest, a blur of white fur.

"I ain't askin' for no help, wolf."

He heard Sleepy Pines Campground before he saw it, heard his daughter's blood crying from the earth, heard the Cherokee roses weeping for their fallen child, heard the Arctic wolf calling for vengeance. The sounds sank into his soul, deep into the place where secrets are kept and pain can eat you alive if you don't do something about it.

Titus reached over and touched the worn stock of his gun.

"Don't you worry none. Daddy's comin'."

The wooden sign over the entrance to the campground hung between stands of thick pines. Titus put his turn signal on and headed that way. Around the bend he eased on his brakes. A van with TV call letters was parked by a silver trailer. A dozen trucks and half a dozen cars littered the parking lot, and people crawled around like buzzards after carrion.

That painted-up redheaded woman he'd seen on TV at the motel was waving her hands and acting important. Grown men pointed cameras at everything that stood still. A bunch of teenagers in red boots and cowboy hats stomped around a pup tent screaming, "Pony, Pon-ee, Pon-ee!"

It looked to him like they'd set up vigil at his daughter's death site. Pony would have told them to go home and sweep the kitchen floor, feed the cat, do something useful. She didn't have no truck with hero worship.

Titus made a quick U-turn. The last thing he wanted was to

be seen by a bunch of nosy folks asking questions he didn't aim to answer. He drove down the road, scanning both sides till he found what he was looking for, a spot where the wooden fence had caved in. The opening was big enough for a man to drive his pickup truck through then hide in the bushes and wait. Wait till they all left. Wait till dark.

Titus was a patient man. He knew how to blend in with nature.

Taking his .44 Magnum, he got out of his truck and chose a high spot nearby where he could hide in a copse of cedars and still see his enemies coming from every direction.

The TV reporter didn't look like the kind of woman who would let anything stand between her and a story. And Sam Donovan hadn't struck him as dumb. By now, the cop would have figured out that Titus wasn't fixing to wait around for the law to fight his battles.

Titus would hear the reporter or the detective coming a mile. Folks born to big-city streets didn't know beans about finding their way quietly through the woods.

But the high hills and deep forests surrounding Huntsville were home to Titus's archenemy. Over the years, Titus had used his rodeo contacts to keep track of John Running Wolf. He would be an old man by now. Still, the Wisdom Keepers and Spirit Guides would already be leading him to Titus.

He reached for his Magnum, sighted down the barrel. He should have shot Running Wolf the first time he ever tried to interfere. This time, Titus wouldn't hesitate.

Suddenly the past sprang from the damp forest floor—sharp thorns that pricked Titus till he bled with memories.

He'd been standing in this very city, his legs bowed from a

hard ride on the back of a Brahman bull, his pants and shirt—
even his skin—covered with dust from the rodeo arena.

Running Wolf had been in his prime, a fierce figure in full
Cherokee regalia. The feathers on his headdress quivered with
rage.

"I forbid you to marry my niece."

"I ain't askin' your permission."

"Morning Star has a bright future. I won't let her throw a
teaching career away on an uneducated mountaineer."

"It ain't your choice. She said yes."

"You're nothing but a has-been bull rider. You can't even
take care of her."

Titus had walked away without a word and married Morning
Star that night. She never complained that they were married
by a justice of the peace without any of her family as witness.

Sitting under the cedar, the truth of Running Wolf's
accusation shot a hole in Titus so big the critters stirring in the
woods around Sleepy Pines could pass right through and he
wouldn't even notice. Winds could howl through him, storms,
and the only thing he'd feel was loss and regret.

What would have happened if he hadn't married Morning
Star, if he hadn't taken her off where the only help she could get
in a difficult childbirth was a midwife with herbs and poultices
and mountain wisdom?

Shattered, Titus walked to his truck, reached into the glove
compartment and took out his daughter's diary. He'd bought it
for Pony on her thirteenth birthday.

With his hand on the cover, Titus hesitated. In all the years
she'd kept it, he had never opened it.

But Pony was gone forever. Murdered. The diary might
hold a clue.

He opened it and began to read . . .

Daddy asked what I wanted for Christmas, and I told him a dog.
I ain't fixing to tell him what I really want. He's a good father, the
best. If I told him what my real heart's desire is, the pain might
kill him. Well, that's exaggerating a bit, but I know he'd be hurt.
I can't even write the words down. I ain't fixing to be the kind of
daughter who breaks her daddy's heart.

The words blurred as Titus's fingers traced the ink on the
pages. He couldn't bear to read on. He couldn't bear to think
that he'd failed his daughter, that she might never have received
her heart's desire.

And that now she never would.

Jo Beth's trailer was dark when she roused herself. She didn't
have to part her curtains to know the TV crew and the teenage
Pony worshippers were still out there. They were a noisy,
intrusive bunch, chattering, stomping around, banging cans
against the side of a cooler that had lost most of its ice in a long
stakeout that had proved futile.

The teenagers now waved lighted candles and occasionally
burst out singing "Home on the Range," apparently the only
cowboy song they knew, while the TV cameras aimed at her
windows. Sharp beams of light pierced the blinds and bounced
off her dark walls.

She didn't have to turn on lights in her trailer to see, either.
She could navigate every inch of it blindfolded. Even in her
current state.

Her stomach rumbled, reminding her she hadn't eaten since

early that morning. She rummaged in the refrigerator, hoping for enough ham to make a sandwich. All she found was half a piece of unidentifiable meat and some wilted lettuce.

She didn't like grocery stores. So many women pushing baskets filled with fresh produce, whole-grain bread and big dreams. Mostly, Jo Beth slunk in at night. And then only when she was down to her last can of peas.

Her cell phone rang, causing her to bump her head on the refrigerator door.

"Jo Beth, you were supposed to be here an hour ago." It was Maggie, getting right to the point and sounding pissed.

"I can't leave. Reporters and Pony fans are camped outside my door."

"Well, I'm sitting in Macaroni Grill with an empty stomach and a waitress who's not too happy that I'm taking up table space and haven't even ordered. Haven't you ever heard of a telephone?"

"I'm sorry, Mags. I forgot."

There was a long silence. Jo Beth wouldn't blame Maggie if she hung up.

"You're drinking. How much?"

Jo Beth looked at the three bottles lined on her table, two of them empty, the last nearly. She picked up the bottle, surprised to see how rapidly the level of liquor had fallen.

"Some."

"You shouldn't be out there by yourself. I'm coming to get you."

"Do you think that will stop them?" Murder and scandal improved media ratings. Jo Beth thought if one more piece of herself was pecked off, she'd be nothing but bleached bones. "They'll hound me wherever I go."

"I'm not worried about stopping reporters, Jo. I'm worried about stopping you from killing yourself with the bottle."

"I'm going to do better."

"When?"

"Tomorrow."

The lie fell between them like poison gas, the noxious fumes covering Jo Beth so completely nothing could find her except her conscience.

As if the poison gas had leaked outside, WHUN's favorite female reporter and her crew put down their cameras and their lukewarm drinks while teenagers blew out their candles. They packed up their gear and candy wrappers and empty coolers and ratings dreams and songs for the dead then scuttled into their vehicles and drove away.

Jo Beth waited until she could hear the sound of nothing except a night owl calling deep in the woods and a few crickets singing because it was summer. Her hand was on the door handle when she remembered what she'd found the last time she'd explored the campground in the dark. Reaching for her gun, she stepped outside and stumbled down the steps.

She leaned against her Silver Streak and breathed deeply. Standing in the solitude of the night, she wondered if she'd been born with some kind of defective gene that had predetermined her capacity for destruction.

Beyond the trees a branch snapped. An animal? The killer coming back to the scene of his crime?

Jo Beth tried to point her gun, but she couldn't hold it steady.

"Who's there? I have a gun."

The Cherokee roses moved, and a tall apparition emerged.

Jo Beth's gun tumbled from her hand and she slid down the side of her trailer.

Sam had been at the rodeo again all day long and not a damned thing to show for it.

He was tired, he was hungry, and he wanted to go home. Grab a couple of beers. Sink into his leather lounge chair, his one big extravagance, and watch the Atlanta Braves kick some serious ass.

If he could stay awake that long.

The jarring note of his phone took care of that.

"Sam?" It was Luther, charged with finding Titus Jones.

"Yo. What've you got?"

"I think we've found him."

"You think?"

"Yeah. He fits the description. Son of a gun checked in at the La Quinta on University under the name of Hunter Lobo."

Hunter Lobo? The significance hit Sam and the back of his neck tingled.

"Bring him in. I want to have a little talk with him."

"He flew the coop, Sam."

"Where'd he go?"

"Nobody seems to know. This man's a ghost. Slips in and out without anybody noticing."

They couldn't afford to waste manpower chasing all over the city for Titus Jones. They had a killer to catch. Still, that didn't stop Sam from following his gut on his own time.

Ignoring his gnawing hunger and the beginning of a headache that signaled he'd had too much coffee and too little sleep, Sam changed out of uniform. He told himself he was being a good cop, going beyond the call of duty to stop a grieving father from vigilante justice.

But Sam was too damned honest to keep up the lies for long. The plain truth was, his house felt so empty and soulless, he might as well have taken up residence in Walmart. The simple fact was, Sam was running from himself.

He stuffed a wad of Juicy Fruit into his mouth, hoping the taste of sugar would replace the taste of regret. Then he climbed into his Mustang convertible and put the top down.

If he was going to chase all over hell's half acre for a mountain man bent on revenge, at least he could feel the wind in his face. Cursing Huntsville traffic, he headed north.

He had a hunch he knew where Titus Jones had headed.

Maggie had left Macaroni Grill in a huff, but it hadn't lasted long. By the time she'd driven home, she was over her snit and had settled into worry.

She kicked off her shoes, slipped out of the size 6 pink linen sundress and into shorts and T-shirt. Who did she think she was going to impress? Jo Beth, who never had cared a flip about clothes?

By the time James got home, she was standing at the kitchen in her bare feet drinking a cup of chai tea, her comfort drink of choice.

"How'd dinner go?"

"She didn't show." Thank goodness James didn't comment, just went to the refrigerator and drank milk straight from the jug, a habit she'd tried to break for seventeen years. Finally she gave up, quit griping about it, and now everybody was happier.

She slipped her arms around his back, tried to inhale him, his steadfastness, his calmness, his sheer goodness.

"Did you ask Roger?"

"He said no."

"Is that all?"

"He had his reasons and they were sound. Let it drop, Maggie."

Her taste for tea gone, she poured the remainder down the drain and put the cup in the dishwasher.

"James, I'm going to drive up there and see her."

"Mags, you promised."

"I know." She sighed. How did he put up with her? How did anybody put up with her? "I won't be gone long."

Thank goodness he didn't call after her when she slid into her clogs and walked out the door. If he had, she would have turned around and gone back. After all, how did she think she was going to accomplish in a few days what she hadn't been able to accomplish in ten years?

Maggie climbed into her car and pushed buttons till she found Patsy Cline on the radio. "I Fall to Pieces." Though she barely knew the words and couldn't carry a tune, she sang along.

It seemed appropriate. Jo Beth was in pieces. That poor dead cowgirl's family had to be in pieces. Maybe even Maggie was in pieces.

Maybe everybody in the whole world was falling to pieces and they just didn't know it yet.

Under a billion glowing summer stars Pony used to call a Christmas sky, Titus stood beside the old camper and looked at the falling-down-drunk woman. That was about what you'd expect from a Dawson.

What he hadn't expected was the dark hair, the tiny frame, the big dark eyes. Something in him tore, a thin curtain he'd stitched around himself after his wife died.

Impossible. The woman at his feet reminded him of Morning Star.

He stared at her till he could restitch his fragile shield, reset his mind. Jo Beth Dawson was no Morning Star. His wife had been shining and pure, full of courage and beauty and pride. This woman was as devoid of pride and courage as a pack rat, living in holes and coming out at night.

All she had was the instincts of a wounded animal. He spat on the ground and kicked her gun that had tumbled to the dirt.

"Can you stand up?"

"Get away from me." She struggled to lift herself on her elbow, and he watched as dispassionately as if she were a turtle trying to climb a log. Defeated, she stared at him from the dirt. "What do you want?"

"I want to talk."

"I don't have anything to say." She inched her hand over the ground, searching for her gun, probably thinking he wouldn't notice. He stood there watching her, granting her mercy. A commodity no Dawson had ever granted his beloved Morning Star.

The smell of liquor and stale sweat, fear and regret rose from the woman on the ground. Pity wedged itself through a small crack in the heart Titus had boarded up and posted with a Keep Out sign.

"I ain't gonna hurt you. I ain't armed." Except for the blade in his boot. He'd left his guns in the truck. He'd never brought harm to a woman and he didn't aim to start now.

"Who are you?" She was still searching for her weapon, scrambling around now. Panic edging out caution.

Titus leaned down, scooped up the gun and offered it to her. "This what you lookin' for?"

She jerked the gun out of his hands, and even in her loose-limbed drunkenness, she knew how to handle it. It made sense, considering what he'd overheard from that pesky pack of TV people while he bided his time in the bushes.

Using both hands, she pointed the gun at his chest. "I'm a crack shot."

"You ain't gonna shoot me."

The gun wavered, and she passed an unsteady hand over her face. "Give me one good reason why."

Something inside Titus ripped apart. Cherokee roses, yellow crime tape, hatred and pity collided, and he fell to his knees.

"I'm Pony's daddy."

They wasn't many women in my life, just the preacher's wife that
come up the mountain every Christmas bringing a pan of corn bread
dressing and a pecan pie, and the truant officer that trudged to our
house every now and then to ask why I wasn't in school.

I ain't never seen Daddy be nothing but nice and polite to a lady.
I ain't never seen him stand over no woman the way he's standing
over Jo Beth, watching her like she's a rabbit and he's just waiting
for her to make a misstep and spring his trap.

Another thing I ain't never seen in my Daddy is hatred. He's
kind to every living critter. One time when I was eight and in love
with fish and snakes and anything else I could bring up from the
creek, I let loose a whole bucketful of frogs in the house. They was
in the cabinets and the wood box and the water pitcher. One of them
even hopped in the refrigerator and set up housekeeping in the milk
jug. A scared frog can jump about a mile. I never seen such a mess.

When Daddy come out of the fields and seen them green rascals
had commandeered our kitchen and looked like they was hunkered
down for the winter, I thought I'd get a whipping for sure. But he
just helped me gather them up while he explained that every living
critter has a place God wants it to be, and frogs is supposed to be
on creek banks.

Now with my daddy full of rage and Jo Beth threatening him with a gun, I step between them and yell, "Put that gun down!"

She don't pay me no more mind than if I was the wind whistling past her ears. Since I can't get no deader than I already am, I reach out and grab her gun, but my hands passes right through.

This makes me stompin', spittin' mad.

"God, if You ain't gonna turn me loose and let me stomp some sense into folks, how come You left me down here? How You expect me to help anybody if I'm hogtied?"

He don't say nothing, and I can't blame 'em. If I'd made the whole word and mankind too, I wouldn't put up with no sass from a dead cowgirl.

Suddenly Jo Beth tries to stand up and passes out in the dirt. In her condition, she can't use her gun on the side of a barn, let alone my daddy.

Maybe God heard me after all. Maybe I owe Him a apology.

Apologies ain't easy for me. I'm in the midst of tryin' to think one up when I hear a engine roaring this way and see headlights turning in the gate. My daddy hears it too. He scoops up Jo Beth's gun, slings her over his shoulder and hotfoots toward the woods.

And me right along with them.

"What are you gonna do with her now, Daddy?" I say, but he don't pay me no mind, just skirts around them Cherokee roses and plunges into the thicket.

About that time a Mustang convertible comes roaring through the gates and skids to a stop beside the Silver Streak. Sam Donovan barrels out looking like he could bite horseshoes in half.

"Jo Beth," he yells. "Jo Beth!" Then he commences knocking so loud it's a wonder her door don't fly off its hinges.

Daddy's running so hard I can hear his breath sawing the air. The last thing I see is Sam Donovan turning toward the woods and yelling, "Titus Jones, if you're out there, give it up. This is not your fight."

Daddy just keeps on running.

Sweet Lord Jesus! He's fixing to get the man that done this to me.

Looks like me and God's got our work cut out for us.

Ten

Sam stared into the woods, listening for the slightest sound that didn't belong. Was that movement in the trees? He drew his gun, took aim. A sound beat upward, wings against the sky, a large bird crying at the moon. He'd almost shot an owl.

Had something flushed the night bird from the trees? A man on the run? A man looking for his daughter's killer?

The instincts that had sent Sam racing to the campground told him Titus was somewhere out there, waiting for his chance to talk to the woman who had found his daughter.

Or maybe he had already been here. Already found her.

Sam pounded on her door. "Jo Beth! I know you're in there." Nothing. Not a sound, not a movement. Something wasn't right. Forget procedure. He was not on duty. With his shoulder to the door, he yelled, "It's me. Sam. I'm coming in."

He sprawled into the trailer and nearly lost his balance. That's what he got for acting like a cowboy. If he'd tried the knob first, he'd have discovered the door wasn't locked.

Even before he found the light switch, he knew he was alone. There was no sense of blood and bone except his own, no hint of flesh, living or dead.

Empty whiskey bottles on the table told their own story. With that much alcohol in her, Jo Beth didn't have a prayer of using whatever skills she had left against Titus Jones. Or anybody else who had come along.

Sam searched for signs of struggle, evidence that someone had been in the trailer besides Jo Beth.

What if it was the killer? What if he thought Jo Beth knew more than she was telling?

If Sam could get his hands on that TV vulture, Sonja Livingstone, he'd wring her skinny neck. Used to be, the press just reported the facts. Now freedom of the press meant license to pontificate and meddle. It meant the public knowing more than they should about murder investigations, and it meant knowledge falling on the wrong ears.

He walked to the back of the trailer, scanning every available surface. He was relieved to find no signs of struggle, no evidence that anyone had been in the trailer besides Jo Beth.

But Titus Jones had an eerie ability to come and go without warning or detection. Sam still smarted at Pony's daddy catching him off guard in his own office.

Parting the curtains at the back of the camper-trailer he saw Jo Beth's bed, the covers wadded and twisted. No surprise there. She'd always been an insomniac. She used to call him on her sleepless nights and he'd drive over, take her to an all-night coffee shop then just listen while she talked.

Lana had hated him for that. One of the many barricades they'd built against each other. If either one had tried to scale the walls, would he still be in a house that smelled of her perfume?

Damning the night that ushered in the ghosts of marriage past, Sam inspected Jo Beth's quarters. Candy wrappers and cracker crumbs littered Jo Beth's bedside table. No wonder she looked like a rack of bones.

His urge to fix things rose to the surface, but Sam battled

it back. He had neither the time nor the energy to fix Jo Beth Dawson. He couldn't even fix himself.

As he walked back to the front of the trailer, headlights cut through the darkness and slashed the windows, shone through the cracks in the blinds. Sam stepped outside. A black Lexus was coming fast and hard. What now?

The Lexus skidded to a stop and a shapely blonde barreled out. "Jo Beth! JOOOO!"

The Carter woman. Jo Beth's friend. What's her name? Legs too short for his taste but great ass. Nice smile that could fool a man into thinking she wouldn't say *boo*. Sam wasn't fooled.

That's all he needed. A righteous little firecracker who'd just as soon serve his balls to the dogs as look at him. She never had cared for him. The feeling was mutual.

Sam didn't even holster his gun. "She's not here."

"What have you done to her this time?"

This time, meaning all the flak that had gone down when Jo Beth left the Huntsville Police Department was his fault. Maggie was typical of her gender. Sometimes he thought he ought to go to church and give a big donation just in case there was a God, just in case Lana got religion and decided to come back. A bribe masquerading as a gift.

"Why can't you just leave her alone?" If the Carter woman had teeth and fangs, they'd be bone-deep in his throat.

Maggie. That was her name.

During Jo Beth's suspension Maggie had told Sam his reservation in Hell was a done deal. Hell was nothing new to him. He went there on a daily basis.

"Shut up and listen. I have reason to believe somebody got here before we did. Tell me what you know about Jo Beth's whereabouts and make it snappy."

"Who? Who got here?"

He didn't have time for this. Sam shoved his gun into the holster and set off toward the woods, knowing in his gut it was already too late. Whatever chances he'd had of catching Titus Jones had been flushed down the toilet the minute Maggie Carter drove through the gate.

"Wait!" She caught up with him, grabbed the back of his shirt. "We were going to have dinner, she didn't show. I called her and she'd been drinking. A lot. That's when I got in the car and drove up here."

"How long ago did you talk to her?"

"I don't know. An hour? Forty-five minutes?" She wrapped her arms around herself, rocked on her heels making a sound you heard in hospital emergency rooms and graveyards.

Was he supposed to comfort her or slap her? He'd never understood women. No wonder Jo Beth thought he had betrayed her. No wonder Lana absconded and left him with a coffeepot and a set of chipped dishes.

"Jo Beth can still take care of herself."

"Did the killer get her? Oh, God!"

"No. Not the killer."

"Who then. For God's sake, *who?*"

If she fainted, Sam would have to deal with it. Why wasn't he home now with a beer, watching the Atlanta Braves? Why had he squandered his off-duty hours charging into the woods?

He had no intention of discussing anything about the Pony Jones case with Maggie Carter. And he certainly wasn't going to waste his time trying to save a woman who was hell-bent on drinking herself to death. He'd tried once, and everybody in Huntsville knew how that had turned out.

If he left now, he might catch the ninth inning of the game.

"I came here to check on Jo Beth, just like you. Looks like we're both out of luck." Sam headed toward his Mustang.

"Wait! I have a key."

"The door's unlocked. She's not home."

Maggie Carter scrunched her face up like she was going to cry. Her perfume got inside him—something sweet and floral, not too strong—and he almost offered her a handkerchief. He didn't, though. He was too old to play hero. He'd tried that twice, and it hadn't worked.

Jo Beth had gone down the tubes and Lana had walked, anyway. For three months after Jo Beth left he found himself listening for the sound of her cowboy boots. He could still follow her scented trail from the locker room to the office to the break room sink where she sometimes stood with her butt hiked up and her elbows on the windowsill.

Had she been looking *at* something or searching *for* something? It was too late to ask now.

Sam climbed into his car and put the key in the ignition. The Mustang fired to life.

"Are you just going to tuck your tail and run?"

"It's dark, I'm off duty and Jo Beth's a grown woman. Go home, Maggie."

"Coward."

She stormed toward the trailer and Sam sat there idling his engine. There were two dozen reasons to leave and none to stay.

Sam cut the engine and climbed out of his car. "Wait." He pulled his cell phone out of his pocket. "What's her number?"

Ten years ago he would have known Jo Beth's number without having to consult his notes or ask. Ten years ago was another lifetime.

·   ·   ·

The woods, thick with cedars and pines, with oaks and hickories and sweetgums, swallowed Titus. Ferns, mosses and fallen leaves layered the forest floor and cushioned his steps. Except for the owl Titus had scared up, the woods were quiet.

The cop was not following. But that didn't mean he wouldn't. Sam Donovan didn't strike Titus as the kind of man to give up.

He changed direction and moved deeper into the woods. Nature's night critters blinked but let him pass without scurrying out of his path. They knew. He was a man of the mountain with a deep love and respect for God's natural world.

What he didn't respect was the men and women who tore down and polluted and trashed God's creation. Including themselves. The woman sagging across his shoulder was a prime example.

Titus stopped under a canopy of blackjack oaks and propped her against a tree trunk. She collapsed like a used-up bag of horses' oats.

"Can you hear me?"

She blinked then tried to sit up straight. "I hear you. What do you want?" Her voice was blurry from whiskey.

"I want to know about Pony. They said you found her."

"I did. But I didn't kill her."

"I didn't say nothin' about killin' her. I just want to know what she looked like. What you saw."

She shook her head. Titus didn't know whether she was trying to clear it, saying no, or trying to remember. He didn't have patience for any of it.

"I just want to find out what you know and be done with you."

Jo Beth's mouth set and her chin went up a notch. She reminded him so much of his daughter Titus was thunderstruck. Pony had that same stubborn, spunky look when she told him she meant to ride the big bulls.

"You doin' good in the rodeo, Pony," he'd told her. "Ain't no use wearin' yourself out tryin' to bust barriers."

"Why not, Daddy? Ain't no rules never stopped you."

As memories of Pony sang through him, Titus waited for Jo Beth's answer, stood in the deep woods with the stillness of a man who knew how to catch a covey of quail unaware, how to catch Rafe Dawson's daughter off guard.

"She was peaceful looking." When she finally spoke, Jo Beth's voice was soft. Titus leaned through a sour fog of whiskey so he wouldn't miss a word. "Not like she'd died hard. Not the way I've seen some."

It was the first shred of light Titus had seen since the roses and wolf had told him Pony was dead. That it had been delivered to him by a woman he'd thought had no decency made the spark all the brighter. He clung to Jo Beth's words with the desperation of a father who could no longer bear to think of the brutal way his daughter had died.

Jo Beth's hand wavered toward him, then dropped back by her side. "I'm so sorry."

Her compassion ambushed Titus. When she looked at him through a veil of tears, history tried to rearrange itself. No Dawson had ever cared about what was his. But then, Jo Beth didn't know what he knew.

Or did she?

"Morning Star." He said his wife's name quietly, watching Jo Beth's reaction.

She shook her head like she might be losing her hearing. "When I found her, there were no stars."

Was it possible Jo Beth didn't know? He wasn't going to be fooled. She was a Dawson. And they knew how to keep secrets.

"What else did you see?"

"She looked like a little kid." Jo Beth swiped at her tears with the back of her hand.

Titus was gut-shot. Once when Morning Star had found a bluebird with a broken wing, Titus had brought it inside, made a little splint and kept it alive in a shoe box beside their bed, all because he couldn't bear to see his wife cry.

He couldn't have told you why it was like that with Jo Beth. He couldn't have said why the sight of her tears crumbled the entire foundation of his hatred.

"Pony was twenty-six."

The stark reminder that somebody had snuffed out his daughter's life with a single blow shored up his foundation, but not much.

He'd seen folks at the foot of the mountain go crazy when they lost young'uns. Titus didn't aim to be one of them. Not yet. Shutting down his softer memories, he clawed his way back to emotions that turned his face hard as a hatchet.

Jo Beth flinched then peered through the darkness, a trapped but cagey animal looking for escape.

"If you run, I aim to stop you."

"You can't keep me captive. That's against the law."

"There ain't no law out here but mine."

"If you're trying to scare me, forget it. I've seen worse than you."

Her stinging words fell on the hard shell of his resolve. It no longer mattered that after he was done nobody would think of him as decent.

"Have you told me everything?"

"No."

"What else?" Jo Beth had been a cop. She'd know what he was talking about.

"There was a white wolf."

"You saw a white wolf?"

"Don't believe me. I don't care. There were roses, too."

Pain ricocheted through him. Somewhere deep in the woods a wolf howled. Titus didn't have to see to know its coat would be snow white.

"What was that?"

"Nothin'. Keep talking."

"Your daughter was under a blanket of fresh white rose petals."

Titus wanted to throw back his head and join Pony's totem in a howl that would shake the stars from the sky, bring down the moon. Instead, he calculated how much head start he had on Sam Donovan.

Not much. Donovan had a whole police department at his disposal. What he didn't have was a father's fierce, grieving heart.

A sound not found in nature split the silence. Squirrels scampered onto the branches and swung to a quieter tree while Jo Beth reached into her pocket and pulled out that ridiculous cell phone folks carried around like a third arm. Titus would have been dead a long time ago if he carried trouble around in his pocket.

"Do you want me to answer it?" She glanced up at him. A winding river. And he could read every turn.

"Yes."

He didn't have to tell her not to mention his name. He'd seen it in her eyes. Whatever her reasons, she didn't plan on betraying him.

I can read the signs of nature like a road map and folks like they was a open picture book. Especially my daddy. But right now, I ain't got a clue what's going on in his head.

He's just standing there while Jo Beth's talking on her cell phone. To Sam Donovan, of all people. One word from her, and my daddy's goose is cooked.

I try knocking that cell phone out of her hand, but my arms fly right through it. They might as well be pinned down like one of them butterflies teachers used to make kids catch and stick on a board. One of the many reasons to give public schooling a wide berth. Butterflies belong on the wind.

"I told you, Sam," Jo Beth is saying into her phone, "I don't have to report to you."

When he says, "Maggie's here with me and she's worried," I see the advantage of being a spirit. It's like I got X-ray ears. I can hear both ends of a telephone conversation.

"I'm with Uncle Mark."

"You're lying."

"I called him. Even I need family."

"Put him on."

"Butt out, Sam. I can watch my own back."

Jo Beth shuts off her phone, then leans sideways and loses her liquor on a bed of wild violets. I'm gonna be pissed if it gets on my boots.

Daddy bends down and wipes her face with his handkerchief, his face as hard as a river rock. He don't cotton to self-destructive habits. He says the good Lord give you only one body per lifetime and it's up to you to take care of it.

When Jo Beth tries to stand up, she topples sideways.

Daddy catches her as easy as he used to catch me when I'd yell, "Geronimo," then leap out of the barn loft.

"I ought to whup your britches, Pony," he'd say. But he never did. That's the thing I remember best about growing up on the mountain. Daddy knew I had a wild heart and he didn't try to tame me.

We walk along in the silver night woods, me and my daddy and Jo Beth, real quiet like, so quiet I can hear the prayers of animals.

Jo Beth ain't passed out now, but she ain't struggling neither. This time Daddy ain't carrying her over his shoulder. He's carrying her the same way he did me the first time ole Rocky Top bucked me off. All cradled up and tender-like, his face open for the first time since I seen him in my room crying because he knew I was dead.

I knew my daddy was a man of compassion, and this just goes to prove it. The one thing he hates more than that woman from Social Services who come prissing up the mountain and tried to take me away from him is a woman who drinks hard liquor. I ain't never touched the stuff, myself. Life is a glorious thing, and I want to see it clear.

"Where are you taking me?" Jo Beth asks my daddy.

"I ain't gonna hurt you."

And he won't neither. I coulda told Jo Beth that in the first place.

But ain't nobody asking me. I reckon they don't even know I'm here.

Eleven

The wolf passed through the trees, ghostlike, keeping pace with Titus as he carried Jo Beth back to his truck. Pony was there, too, her body a mere shadow, her spirit light as dandelions borne through the night on a rose-scented breeze.

He accepted all of it without question, tethered himself to the visions that were his only link with his wife and his daughter.

But he was relieved Jo Beth had passed out again. She'd seen the wolf once, seen the roses. A woman of her spunk would ask a dozen questions, even if she was still addled with alcohol.

Toting a dead-weight drunk woman was a sight easier than explaining signs and totems and the mysteries of the universe to her. It was better than carrying a wide-awake woman who kept looking up at him with Morning Star's dark eyes.

He didn't know why he was still holding onto her. She'd told him what he needed to know. He ought to dump her in the woods and leave her, forget she'd ever existed.

But that would make him like the Dawsons.

Titus walked doggedly on, trying not to look at her. But the moon was a magician, the deep night a trickster. Holding a woman, even a Dawson, reminded Titus he was still a man.

In the pale light he could see how Jo Beth had once been a

beautiful woman, how she might be again if somebody would save her.

That somebody would not be Titus Jones. As his truck came into view, he picked up speed. He'd let her sleep it off tonight then take her back to her trailer and be done with her.

Jo Beth weighed no more than Pony had. The sudden memory of his daughter, cold and still, bowed Titus's head. With his face almost touching Jo Beth's hair, he breathed in the scent of her. She smelled of whiskey and floral soap and something so alive, so uniquely *woman* it jerked him upright.

Shifting her slight weight to one arm, he yanked open his truck door and dumped her inside. She moaned once, then curled into a question mark and sank into a stupor.

Titus watched long enough to satisfy himself she wouldn't be trying to run off then he climbed into the back of his truck, pillowed his head on his backpack and lay there looking up at the stars. Pony was all around him, shining through him like the stars overhead.

He lifted his arm to point out the Little Dipper with its navigational star.

"Look at that, Pony. The North star will always guide you home."

I ain't never seen nothin' so beautiful, Daddy.

Was it Pony he heard or was it a breeze passing through the cedars?

"I wish you was here."

He waited, but all he heard was the wind picking up. It was a sound that would tear a man apart if he'd let it.

He pulled his coat closer. Soon the cab would cool down and Jo Beth wasn't wearing a coat.

What did he care?

Titus shut his eyes but it wasn't that easy to shut off his conscience. He unfolded his long legs, climbed out of the truck bed and took off his coat.

Easing open the door so as not to wake her, he placed his coat over Jo Beth.

Saving her.

Or was he saving himself?

Some things never changed. The east giving birth to morning, Venus shining through the dawn, anvils pounding her head after her latest binge.

Jo Beth didn't know where she was, but that wasn't unusual. She knew better than to sit up fast. Instead, she lay still trying to get her bearings.

A man's denim jacket covered her, a steering wheel punched into her left shoulder, a hard seat spring jutted into her back. It all came back. All those bottles. The woods. The battered pickup truck. Pony's daddy.

"You're awake."

He was standing at the open window, as lean and hard as one of those wooden Indians she used to see in storefronts when she and her granddaddy traveled to Arizona for a rodeo. Jo Beth wanted to touch the face that looked like a carving, to assure herself she hadn't dreamed the man who said he was Pony's daddy.

"Who are you?"

"My name don't matter. I'm takin' you home."

He opened the door, and she scooted out of his way, aching and miserable. He was right. His name didn't matter. The news media would broadcast it soon enough, but she had no reason to know. All she wanted was to hole up in her trailer till her head quit pounding, then go someplace different. Any place that was not Sleepy Pines Campground.

They lurched through the woods till Jo Beth thought her head would explode. Even if she'd wanted to find where he had taken her, retracing the path would be impossible. Unless you were a bloodhound or Pony Jones's daddy. All the trees looked alike.

The sky was still pink when he shot onto the road. Finally he stopped at the entrance to the campground.

"Can you get home without fallin' down?"

"If I do, I know how to get up."

That was a lie, but he'd never know. She planned to wait till he was out of sight before she started walking back to the Silver Streak. If she fell, she'd crawl. Over the years, she'd perfected crawling to an art.

She climbed down from the rusty old blue truck, then stood on the graveled road trying not to inhale too much fresh air. In her condition, an overdose just might kill her. On second thought, maybe she ought to gulp it down. Today was as good a day as any for dying.

The old truck engine idled and he sat there watching her.

"Ain't you goin'?"

"I'm just catching my breath. Go on."

He sat there awhile longer, but she didn't budge. She had all day. Finally, he said, "Suit yourself," then headed down the road, his truck kicking dust.

She made it to the Silver Streak upright, then fell into her bed.

The sun was up when her cell phone woke her. It was Maggie. Worried. And mad.

"Where *were* you last night?"

"I told Sam where I was."

"I don't believe you and neither does he. Stay put. I'm coming out there to get you and don't you argue."

"I need some time alone, Mags."

"You'll just get drunk again."

"I can't."

"Why?"

"I'm out of whiskey."

"Well, all right, then. I won't come today. But I'm warning you, Jo Beth, I'm not letting you throw yourself away."

"What self?"

"I'm not kidding you. I'm not above an intervention."

Was it possible for a friend's generous opinion of you to take root and sprout like strong stalks in Alabama red clay? Was it possible for a stranger's brutal opinion to rip off your protective shield and reshape who you are?

Waiting on the edge of her bed until the world tilted upright, Jo Beth sifted through last night's fractured memories. She'd been drunk but not too far gone to notice the conflicted feelings of a man who wouldn't even tell his name. Except for his relationship to Pony, she didn't have any idea who he was, and yet the hatred he'd felt at his daughter's killer had also been directed at her.

"Who are you, Pony Jones?"

Git up.

Jo Beth nearly toppled off the bed. Hangovers were bad enough, but if she was going to start hearing voices, too, she'd have to find something stronger than Jack Daniel's.

"Leave me alone."

Until now, Jo Beth and the wrongful dead had a pact: they

stayed out of her business and she stayed out of theirs. But the spirit of Pony Jones was breaking all the rules—not surprising considering that's the way she had lived.

Where's your spunk?

You hidin' from somebody or from yourself?

Jo Beth leaped up, fumbled with the clock radio till she found a station playing music, then turned the volume on high. Willie Nelson's whiskey voice boomed through her small trailer, drowning out everything except Jo Beth's thoughts.

She'd parted company with regret a long time ago. But with Willie Nelson crooning "Angel Flying Too Close to the Ground" and Pony Jones whispering barbed commands to find her sass, Jo Beth thought of the one person she'd never wanted to disappoint. Clint Dawson. What would her grandfather say if he could see her now, a sour-smelling drunk whose only talent was in knowing when to run?

She went into the kitchen, put on a pot of coffee and told herself she was going to do better, she was going to hold it all together.

When her cell phone rang again, she snapped, "Maggie, I told you, I'm okay."

"I'm coming out there to make sure." It was Sam, shattering what little control she had left.

"Like you made sure when I was wearing a badge?"

She hung up, then sat down at the table and reached for the bottle that still had two inches of whiskey. It was a start. Her hands shook as she lifted it to her mouth.

Ain't you got no pride?

The bottle crashed to the floor, spewing glass and lukewarm Jack Daniel's across the linoleum. She put her hands over her ears, but Pony Jones was in her head and wouldn't go away. Or was it her own conscience? Was it possible there was still a single, hopeful part of herself that Jo Beth hadn't stomped out, cussed out, and outrun?

She dumped the bottles into the garbage can, then cleaned up the floor. Taking a deep breath, she steadied herself and reached for a cup. As she stepped outside with her coffee, she glanced at the spot where she'd found Pony. The sun had burned away the last of the rose petals, leaving behind yellow tape and an unsolved crime.

Why couldn't Jo Beth let it go? Something about this case was a briar under her skin, one she couldn't see to remove and find relief.

When she'd been part of the Dawson and Donovan team, Sam used to say he did most of the legwork while Jo Beth did all the head work. Nudged by the caffeine kick of coffee, the sight of crime scene tape and the ugly truth of herself as a woman who searched for disaster till she found it, Jo Beth replayed the facts of the Pony Jones case.

Not that she planned to solve it. That was Sam's job. But there were angles he didn't know—that Pony's daddy was hiding in the woods, that he was out for revenge, that he obviously had a vendetta against the Dawsons.

Something Pony's daddy had said last night nagged at her. Something about the stars that were out the night she found Pony.

Why would he ask if the stars were shining?

Her mother's voice answered her, drifting up through a tunnel of time. *What about morning star?* Jo Beth had been standing outside her mother's bedroom door clutching a dollar in her grimy little hand, waiting for . . . who? Her grandfather? Her uncle? She'd been seven, maybe eight, and she'd been anxious to get ice cream.

As the truth came to her in bits and pieces, Jo Beth's blood became a river that washed every single thought from her head except the truth.

Pony's daddy had not asked about celestial objects. And neither had her mother.

Jo Beth pulled out her cell phone and scrolled till she found the number she called once a year. On his birthday.

"Uncle Mark? Where are you staying?"

"The Marriott. On Tranquility Base. Why?"

"I'm coming to see you."

She hung up before he could make excuses. She hung up before she could change her mind. If she hurried she could be out of there before the media circus came.

Jo Beth spent three minutes in the shower and two trying to decide between the pink blouse that put some color in her face and the yellow one that put the illusion of meat on her bones. In the end she went with the pink. She even put on lipstick. Maggie would approve, never mind that it took both hands to paint within the lines.

When Jo Beth gave herself a final inspection in the mirror, she saw a double image—her own washed-out looking face and that of a grinning young woman with a long, black braid.

Pony winked at her.

Grabbing a cloth, Jo Beth scrubbed at the fog steaming up her mirror till she'd erased the disturbing vision.

From somewhere over her left shoulder, Jo Beth heard the young cowgirl laughing.

If it was me, I'd be eatin' instead of primping.

As if it weren't enough that Maggie tried to boss her around, now Jo Beth had a sassy, opinionated ghost telling her what to do. She couldn't get out of her trailer fast enough.

On the way into Huntsville, she stopped at Hardee's, but not because Pony told her to. She ordered a sausage and biscuit. With orange juice. And jelly. She couldn't remember the last time she'd had a real breakfast.

She couldn't remember the last time she'd wanted to find out anything except directions to the nearest liquor store.

Twelve

The Braves had won and Sam was celebrating with a Hershey bar. He was determined not to let last night's wild goose chase and this morning's ill-fated call to Jo Beth spoil his day.

"Is that your breakfast?"

Luther pulled up a chair and put his feet on Sam's desk, nearly overturning his coffee cup.

"Hey, watch that." Sam moved the Styrofoam cup. "Yeah. It's breakfast."

"Ever thought of trying bacon and eggs?"

"Lana took the frying pan."

"That's why God made IHOP." Luther plopped a piece of paper on the desk. "Here you go."

"What's that?"

"List of everybody who participated in the rodeo and list of people who were last seen with or were looking for Pony Jones."

The first name on the second list leaped out at Sam. "Brick Farraday? The saddle bronc champ?"

"Yeah. Rodeo talk is he and Pony were an item."

"Lovers' quarrel?"

"Maybe."

Sam wadded up his candy wrapper, threw it at the waste can and missed.

"You having an off day, Donovan?"

"Not that I've noticed."

"You used to hit the can every time."

Luther was right, but Sam didn't care to get into that. Luther was one to twist and stretch a point till not hitting the wastebasket translated into making a major screwup and getting shot.

"What's Buckin' Billy Rakestraw doing on this list?"

If you questioned somebody more than once, they'd wise up, start asking for a lawyer. The next thing you know, three-piece suits would be all over your back and word would hit the streets you had a suspect. Maybe even a killer. The press would catch wind, interview irate citizens who would get on public TV and say it was high time the Huntsville Police Department did its job.

Sam didn't like hauling Buckin' Billy down to the station twice.

"He tell you he tried to horn in on Brick Farraday's territory?" Luther hitched up his pants. Sarah, his wife of thirty years, had him on the Atkins diet and he'd lost his belly. In spite of the doughnuts he sneaked while she wasn't looking.

"He wanted to date Pony?"

"That's the way I heard it."

Most folks would say that not telling the whole truth put Buckin' Billy into suspect territory, but murder was never that simple. Sam stared at the last name on the list. "Who's this John Wolf?"

"Some old Native American guy."

"Blue denim jacket? Turquoise watchband?"

"Beats me."

Sam got the twitch in his eye that used to mean he was onto a good lead. Nowadays, though, it could mean just about anything, including that Jo Beth was in town and Lana had called out of the blue at midnight and he hadn't had much sleep.

Just to talk, she'd said. What did they have to talk about after all these years?

Sam fired his empty cup at the garbage can and missed again. He was losing his touch with coffee cups but he hadn't lost a damned thing when it came to ignoring voices in his head.

Jo Beth's uncle was waiting for her in the lobby. Sitting in a plush chair near the TV, Mark Dawson looked shrunken, old, not at all the commanding figure he'd presented at the rodeo.

Why wouldn't he, though? He was seventy-five. Strange that he was the closest family she had and she knew little about him except his age and bits and pieces of his marital history. He was married to a doughy-faced woman, Aunt Julia, who tolerated their arrogant expatriate son, Mark Jr., and loved her cat.

She also knew Uncle Mark had money. He still lived on Dawson family land just east of Tupelo. You couldn't run a three-thousand acre spread and support a son in Paris without money.

He hadn't seen her yet, so she had the advantage. You could learn all kinds of things about a person if you caught them off guard. Polished boots, starched shirt, creased pants said he was neat. Deep grooves around his mouth and the way he sagged in his chair said he was tired. Creases between his eyes said he worried a lot. That he'd chosen to meet her in a public place said this was not a reunion: it was all business.

Jo Beth would rather be struck by lightning than place herself under the scrutiny of the uncle she wouldn't even recognize if he didn't make the news with regularity. Except for the recent rodeo parade, the last time she'd seen him was the day after she'd been booted from the Huntsville Police Department.

That day so long ago, she'd awakened to the familiar feeling of being dragged behind a John Deere tractor over ten miles of bad gravel roads and the sound of pounding on her door. When she'd swung it open, Uncle Mark had been on her front porch. The way his lips curled down reminded her of a door-to-door vacuum cleaner salesman who hated his job.

"Jo Beth," he'd said to her, "you've made the news and disgraced the family."

"Did you drive all the way from Tupelo just to tell me that?"

"I came to tell you not to expect me to bail you out and fix this mess you're in."

"I didn't ask you for anything."

"You'll change your mind and come crawling to me."

"I wouldn't ask you for help if you were the last person on earth. And for your information, I don't crawl. I walk in boots like Granddaddy taught me."

"Daddy spoiled you rotten. Just like he did Rafe. And both of you a shame on our family name."

"Leave my daddy out of this."

"Gladly. As far as I'm concerned, neither one of you is a Dawson."

If you dwell on the past long enough, the memories can become blackbirds that will peck your eyes out. They can blind you to the truth staring you right in the face.

Uncle Mark was going to humiliate her again. That was the truth.

But the deeper truth, the one that coursed through her like a river, was that Jo Beth could no longer distinguish herself from the spirit that refused to leave. Sometimes she imagined she was the one lying dead underneath the roses, crying out for mercy. Sometimes she'd have a thought that was as foreign to her as sobriety, and she'd swear Pony Jones's blueprint was burned into her bones.

Jo Beth smoothed the front of her blouse and stepped from behind a marble column. Uncle Mark saw her and the change was instant. Without effort, he transformed to a regal, slightly arrogant public figure.

He stood. "How good to see you."

Good to see you usually meant a hug. His hand was callused, his handshake firm. But he didn't even look her in the eye as he sat in an overstuffed armchair. There would be no affection in the lobby of the Marriott.

"What brings you here, Jo Beth?"

What had brought her here? A vaguely recalled remark from an alcoholic mother? Desire for humiliation? She tucked her hair behind her ears. It felt limp and dry. Cheap shampoo would do that. Soap was even worse.

On the TV behind her, Sonja Livingstone, who apparently never slept, turned the program over to the weatherman. He was predicting thunderstorms.

"If you're here for money, I'll write you a check." Mark Dawson reached into his pocket and Jo Beth was suddenly alone. Worse. She couldn't feel her bones, her blood, her skin. Jo Beth Dawson didn't even exist.

"How much?" His checkbook was in his hands.

She wondered what she was worth. Fifty dollars? Fifty cents? How could you put a price on life? On hers? On Pony's?

"I don't want your money."

"There's no need for embarrassment. I've put the past behind me. After all, we're still family."

"Since when?"

Maggie's family shared holidays and vacations. The dinner table, for God's sake.

"I don't have to listen to this. If you can't control yourself, I'm leaving."

"Who is Morning Star?"

Mark Dawson didn't even blink at her question. "Pony Jones's mother."

"How do you know?"

"The news." He nodded toward the TV. "They've been covering her story all morning."

Sonja Livingstone's image filled the screen again as she leaned forward, sharing secrets with her TV audience. "For more on rodeo icon Pony Jones, we have a live hookup to Tom Abbott in Doe Valley. Tom, are you there?"

"I'm here, Sonja, with Sheriff Jim Buckley. And, boy, the rain is coming down in Tennessee." He was wearing a yellow slicker with the collar turned up. Behind him, a dozen young women in dripping cowboy hats milled around waving signs that read, *Pony Jones Lives!* WHUN's roving TV reporter looked as if he'd rather be anywhere except where he was.

Jo Beth empathized. As much as she wanted to leave her uncle without another word, her stubborn streak held her to the floor. And something else, too. There was a little girl inside her lost in a howling jungle, a child hungry for things she didn't dare name, crying *Look at me.*

"You're lying."

"Why would I lie?" Her uncle never changed expression.

Jo Beth knew stonewalling when she saw it. She also knew the only thing to break a stone wall was a battering ram.

"I heard Mother mention Morning Star. What was she to the Dawsons?"

"Nothing. She was just another Indian at the rodeo. Sit down, Jo Beth, before you fall down. You look like you need a drink."

The thought of cool, dark whiskey almost brought Jo Beth to her knees. The memory of her mother's closed door kept her upright. There had been two voices behind that door.

The memory clicked, slid into place.

"It was you. Mother was talking to you about Morning Star."

"Your mother was crazy. This family would have been spared a lot of grief if Rafe had never married her."

"I'd never have been born."

"Precisely." Mark Dawson stood up. "Now if you'll excuse me, I have important people to see."

Somehow she made her way out of the hotel and across the parking lot. Sitting in her truck with her shoulders hunched and knuckles white on the steering wheel, Jo Beth longed for a drink, a rock to crawl under, anything to diminish the humiliation of her encounter with Uncle Mark.

If it was me, I'd a stomped him till he was flatter than a cow patty.

That voice again. The words ricocheted through her like a shot of adrenaline. Was she hallucinating or was the spirit of Pony Jones so strong it could communicate with the living? Get too much alcohol in your blood and there's no telling what would happen.

In her peripheral vision Jo Beth saw two young girls strolling through the Marriott's parking lot, their heads together, one of them saying in a loud voice, "You shouldn't let him treat you like that, Jill."

Desperate to find logic in a world suddenly turned upside down, Jo Beth latched onto the first thing she could find that made sense. She'd been merely overhearing a conversation that had nothing to do with her. Nothing to do with Uncle Mark and Morning Star. And yet the words felt personal. She couldn't get them out of her head.

Who was Jo Beth Dawson to stomp anybody?

Need rose in her again, but this time it wasn't a need for liquid courage. It was a raging river that would drown her if she didn't find out the truth.

And she knew where she might find it. Firing her truck to life, she headed to the rodeo.

Thirteen

Titus wondered if grief made a man invisible, if sorrow changed a man to a dragonfly, devoid of bones and blood, so transparent he could float among the rough stock-holding pens and dusty cowboys and never be seen.

Or maybe it was Pony's energy that allowed him to glide through the rodeo crowd undetected. Her indomitable spirit was everywhere, in the smell of sweet hay and plaited leather ropes, in the shadowed faces and hushed tones of her peers, in the toss of a stallion's head and the challenge of a bull.

He wanted to reach out and gather her close, sit on a bale of hay and rock her in his arms while friends gathered round to tell how she could make you laugh without trying, how she could put a hand on your shoulder and you'd feel comforted for days, how she could blow into a room and you'd swear she'd sprinkled some magic potion on you. You'd vow she'd cast some kind of spell that made you remember who you'd wanted to be before everybody said you were too short, too tall, too broke, too uneducated, too unsophisticated. Until finally you were just plain too scared.

He wanted to stop people and say, "Do you remember my Pony? What was she doing the last time you saw her?"

Titus wiped his hand over his face. Swiping at tears that

wouldn't come. Trying to remember Pony exactly as he'd seen her when she left Doe Mountain.

She'd been wearing red boots, her Stetson at a jaunty angle, her black braid shining in the sun. He'd been in the barn raking hay.

"Daddy, why don't you come with me?"

"Can't, Pony. Got too much to do around here."

"I'm gonna win."

"Don't you always?"

She'd walked over, put her arms around him and kissed him on the cheek.

"See you later, Daddy."

He'd gone on raking his hay. He hadn't even watched her walk away. If only he'd known. And yet, wasn't that part of God's grace? That you didn't see tragedy coming, even when it was roaring at you with the speed of a runaway train? That you went about your business expecting the best?

Titus slid between the horse trailers looking for the man who had cut her down. Specifically, he was looking for Buckin' Billy Rakestraw. There was talk about him and Pony—lots of it. Titus had expected to hear of the grudge he bore her for taking his bull riding title. Buckin' Billy was the first man his daughter took it from, and she hadn't stopped outscoring the cowboys until somebody put a permanent end to the threat of Pony Jones.

What Titus hadn't expected to hear was that Billy had tried several times to date Pony. Talk was, the last time she'd turned him down, he'd vowed to make her pay.

Titus was headed around the biggest trailer on the lot when he spotted Jo Beth talking to a beat-up looking old cowboy. If there was a Dawson about, trouble wouldn't be far behind. He eased along the periphery of the trailer till he was close enough to overhear.

"I'm trying to find Titus Jones," she said. "Have you seen him?"

Titus Jones stepped backward into the shadow of the horse trailers. He didn't want another encounter with Jo Beth Dawson.

For more reasons than he cared to think about.

Sam was hot and tired and hungry. A candy bar didn't last long when you were chasing all over the rodeo for a killer.

If you asked him, this whole case was a killer. In all his years of police work he'd never had a victim get under his skin the way Pony Jones had. He was taking her murder personally. A dangerous thing for a man in his line of work. Because of a little slip of girl with the heart of a lion, he was making foolish mistakes, squandering his off-duty time chasing after Titus Jones, wondering about Jo Beth Dawson, trying to remember what it had been like with a woman in his house.

Shoot, he was even trying to talk Jo Beth into a cup of coffee and picking up the phone every time Lana called.

Before the Pony Jones case, he'd screened Lana on his caller ID. Now he was letting her through with the regularity of a man who was losing his grip.

Maybe he was.

Sam might as well eat a hot dog. No sense starving himself just because he'd cracked open the door to the past and was now trying to dig himself out of the avalanche.

He'd headed to the hot dog vendor when his cell phone rang. With his stomach rumbling and his hot dog quest on hold, Sam answered.

"Yo. Luther. What've you got?"

"The Indian."

"Bring him in."

Sam hurried to the hot dog vendor and bought three foot-longs, one for Luther. He wasn't about to question John Running Wolf on an empty stomach.

Standing in the interrogation room, Sam's half-digested hot dogs rolled around in his stomach, causing him to regret his gluttony. While he fidgeted and squeezed his sphincter muscles to prevent exploding gas, the ancient Native American sat so still he looked like he'd died in his chair. So far he'd told them nothing except his name, address, age and rank. John Running Wolf was a veteran of the Korean War.

"Let's go over this again." Sam leaned across the table that separated them. "Why were you asking about Pony Jones at the rodeo?"

"She's famous."

"But you wanted to see her personally. Outside the rodeo ring."

"I wanted her autograph."

Sam swiveled to Luther, who was standing against the wall looking as solid and uninviting as a brick shit house. "Luther, do you buy it?"

"Naw." Luther lowered his toothpick and flexed his shoulders. "He's lying. Take a break, Sam. I'll get the truth out of him."

John Running Wolf didn't blink, didn't register a single change in body language or expression. Any other time, Sam would have admired him. The old man wore dignity like a tailor-made coat.

Today, though, he just wanted to shake some answers out of him so he could make some progress on his stalled case. Sam leaned across the table, the good cop full of sympathy, ready to make a deal, versus the bad cop who was about to shove himself away from the wall and use John Running Wolf the way Oscar De La Hoya used a punching bag.

"John, I'm just trying to get a few things straight here. My partner doesn't believe you. He doesn't even like you. But I do. I don't think you had anything to do with Pony Jones's murder." Sam leaned closer, dropped his voice. "Did you, John? Did you kill Pony Jones?"

"I am not a murderer."

Luther separated himself from the wall and slapped the table. "Did you kill her?"

"I honor all living creatures."

Luther got in his face. "You wanted to find her because you had a beef. She put up a fight and you hit her over the head."

"No."

"Don't give me that shit." Luther's face turned red. Sam was going to have to remind him, he was too old to play tough cop. He had to be careful of his blood pressure. "You're a war veteran. Trained to kill. You came down that ridge armed to the teeth. You found her and you killed her."

John Running Wolf had been packing a Buck Knife with a big, carved-bone handle inlaid with turquoise stones. Big enough to hit a small woman in the back of the head. Big enough to kill her if you hit hard enough.

Sam studied his opponent. In spite of his age, John Running Wolf had the closed look of a man full of dark secrets and pent-up rage, a trained warrior who could kill, then walk away and eat jalapeño peppers straight from the jar without upsetting his digestion. Even worse, he had the look of a man with nothing to lose.

Of all the people Sam faced—desperate, despairing, defiant—a man with nothing to lose was the most dangerous.

They would get nothing from John Running Wolf. Not today. Not any day.

He nodded at Luther, and the two of them walked out, leaving the old man in the room alone. They stood awhile looking at him through the one-way glass. John Running Wolf didn't move, didn't blink. He looked as if he were meditating.

"He's lying," Luther said.

"Yeah. But lying doesn't mean he killed Pony Jones."

In fact, they didn't have a clue who had killed Pony Jones. Maybe it wasn't hot dogs that had his gut in turmoil: maybe it was the case. Whatever the reason, on his way home, Sam planned to stock up on Gas-X and Pepto-Bismol.

Not that it would solve the problem. All it would do is mask it, coat his angry gut so he could sleep at night. What he needed was a break in the case. What he needed was some peace with his past. What he needed was a miracle.

"Luther, Pony Jones was part Native, right?"

"You think there's a connection? I'll go back in there and get it out of him."

"Save the Rambo posturing. Wolf's not going to tell us jack shit."

"Donovan, you wouldn't be suggesting we have to dig the dirt ourselves?"

"Get ready to soil your lily whites, Lu."

·   ·   ·

Running Wolf knew they were watching him. Closing his eyes, he removed himself from the sterile room with the cold, gray walls.

He was in the deep forest, lying on a bed of pine needles, the sun shining on his face and the wind lifting his hair, lifting the wings of the eagle that soared above him. He could hear the sound of water running clean and clear.

Or was it his sister's laughter? Her voice that made you think she was filled with bubbling brooks and gentle breezes?

What was she saying? What was she trying to tell him?

Hurry.

What was the hurry? Pony was dead.

The heavy door opened and a cop in uniform came to escort him out, gave him the knife with the bone handle carved by his grandfather. The bone burned his hand and called to him in the voice of his ancestors, while the diary, locked safely away in the toolbox of his pickup truck, cried to him with the tears of his sister.

Hurry.

Running Wolf knew what he had to do.

Surrounded by the muted roar of rodeo and the thin gray curtain of dusk, Titus sat in the shadow of the rough stock-holding pens with his tired head in his hands, trying to imagine what Pony would have looked like in ten years. Would she still have been riding the bulls? Be married? Have kids?

Titus felt the loss of Pony's unborn children as acutely as if the murderer had taken a blunt object and felled them, too. Three boys with Pony's grit and a little dark-haired girl who would have looked just like Morning Star. Titus would have taught them the names of wildflowers, all the flowers on Doe Mountain that their grandmother had loved. He would have told his grandchildren how the moon let you know when it was time to plant corn and how migratory birds taught you about the coming of winter and the greening of spring. He would have built a tire swing underneath the old hickory tree in his front yard so he could sit on the porch with Dog and watch his grandchildren laugh.

And he'd have dared Pony to introduce them to rodeo.

Suddenly John Running Wolf stood in front of him, ancient as the mountains and inscrutable as the sea. Titus had not even heard him coming. He was not surprised, considering that he was the age of diminished capacities and John Running Wolf had been born stealthy.

"I'm John Running Wolf."

"I know who you are." Titus never forgot his enemies.

"I'm sorry about Pony."

"I don't need your sympathy." John Running Wolf had tried to take Pony from him. Titus didn't want anything the man had to offer.

"I came to talk."

"Whatever you have to say, leave her out of it."

The old man hung his head as if he were suddenly ashamed, as if he couldn't face Judgment Day and Titus Jones without confessing his sins.

Titus had nothing left for him to take. And so he waited, coiled and dangerous.

Finally John Running Wolf lifted eyes that had turned tragic. "I killed her."

The air became thick and red, thick enough to smother a man. Titus tried to find Running Wolf through the bloody haze, but all he could see was a shadow, a vague outline of his archenemy, and behind him, an image of his daughter.

"Pony?"

Titus whispered her name, and she stared at him through the swirling red mist.

I want to go home, Daddy.

Titus's heart clove in two. With a wisdom born on the mountain and honed by love of a Native wife, he understood as few men did: his daughter was caught between two worlds and belonged to neither.

Looking at her sweet, proud face, his blood felt too hot, his bones too heavy. It was up to him to find her killer so Pony could find peace. Titus tried to tell her but the words turned to stone in his mouth.

The wind picked up, hinting of storms, but Titus didn't move. He strained his eyes through the swirling mists until Pony began to dissolve. He tried to say *Don't go,* but his plea turned to a boulder in his chest. A lesser man would have been crushed, but Titus remained upright, his eyes fixed on his daughter until the mists lifted and she vanished.

John Running Wolf had not killed his daughter. If he had, Titus would know.

With the haze lifted, Titus saw him clearly, a stooped old man who bore little resemblance to the strong, proud Cherokee he'd once been.

John Running Wolf had never brought Titus anything except trouble. And now he was back with the foolish ramblings of an old man.

"Leave me." Titus had no time to waste on him.

"This was meant for Morning Star and Pony." Running Wolf pulled a flat, crumbling book from his jacket and placed it at Titus's feet, then turned and walked away, despair in his steps and dignity in his bones.

Titus wanted to call after him. *Wait*, he wanted to say. *I don't want anything that belongs to you*. But the small parcel at his feet gave off a scent as seductive and sad as fallen roses.

He picked it up. The book was elaborately beaded with white, green and gold in the design of the Cherokee rose, the yellowing pages held together with faded ribbon.

Titus untied the ribbon and read the fine script on the cover page: *They call me Cherokee Rose and this is my story.*

He closed the diary. Titus knew this story by heart. It was the one Wolf had told when he'd come up the mountain for Pony. It was a story that had settled in the bones of those involved like soot, staining their lives for three generations.

In the distance, thunder rolled and a streak of lightning split the sky. Titus prayed for rain, a torrential baptism from the skies that would wash them all clean.

When the storm hit, Jo Beth was spreading mustard on a corn dog she'd bought from a rodeo vendor, wondering why she was even bothering to try to piece together bits of her past. What good would it do?

Within minutes she was soaked by rains so dark and fierce she was left standing in the parking lot with beating heart, skeleton and sinew exposed. Even her thoughts and her fears were visible to curious passersby.

A middle-aged woman, holding a soaked newspaper over her head as she dashed to shelter, was stopped in her tracks by the sight. "Say, aren't you Jo Beth Dawson?"

"No." Jo Beth thought about having her name legally changed. People did it all the time.

What was not so easy was changing yourself. If she were a snake she'd shed her skin, emerge sleek and brand new. She'd become Somebody Else. Anybody except the woman who knew the names of every liquor store in Mississippi and Alabama but could barely remember the color of her mother's eyes.

As she dashed through the parking lot, a piece of debris flew into Jo Beth's eye. Inside her truck she found a crumpled napkin in the glove compartment then pulled down the rearview mirror and set to work.

Suddenly her passenger door opened and Sam Donovan slid into the seat. "Let me."

He grabbed the napkin and had the cinder out in seconds.

"I didn't ask for your help."

"I don't need a *thank-you*. I just want to know what you're doing at the rodeo."

"You know how I am about rodeo, Sam."

"I'm not buying it. Who are you looking for? Titus or the killer?"

"If you want a formal interrogation, you're going to have to take me in."

"Dammit, Jo Beth." Sam spat out his gum, cracked open the door and tossed it. "If you're withholding information, I'm going to forget that I once tried to save your butt."

"You never tried to save me, Sam. You covered my mistakes to keep your own reputation safe. Dawson and Donovan, the best detective team in the business."

He stared at her so long she began to sweat. "Once upon a time, you were a crusader, Jo."

"That woman no longer exists, Sam."

"Dammit. Don't you lay that guilt trip on me. I'm not the one who killed her. You did."

He slammed out of her truck, said a heartfelt *Shit*, then stalked off, occasionally stopping to swipe the gum from his shoe.

"Serves you right," she yelled.

A female voice yelled back at her, *Atta girl. Cowboy up!*

Jo Beth was so startled she cracked her head on the rearview mirror. The voice had come out of nowhere, as clear as if the speaker were in the truck with her. For a crazy moment the face staring back at her was not her own.

She peered through the driving rain, but she couldn't see a soul. When the voice whispered through her mind once more, *Cowboy up*, the truth took root in her like fierce dandelions. She took a deep breath, fighting her familiar response of *drink and run*. Who would care?

The stubborn spirit who refused to leave answered her. *I would*.

With her hands shaking, Jo Beth picked up her cell phone and dialed.

"Mags? I need to talk."

I'm split in half, standing in the middle of the rain, dry as a bone, my throat parched from yelling at Jo Beth to put on her boots and spurs and at the same time yelling at Daddy for explanations.

Not that I need much. I ain't dumb. The Indian man who calls hisself John Running Wolf is some of my people. I feel my bones attached to his.

And that diary . . . The only time I ever felt the kind of excitement I had looking down at them beaded Cherokee roses and then reading over Daddy's shoulder when he opened the diary was when I rode my first bull against the men.

"Go on," I'm yelling. "Turn the pages. I want to know."

But Daddy has shut his mind to me. He just sets there, planted firm as a rock without any intentions of moving.

When I was alive and kicking, riding the bulls and beating the pants off everybody that come along and tried to take my title, I had such good instincts I could tell you when it was going to rain even before the first cloud appeared in the sky. I could predict the sex of unborn babies and tell you to the day when they would be born. I could even tell you down to the exact month when you was going to fall in love and get married, and whether the marriage would last.

One time I asked Daddy if they was any shamans in my mother's family, and he said, "The past don't concern us, Pony. Just the future. And we gonna make it a good one."

We did, too. But, oh, I missed the comfort of women. That's the one thing Daddy never give me. My female relatives. If he'd kept turning the pages of my diary while he was setting in the woods, he'd a understood that.

I'm crying but I can't feel my own tears, just a void so deep inside me I might fall in and disappear.

"Pony." My mother's hand is soft on my shoulder, her voice a whisper in my ear. "In time your daddy will understand what you needed, but it's too soon. If he adds regret to grief, it will kill him."

"Is John Running Wolf my grandfather?"

"No, Pony. He's my mother's brother."

"Who is Cherokee Rose?"

"My mother."

I reach down and try to snatch my grandmother's diary away from Daddy, but my hand passes right through. I ain't never been one to give up. Even if I am dead. So I try it again.

When my mother laughs, I whirl around trying to catch her unawares and see her face, but I don't see nothing except the rains beating on the rodeo parking lot.

If it would do any good, I'd commence having a screaming, kicking hissy fit. I'm tired a being stuck without no control over my body.

"Be patient, Pony. 'Now I see through a glass darkly, but then face to face.'"

Her leave-taking sounds like the sigh of the wind.

I'm glad she come, but I coulda done without the Bible quotes.

I guess my mother don't know me and organized religion split the sheet years ago. We got lots a catching up to do when I get wherever I'm headed.

Heaven, the preacher used to say when I was still going to church and listening. Accordin' to him, if we was good, we was all headed to a place called Heaven.

But I've growed up a bit since then and it seems to me, folks makes they own heaven and hell right here on earth. It seems to me that hanging around streets of gold, twanging on a harp ain't no way to spend eternity.

I'm hoping there's a barn somewhere in my future. Horses and cows and cats and dogs and every kind of critter you can name. Even bulls. Maybe there's a big rodeo where I'm a heading and I'll get to strap on my spurs and show them saints what Pony Jones is made of.

But most of all, I just want a chance to lay my head in my mama's lap.

Fourteen

Maggie stood in her bare feet staring at the storm from her kitchen window. Jo Beth didn't go anywhere voluntarily. At least, not in the last ten years. So why now?

The rain pounded the windows and cut a visible path through Maggie's zinnia bed. Jo Beth must be desperate to go out in that downpour. Maggie just hoped she was sober.

She poured cream into a silver pitcher, then added two slices of apple pie to the serving tray. She always bought Mrs. Smith's, transferred it to her blue stone pie plate and told her family it was homemade. Some people would call that a deception, but Maggie preferred to think of it as a time-saving device that did no harm, but caused guests to compliment her cooking and her husband and children to worship the quicksand she walked on.

When the doorbell rang, Maggie put on her shoes and went down the front hall to let Jo Beth in. Soaking wet, she looked like she weighed no more than the occasional stray cat that showed up in Maggie's backyard during the harvest moon, when the air was so motionless every word you said got trapped and hung over your head like a cloud.

Maggie leaned in close to hug her. Regret clung to Jo Beth's skin like the fine dusting of compost Maggie got when she repotted her dragon wing begonias.

She lingered over the hug long enough to determine if Jo Beth had been drinking but not long enough for the scent of unspeakable secrets and dark thoughts to rub off on her. Maggie was too light to endure such burdens. She knew that about herself. Though she was feisty and defiant, she was not built with the same strong fiber that kept Jo Beth from disintegrating, that let a tiny-boned young woman like Pony Jones ride the bulls.

Tonight, when Maggie was tucked safely in bed, she would tell James that Jo Beth had been stone cold sober today. She needed to do that, needed to justify her actions to her husband. Another example of her own soft nature. She'd be willing to bet that women like Pony Jones didn't justify themselves to any-damn-body.

Last night James had complained that having Jo Beth in town changed Maggie, took too much out of her, made her do foolish things. He'd suggested Maggie ought to back off till Jo Beth straightened out. His very words.

Standing in the hallway now, she said to Jo Beth, "Get out of those wet clothes and I'll throw them in the dryer. There's a robe hanging in the downstairs bathroom."

"What about James?"

"He's working late tonight. Some big corporate case that's driving us both crazy."

After she'd put the clothes into her Whirlpool dryer, Maggie carried her heavy silver coffee service to the living room. While she waited for Jo Beth, she thought of apple pie and white lies and regret so wide it took up all the space in a room so you had to walk out onto the front porch to catch your breath.

She would not back off, as James had so impolitely put it. She was not about to spend the rest of her days on the front porch trying to breathe and wondering how Jo Beth would have turned out if she hadn't abandoned her.

"Is something bothering you, Mags?"

Jo Beth was back, dressed in Maggie's blue flannel robe that hung from her shoulders like the clothes you put on scarecrows to ward off birds that were stealing your corn.

"Who? Me?" Maggie recovered her equilibrium. "Sit down. Here. Have a cup of coffee. It'll warm your bones." It was her best cheerleader imitation.

"Cut the cheering section and give me the truth."

She should have known Jo Beth would see right through her.

"Just a little argument James and I had."

"About last night?"

"Yep. I let him rant and rave then I sewed him a new frock, as my grandmother would say. It'll be a cold day in August before he tries to tell me what to do again."

"Don't let me be the cause of problems between you and James."

"Any problems I have with him are my own doing." Maggie offered a slice of pie. "Your call sounded serious, Jo Beth. What's on your mind?"

"Mendacity."

"Have you been reading *Cat on a Hot Tin Roof* again?"

"I've been living it. My mother and even my grandfather told me only what they thought I needed to hear. Now Uncle Mark's skirting around the truth and so is Titus Jones. It's like we're all caught up in some alcoholic fog."

When she set her cup on the table, Jo Beth had to hold it with both hands to keep from spilling coffee.

"I can't get Pony Jones out of my mind, Mags. She's stuck in there and won't go away. It's like she's part of me. It's like she's telling me if I don't deal with my past, I'm never going to have a future."

Maggie hid her astonishment behind the coffee cup. Over the years, Jo Beth had become a tambourine in a tornado, jangling tunelessly with the gusts of every whirlwind. For the past few days, though, Maggie had felt Jo Beth was standing at a crossroads. Any little thing could tip her one way or the other.

Now Pony Jones had reached from the grave and shoved her upward.

Maggie thought that sometimes, suddenly, there was God. At the moment you despaired, even to the point of giving up, a miracle took place in your own living room, and all you could do was sit there hanging onto your coffee cup while random words whirled around your brain—*please* and *thank you* and *yes*.

"Well?" Jo Beth studied Maggie over the rim of her coffee cup. "Aren't you going to say anything?"

"Do you want more pie?" Jo Beth shook her head no, but Maggie stood up and hurried to the kitchen anyway. She grabbed a paper towel off the rack and wiped her eyes, honked her nose.

Nobody ever understood why she cried when she was happy. The more hellish the problem, the harder she cried when she saw the resolution. She stuck a wadded piece of paper towel in her mouth to cover the sound of her vast relief, then finally had to use the dishcloth.

"Mags?" She jerked around so fast she nearly knocked over the coffeepot. Jo Beth was standing in the doorway. "What's wrong? Is it James?" Maggie could do nothing but sniffle. "If it's James, I'll shoot his balls off."

Maggie started to giggle and ended up with the hiccups. Jo Beth pulled open cabinets, searched till she found a plastic sandwich bag.

"Breathe into it."

Maggie covered her mouth with the bag. Sometimes, all you needed to breathe again was a little help from a friend.

"Good grief, Mags. I thought I was going to have to call 911."

"You know me. I cry as hard at good news as I do at funerals." She threw the plastic bag and the paper towels into the garbage can. "You don't have to worry about doing this on your own. I'll go to the meetings with you."

Jo Beth narrowed her eyes. "If you think you're going to drag me to AA meetings, forget it."

"But you said you wanted a future."

"I didn't say I wanted one. I said Pony Jones wants me to have one."

What were the liquor companies doing now? Making alcohol you couldn't smell. Good lord. Maggie felt like throwing the coffeepot.

"See?" Jo Beth raked her hands through her hair. "Even you think I'm going crazy."

Maggie didn't point out the obvious, that Jo Beth was talking to a dead cowgirl. Instead, she started tossing flour and eggs and sugar into a mixing bowl.

"Maggie, what in the heck are you doing?"

"Making a cake. When I'm upset, I cook."

For a minute, Jo Beth looked like she might bolt, blue bathrobe and all. Then she started laughing.

"While you're at it, make it a bourbon cake."

"I'll do no such thing." Maggie dumped chocolate and nuts into the mixture. "You sit right down, missy. You're going to tell me what's eating at you, and I don't care if it does involve a talking corpse. I'm going to get the truth even if it takes all night."

Jo Beth sat in a chair with the same air of a third grader Maggie had scolded. She considered that a small triumph.

"I don't know where to start, Mags."

"Start any-damn-where you want to. Just *do something*, Jo Beth."

Jo Beth jumped back up so fast her chair clattered to the floor.

"It's not like I have options, here. For God's sake, Maggie. I'm a sorry-assed drunk."

"You are *not*. If I ever hear you say that again I'm going to"—Maggie wadded her hands into fists—"beat you with a broom."

They glared at each other across the length of Maggie's kitchen. Suspicion was so thick it coated Maggie's skin and curdled the milk in her cake.

"I mean it, Jo Beth. I am tired of you pitching yourself headfirst into whatever garbage can is convenient."

When Jo Beth's shoulders sagged, Maggie was struck at how small she was. Not just skinny, but petite. Had she always been so tiny? Was it the cowboy boots she used to wear that had made her seem larger? Or had it been her swagger, her *take no prisoners* attitude?

"I'm sorry, Mags." Jo Beth poured herself a cup of coffee, righted her chair and sat back down. "Ever since I found the body of Pony Jones, my life has been turned upside down. I don't know what to do anymore."

Maggie pulled her chair close and took both Jo Beth's hands. "I'm here, Jo. Let's figure it out."

"A part of me wants to know what happened to Pony."

"That's a good thing. You were once a great detective. You could be again."

"It's not my case. Still, I have this nagging feeling that my family is somehow connected to Pony Jones."

"Not to mention that the victim told you so." Maggie was glad to see Jo Beth's grin.

"Go back to your cake before I swat you."

"I've lost interest in the cake."

"When I was little, I overheard Mother and Uncle Mark talking about Morning Star."

"The dead girl's mother?" Maggie had heard it on the morning news. "Why do you think there's a connection to your family?"

"Uncle Mark lied to me about her. And I have this gut feeling."

Gut feelings were good. That meant Jo Beth was coming back, didn't it? Maggie was almost afraid to get her hopes up again. But she always had the cake to fall back on.

"I could research Pony and Morning Star on the internet, Jo. And there's the Native American Cultural Center."

Jo Beth sat still for so long Maggie thought she was backing out of her newfound resolve. All she could do was shut her eyes and silently beg, *Please.*

"Where are my clothes?"

"In the dryer, and it's still running."

When Jo Beth headed toward the laundry room, Maggie would have sworn she stood two inches taller.

"They're not dry yet, Jo. Stay for supper." Maggie followed along and found Jo Beth struggling into a pair of damp jeans. "Does this mean you're going to take names and kick butt?"

"Don't get your hopes up, Mags. I'm just putting on clothes. Last I heard, you can get arrested in Huntsville for going about the streets naked."

The storm clouds had blown over by the time Jo Beth left. A few stars straggled across the sky and a moon straddled the topmost branch of Maggie's magnolia tree, looking like it might topple out of the heavens if you weren't careful.

Maggie held her breath, not wanting to be the one who caused the fall of the moon. She'd lived her whole life *careful*. What would James say if all of a sudden she turned into somebody else, somebody who could dig up the dirt about Morning Star, somebody who could help solve the mystery of Jo Beth's past and a rodeo cowgirl who wore red boots?

Titus had not meant to read Cherokee Rose's diary, but no matter where he put it—in the glove compartment of his pickup, underneath his folded-up jacket on the seat, in the toolbox attached to the truck bed—it gave off a fragrance that sucked him in, seduced him as surely as if Morning Star were standing in the deep, rain-soaked woods beside him, unbraiding her hair.

With the deep green smells of earth and forest surrounding him, Titus lifted the beaded diary from the folds of his jacket. When he opened it, the sky turned vicious, while the scattered stars and the moon glowed a bright, angry red.

Was there a warning in the book? A finger pointing to his daughter's killer? An answer to why John Running Wolf had said he murdered Pony?

Using the tiny penlight he kept in the glove compartment, Titus scanned the pages. The story was all there just as

Running Wolf had told him that day on the mountain—the tangled family roots, the betrayals, lies, and secrets.

He retied the frayed ribbon, laid the diary on the seat of his truck, got a can of pinto beans from his stash and opened it with his knife. He wouldn't risk building a fire. Instead, he ate the beans cold, off the tip of his knife, then chased the heavy, sticky taste with water from the cooler he'd brought from Doe Mountain.

If he didn't find the killer soon, he'd have to replenish his supplies. Titus threw the empty can into the plastic trash bag in the back of his truck, poured water over his knife blade, wiped it on his pants, and put it in his pocket.

Tomorrow he'd have to put on a clean pair. These would do for now. You didn't need clean clothes for a few hours' sleep in the back of your truck.

Titus looked at the sky, judging whether the storm was over, whether he should lay his bedroll under the stars or if he needed to sleep in the cab, where he'd have to bunch up his knees and likely get a cramp in his legs.

A sound that didn't belong in the woods came from his far right. Titus dropped his bedroll and reached for his knife.

The sound came again, the forest floor crackling underneath clumsy footsteps. Whoever was tracking him didn't know the least thing about stealth. That let out John Running Wolf. And probably Sam Donovan, too. The cop didn't strike Titus as a man who blundered about, announcing his presence to anybody with sense enough to be still and listen. He might as well send out calling cards.

Keeping low, Titus slid from cover to cover, thankful to the universe for thick bushes and a cushioned forest floor, for years of living in harmony with nature and its critters. Squirrels and birds watched him glide by without startling off and betraying his presence.

A quarter of a mile from his hidden camp, Titus saw his stalker. She had mud up to her knees, wet leaves and brambles caught in her clothes and twigs in her hair. If it had been any other time, any other woman, Titus would have laughed. But this was Jo Beth Dawson.

She started right, then stopped, said *Shit* under her breath, then turned left. If she aimed to find him, she was going the wrong way. The trees thinned in that direction and he could see her for a good long while, thanks to Orion, the Hunter, putting in a late appearance.

Jo Beth took another turn and headed back toward him. The woman was going in circles. She didn't have a clue where she was heading and probably didn't even know which direction she'd come from.

Titus pocketed his knife. He could walk away. He could go back to his truck, get in his sleeping bag and rest easy that he wouldn't be disturbed by her. At the rate she was tracking, she'd be lost in the woods the rest of the night.

But ingrained decency and years of treating every one of God's living critters the way he'd want to be treated propelled Titus down the open path.

"Are you looking for me?"

She spun around, both hands holding her gun, the weapon pointed straight at him. There was no unsteadiness in her now, no sign of the heavy drinking he'd seen the last time he confronted her.

As her eyes adjusted to the dark and she recognized him, she lowered her gun.

"Yes. I want to talk to you."

"About what?"

"Everything. I want to know about Morning Star. The whole truth. And after you've finished telling me that, I want to know why you hate me."

Sam desperately needed a break in the Pony Jones case. Up until now he'd been the detective who could wrap up ninety-nine percent of his cases before they got cold. He could deliver the perp before the public lost faith and the news media turned nasty.

Sonja Livingstone's latest report on the Pony Jones case was borderline nasty. One more day and she'd be out for blood.

His coffee had turned cold, but he didn't pour it out and refill his cup. He'd be out of there in ten minutes. He planned to go home, put on a fresh pot, then sink into his sofa with a bag of Fritos and a jar of cheese dip and watch the Braves. Chipper Jones was due for a homer.

Sam massaged his temples and watched the clock. And then Chief of Detectives Carl Madison stuck his head out of his office and yelled for him.

"Yo?"

"Some kid found a bloodstained blunt object out in the soccer field near Mill Village."

Sam started strapping on his shoulder holsters. "You think it's the Pony Jones weapon?"

"Could be. It's close enough to the rodeo." Carl popped a Tums into his mouth. "You and Luther get out there before some idiot screws up the evidence."

Within two minutes Sam and Luther were barreling toward Mill Village, Sam driving while Luther blew into his Styrofoam cup to cool his coffee.

"Did you get me a cup, Lu?"

"Who do you think I am? Your wife?"

"My wife never brought me coffee."

"Then you'd think you'd have learned to get your own by now." Luther took a sip, then smacked his lips just to get Sam's goat. "Good stuff."

"Shut up."

"Caller say what the blunt object was?"

"Carl didn't say."

"That's odd. Don't you think they'd say a hammer if that's what they found?"

"Maybe it wasn't."

"Then what was it?"

"How do I know? Do I look like Houdini?" Was getting snappish a sign of pressure or old age?

"Naw, you look like hell."

Sam might have to kill Luther before the night was over. But first, he had to find out about the blunt object.

If it was his lucky night, they'd get a blood match and fingerprints. If they were very lucky they'd wrap this case up in a couple of days.

Sam planned to go fishing. Maybe down to the Alabama gulf coast. Not Gulf Shores. Too fancy; too close to Lana.

He'd go to some out of the way hole-in-the-wall where he wouldn't shave for a week and could get a good hot dog for a buck and half. He'd go someplace where memories of his failure with the only two women he'd ever cared about—Jo Beth and Lana—didn't waylay him around every corner.

Standing in the deep woods, pointing her gun at Titus Jones, Jo Beth found herself looking at sorrow so deep you could dive in and end up at the bottom of the ocean. What right did she have to witness another man's grief, even in the dark when the pale light of the North Star turned the shadows to silver?

Dampness rose from the forest floor and seeped through her skin, settled in her bones. She should be in her Silver Streak facing the choice of bed or bottle instead of confronting a man who looked more like a battle-scarred wolf ignoring the pain of a mangled leg than the father of a young woman whose body had been buried under roses.

The gun grew unsteady in her hands and she wanted desperately to sit down, to wrap herself in something dry and comforting, an old bathrobe, a quilt made by Maggie's grandmother, the arms of somebody who saw her for what she was and loved her anyway.

Now that she had found Titus, what was she going to do with him? She had been a cop too long ago and sober too short a time. How did she think she could pry information from a man who looked and acted like a piece of granite loosened from a mountain?

"I ain't telling you nothing."

When Titus spoke, Jo Beth couldn't have been more surprised if she'd heard a rock start talking.

"I'm not leaving till you do."

"I can stand here all night."

"So can I. And I'm the one with the gun."

From the woods on her left, Jo Beth heard a girlish giggle. Out of the corner of her eye she caught a glimpse of Pony Jones's red shirt and long black braid, then the cowgirl herself, boots planted wide, hands on her hips. She winked at Jo Beth, then pumped her fist in the air.

The single gesture was such a powerful affirmation, Jo Beth

raised her own fist in a signal of victory. Birds hushed their singing. Tree frogs fell silent. Even the wind got so still you could hear the thoughts of trees, the prayers of squirrels and rabbits and owls.

In the sudden silence, Jo Beth and Pony assessed each other. Did Titus see her too?

A quick glimpse told Jo Beth *yes*. He had the look of deep ocean calm after a raging storm.

One by one the woodland creatures took up their nocturnal songs, and Pony began to dissolve. First her boots, then her jeans-clad legs, her red shirt, her gleeful face. At last there was nothing left but a Stetson. And then that, too, vanished.

Were did she go? Into the deep woods? Into another realm? Into the far reaches of Jo Beth's and Titus's minds?

Pony's voice, borne back to her on the scent of Cherokee roses, said, *You two need to set down and act sociable. Ain't neither one of you as tough as you pretend.*

Jo Beth fell into the hope and stillness of scent and sound. For a moment she felt a blessed sense of peace, of belonging, of coming home.

She could float there. She could close her eyes and imagine herself free of her past, free of her cravings and, most of all, free of her low opinion of herself.

"Are you comin' or ain't you?"

When Titus turned and walked into a thicket, Jo Beth shook off the magical visitation and followed. Brambles tangled her legs and thorns scratched her arms, but she didn't complain, didn't call after him to wait. She forged ahead while bits and pieces of herself flew off and scattered like confetti on the trail blazed by Titus Jones.

He never looked back. But every now and then he stopped, waiting for her to catch up, judging her progress, she supposed, by the labored sound of her breathing and the thrashing of fallen limbs and overhanging branches.

"Where are you taking me?"

"You'll see."

The rains started again, not fierce but hard enough to make the forest floor slick and treacherous. At least to her. Titus plowed forward, unchecked and unfazed.

When his old truck materialized and he opened the door and told her to get in, Jo Beth climbed inside, grateful to be out of the rain, grateful not to be lost, grateful to put her hands on her own arms and feel her flesh still attached to her bones.

Titus got in on the other side and sat there with his hand gripping the steering wheel. She wondered if he was planning to take her back to the campground entrance and put her out. If he was, there was nothing she could do about it. She certainly wouldn't use her gun. She'd only brought it in case she scared up a snake in the woods.

Or a killer.

"It's wet out." Titus still had his hands on the wheel, staring straight ahead. "You shouldn't have come."

"I had no choice."

"I reckon ever'body's got a choice."

"Pony's death changed that for me."

Titus looked at her then, looked at her with naked eyes she could see right through. And what she saw made her think of a night so cold you couldn't feel your hands and feet, you couldn't even feel your own heart pumping blood. This man knew about choice. He knew about cowards who chose to knock an innocent girl in the back of the head. He knew about a father bowed from grief who would never stand upright again unless he avenged his daughter.

"I don't know what you're looking for, but you leave my daughter and wife out of it."

"I can't."

"Leave it be."

"I've made up my mind."

"Then unmake it."

"Why? I was once a cop. A good one. I can still tell the difference between a lie and the truth. You've been lying to me, Titus."

She was aware of movement, of cold wind rushing across her skin, a blur as his arm snaked across her and flung open the door.

"Get out."

"Do you know something about my family that's triggering your hatred, or do you just plain hate women?"

"Leave me and mine alone. Go on. Get out."

"I don't know the way back to my trailer."

"You a Dawson. You'll figure it out."

And so they were back to that, the wolf that stood between them, claws and teeth bared, snarling. It was the image of the Arctic wolf that came to her, the wolf she'd seen the night she found Pony.

Why an Arctic wolf? Why not any old wolf? A regular timber wolf? Or a tiger?

"Why do you hate the Dawsons?"

"You go diggin' in trash, you're gonna get dirty."

"I came to get answers. And I'm not leaving this truck until I do."

The change that came over him was a wind, sweeping

through the truck. And Jo Beth knew it was a changing wind, one that would howl through her, howl through both of them, the rest of their days.

"Pony was your niece."

The wind crooned, long and low, and the moon vanished, leaving them the only two people on the earth.

Our
FOREFATHERS'
BONES

⊱⊰

The Past Revealed

Their bodies must be formed of the
dust of our forefathers' bones.

—*Chief Luther Standing Bear, 1868–1939*
OFAKTE (PLENTY KILL)
OGLALA SIOUX

If my heart was still beating it woulda come to a screeching halt when my daddy said them words. "Pony was your niece." I commence kicking and screaming and tearing out my hair, but don't nothing come out, not even a peep, not even a single strand of the long black braid that hangs down my back. Hair the color of the woman daddy said is my aunt.

I think of all the years I longed for a female relative who belonged to me, somebody who knew how to comb a little girl's hair and tell her the secrets only a mother and daughter can know.

How come my daddy kept Jo Beth from me? It don't make no sense. Didn't he know I was only half myself without a woman to fit the other parts of me in the right place? Didn't he never hear me wishing on stars? Didn't he never find one of them bottles I sent down the creek with messages for God to send me somebody who wore pleated skirts and smelled like rose powder?

No wonder I grew up in overalls and ain't never wore nothing but britches since. No wonder I can spit like a boy and fight like a man. No wonder I know more about bulls than I do about girlfriends.

This is new to me, this feeling that my daddy ain't the saint I thought he was. I keep telling myself he musta had a good reason. My daddy ain't no mean man. He ain't got a mean bone in his *body. But I can't think of no reason good enough to keep a little girl from knowing she had a aunt who woulda taught her how to have tea parties with dolls and girly conversations with boys.*

I want out of this mission that's got me earthbound. I want relief from this strange woman who is supposed to be my aunt. A aunt is somebody who comes to your birthday party and sends you Christmas presents. A aunt is somebody who fills up the holes your mother left so you only feel her loss when the moon turns so full and heavy it falls from the sky and through your bedroom window. A moon that makes you think of getting your first kiss and driving down the mountain in a open-top convertible and coming home to find your mother waiting up to hear every last detail.

"How could that be?" Jo Beth is saying to my daddy. "How is that possible?"

"You didn't know?"

"How was I supposed to know? Nobody ever told me. Including you."

Jo Beth looks like she's fixing to haul off and sock my daddy, and I ain't got the least inclination to stop her. Matter of fact, I'm balling up my first fixing to help her. And that ain't right. I know it ain't.

If I was alive, I'd grab my daddy by the arm and drag him out to the front porch and he'd set down in his rocking chair and tell me the truth, gentle-like. Which is his way.

Or so I thought.

They ain't nothin' gentle about my daddy now. When he speaks, his words comes out hard and sharp, nails he's hammering on a falling-down barn wall.

"I got my reasons."

"What could possibly be reason enough to keep Pony from me?"

Daddy don't say nothing. I reckon he ain't got no answers. Instead he reaches into the glove compartment and takes out my grandmother's diary. The minute I lay eyes on them beads, they commence glowing and burning. I feel like stars has fell out of the sky and scorched all my hide off. Right down to the bone. Right down to the center of my chest where my heart is, lying still as a newborn kitten, as still as them two setting in Daddy's truck staring at each other.

"You might as well have this." Daddy hands Jo Beth the book. "I ain't got no use for it now."

Then he cranks up the truck and heads out of them woods like wolves is after 'em. And I guess they are. Out of the corner of my eye I catch a glimpse of white fur in the dark woods, a glimmer of yellow eyes. My Arctic wolf.

What's my totem trying to tell me? To forgive my daddy?

Or that there ain't nothing to forgive?

Fifteen

The night was something Jo Beth had dreamed. She'd wake up on her bunk in the Silver Streak with her boots unmuddied and her head pounding from too much liquor and too little sleep.

Except she hadn't had a drink all day and she could smell mud from the loamy forest floor on her boots. She could taste truth in the damp, close air of the pickup truck. She could see it in the deep-river eyes of the man who sat opposite her, feel it in the colored beads stitched into the cover of the book.

She had come into the woods looking for answers. Would she find them between the pages of a book?

Titus cranked the truck and headed out of the woods, onto the road that led back to the campground. The rains had stopped and the clouds had rolled back revealing a sky burning with stars. Antares, the angry red heart of Scorpio, scorched a path over the beads and Jo Beth recognized the pattern. A Cherokee rose. Something inside her lurched, as if someone had taken a battering ram to her chest.

When the old truck ground to a halt at the gates to the campground, Jo Beth and Titus sat facing forward, the only survivors on a boat lost at sea. Jo Beth felt strength gathering in her bones and a glimmer of something so fragile she was scared to give it a name, afraid that any attempt to make it concrete would cause it to disappear.

"This is where you get off."

Titus didn't look at her, and she was glad. At night, the soul's windows are wide open, and if you look too deeply, you can get trapped in the darkness and never find your way home.

Jo Beth stumbled down and headed to the Silver Streak without looking back. Fatigue weighed every step. By the time she got to her trailer, she was falling-down tired.

The trailer smelled closed up and stale, as if it had been uninhabited for years. And maybe it had. In many ways Jo Beth was a ghost, a child's stick-figure sketch of the woman she had once been.

She started taking bottles out of the cabinet, all of them empty except one. If she nursed her drink long enough, there was enough Jack Daniel's to ensure a night of oblivion. Her hand shook as she poured the liquor.

Our of nowhere she saw Maggie's face, hopeful as she turned from the cake. She heard Pony's voice, young and fierce and strong, saw the fist pumping in the air.

When Jo Beth threw the glass, it shattered, sending up a spew of whiskey.

She stumbled toward the window and flung it open. Night sounds filtered in—cicadas singing in the trees because it had rained, crickets playing their harp legs in the night, an owl calling somebody's name. A light breeze rattled the Venetian blinds. Jo Beth stood in the window and took deep breaths.

When her awful need was under control, she turned on the light, sat on the edge of her bed, opened the beaded book and began to read.

They call me Cherokee Rose and this is my story.

The first entry, dated 1945, was printed with a child's block letters and misspellings. Obviously, the title page had been added at a later date.

I danct in the rodeo parad today. It's a importunt time. the rodeo ust to be Cowbois Turttle Asoceashun. Now its Rodeo Cowbois Asoceasshun. A man at the nuwspapur tuk my pitchur, he sed I was a Cherokee Rose. I write my name lik that now and my Mothers mad, But I am 7. prakly a womun.

What had any of these childish ramblings to do with her? Jo Beth started to close the diary and go to bed, but the faint scent of roses came through her window and settled into cracks and crevices, ceiling and floor, teacups and bedsheets. It was the scent that had propelled her from Hot Coffee, the same scent that had surrounded the flower-strewn body of Pony Jones.

Jo Beth closed her eyes and let herself breathe, simply *breathe*. She felt as if she'd stepped into the shade of a deep green tree where a hammock waited, a pillow, a patchwork quilt and a good book to get her through a long, cool evening.

Opening her eyes, Jo Beth scanned the yellowed pages of the diary, skimming, speed-reading, looking for a connection between her and a Native American who called herself Cherokee Rose. She read of a little girl fishing and swimming with her older brother, John Running Wolf, growing up in the Alabama ridges with a strong sense of her heritage but also filled with a romantic longing for something more, something different, something cataclysmic that would transform her. She found it on June 13, 1955.

Boston. Red letter day. I was wearing my white leather skirt with the bells. Flashbulbs were going off in my face everywhere, and why not? Cherokee Rose always leads the rodeo parade. My escorts are selected for me. Usually it's a current champion, mostly a rough stock champion. The danger lends these cowboys an aura of heroism and glamour, they say. I'd never thought so until today, until I met a bull rider of extraordinary good looks and killer charm. He was larger than life, a mythic figure clothed in jeans and a Stetson. I was charmed. I was enchanted. And I fell instantly, utterly and irrevocably in love with RD.

Jo Beth felt light-headed. Was it lack of sleep or premonition? She hadn't paid attention to her feelings in so long, she could no longer read her body's signals.

The date, the bull rider, the good looks, the city. Everything fit. But logic told Jo Beth there would have been more than one handsome rodeo cowboy with the initials RD at the rodeo that day. She read on.

June 14, 1955. Running Wolf says I am betraying my people, disgracing our name, courting trouble. Nothing my brother says can sway me. RD and I can't stay away from each other. It's like we're both caught up in an electrical storm, and if either tries to leave, both of us will be struck down by a bolt of lightning. Mother says I am too romantic, that I will bring trouble on us all.

June 16, 1955. I am a river and RD swims endlessly in my silver waters. Love overflows my banks.

Jo Beth read a string of similar entries, the romantic outpourings of a love-struck seventeen-year-old girl. Then, on August 15, 1955, Cherokee Rose wrote the entry that irrevocably changed Jo Beth's past, her present and her future.

August 15, 1955. I am pregnant. Running Wolf is furious, somebody I don't even know. And Mother's tears would fill the creek that flows behind our house. I can't stay in this house. When I tell RD about the baby, he'll come and get me. Mother says I am being foolish, that RD will never take me to Mississippi, never make me part of the elite, powerful family who founded the rodeo.

Jo Beth's entire history rearranged itself. Everything she'd thought to be true became myth, a hoax perpetuated by the people she'd loved and trusted. Her mother, her grandfather, even her uncle Mark.

Her mother, a Beacon Street socialite, had met Jo Beth's father, a handsome, bull-riding cowboy, at the spring rodeo in Boston. They were married four months later—September, 1955—and he brought her back to his family home in Mississippi.

RD was Rafe Dawson. Jo Beth's father.

Sometimes it was possible to vanish while you were still sitting on your bed. It was possible for the person you'd been to so completely disappear, you could walk across the room, look in the mirror and not even know who was staring back at you.

Ordinarily John Running Wolf didn't like driving at night, but he'd stayed late at the rodeo and the rains had delayed him. Then he'd wanted to simply drive, an urge he hadn't had since his youth. It didn't matter where he was going as long as he was on the move, the darkening world passing by outside his window.

Martha Running Wolf was anxious. She had already called three times to ask about his plans. And now, as he was negotiating his truck around a particularly sharp curve on the mountain road, his cell phone rang again.

"John? Stay in a motel tonight. The roads are wet and dangerous."

"I'm on the way home." He wasn't even going in the

direction of Cherokee Ridge, but his words tasted of truth. "I'll be there soon."

"You're too old to drive at night. You can't see."

"Pshaw."

"What does that mean? *Pshaw* is not even a word." Martha got schoolmarmish on him when she worried.

"Pshaw is what I said and pshaw is what I meant." It was better to have his wife mad over an inconsequential thing than to have her asking what he'd done at the rodeo, who he had seen, what had taken him so long. There was no use upsetting her by recounting his grilling at the police station and his conversation with Titus Jones. Words would never pass his lips about the diary and his part in killing Pony Jones.

The diary was out of his hands now. The last link between him and a history that scarred his soul was lying in the police morgue. He had rid his house of the wolves that raged at the door.

It was not so easy to rid his soul. Wolves lurked in the shadows, their sad eyes and broken hearts testament to his betrayal.

The wolves were with him now, coming out of the shadows and collecting along the sides of the road, his judge and jury.

Martha's voice at the other end of the line made them dim, but they never completely vanished.

"John, you be careful. You're an old fool but you're my old fool."

"I love you, too, Martha."

He laid his cell phone on the seat of his truck and rounded the curve of the mountain. The wolves were waiting.

The diary in Jo Beth's hand is calling to me like a mourning dove on Doe Mountain. While she's setting up reading, I'm soaking in the words like they was a God-song composed just for me. I am full of contradictions. I feel mysterious and grounded, curious and off-balance, happy and heart-broke.

From the looks of things, this conflicted skinny woman I will never know as my aunt is fixing to set up all night, and I hope she does. If she gets tired and shuts that beaded diary, I don't how I'll finish reading.

Suddenly she throws the book down and stalks to the bathroom then just stands there staring at herself.

"Who are you?" She sounds lost and scared.

I touch her hair, feeling sorrow in each neglected strand.

She looks startled and puts her hand over mine. Does she feel the currents running between us? Like the soft yellow light of a front porch bulb left burning so you can find your way home through the dark?

I try to tell her I wish I'd known her when I was alive, but she don't hear me. She trudges back to the bed, her steps heavy. She's tracking mud all over her trailer, but she don't seem to care.

She opens the diary again and I start reading.

August 25, 1955. RD is not coming. He will never come; he is getting married to a proper socialite who will bear him legitimate heirs. Running Wolf says I am to forget him, never speak his name in this house. We will take care of our own son. We'll raise him Native and he'll learn the ways of dignity and respect for the land. I don't tell my brother, but the child in my womb is not a son. It's a daughter, and I will call her Morning Star.

Jo Beth cries without sound, but I am gut-shot, speechless. A whole 'nother set of relatives has rose up off them diary pages to greet me. Looking backwards I can see how some things I never give a second thought when I was a kid is now full of meaning. Daddy telling me about my mother, saying she was half Cherokee. The time I asked him who Running Wolf was after I overhead Daddy talking to the sheriff.

"Nobody, Pony. Don't ever speak that name again."

But most of all, I understand about all them roses.

I am surrounded by roses, I am defined by roses, and every one of them is my Cherokee grandmother watching over me.

⇒ Sixteen ⇐

Sam parked the patrol car in a treacherous curve of Cecil Ashburn Drive beside the other emergency vehicles. Orange cones had already been set up and two cops Sam barely knew were directing traffic.

Halfway down the mountain the black Ford F-150 Lariat rested on its side, folded up like an accordion, almost swallowed by a thicket of vines. The Jaws of Life crew was already at work extracting the victim.

Sam knelt to inspect the road and Luther came up beside him, brushing doughnut sugar from his pants.

"See anything, Sam?"

"No skid marks."

Luther squatted down. "Looks like he just drove off the road."

"Or had some help."

"From Titus Jones?"

"We'll know soon enough."

They picked their way down the mountain, Sam feeling every jolt to his joints like he was sixty-five instead of not quite fifty. It was all that greasy food, his doctors told him, but he had a different theory. It was the women in his life—tough-talking, self-destructive Jo Beth and screwed-up, needy, beautiful

Lana, who had run off for something better, then couldn't make up her mind if she'd run to something better or if she'd left it behind.

She'd called again last night. Asking to come home. Just to talk.

And he'd said no, he was busy, the case was killing him, they didn't have anything to talk about, and why now, after all these years, for God's sake. Everything except what he should have said. Don't call me again. Ever. We're finished. Over. Done with.

All the lies he'd told himself for years.

"Sam?"

"Yo."

"I called you twice. Are you going deaf?"

"Indigestion."

"Again?"

"Yeah, man."

Sam smelled the roses before he saw them. At the bottom of the rocky incline, the truck was buried so deeply in a thicket of vines it looked as if it had been there all summer while the roses grew around it.

It wasn't the sight that stopped Sam cold, but the scent. Trapped in a net of fragrance, he felt his truest nature rise. What surprised Sam most was not that he tasted regret, but that he tasted hope. As if the roses had unearthed his past and dumped it at his feet, Sam stood on the edge of the thicket filled with kaleidoscopic images and emotions.

He no longer saw the dissolution of his marriage as one person leaving but as two people veering in different directions, each helpless to stop the momentum. He saw Jo Beth's downward spiral not as alcoholic weakness but as a strong woman systematically destroying herself.

In each case, he might as well have been a bystander. To give himself credit, he'd thought he was protecting them by covering up their flaws. But his head-in-the-sand attitude had done nothing to stop them—Lana from leaving and Jo Beth from smashing herself to pieces against the stone wall she'd erected.

The roses called him to a higher plane. They peeled back the layers of regret to reveal a glimmer of something better. The question was, did he have the courage to embrace his nobler self?

"Sam?" Luther's voice caught hold of him and pulled him back from a rose-scented precipice.

"Yo?"

Luther was standing slightly above Sam, scratching his head. "Have you ever seen anything like it?"

"I've seen something similar. And you have, too."

"Holy shit. Sleepy Pines Campground." Luther cracked his knuckles in that irritating way he had when he was trying to make sense of the unthinkable. "Look at the size of the suckers, Sam. These bushes have been growing here awhile."

Sam had driven this road a thousand times and had never seen them. He considered himself an astute observer. Not perfect, but good enough to have seen a bank of rosebushes that big.

You could be certain of one thing: the roses would not go into his report. That was all the HPD needed, a bunch of magic roses that would send the media into a frenzy of speculation. Next thing they knew, the Pony Jones killer would be some kind of vengeful spirit running amok through Huntsville, and the growing cult of Pony worshippers would be planting rosebushes on every corner.

"Yeah," he told Luther. "The roses have been here all along."

Sam had spent too much time on stakeouts enthralled by Jo Beth's legends of the Wisdom Keepers and others passed along by her grandfather to believe the lie he'd just told Luther. Luther probably didn't believe it, either.

But lies were sometimes less complicated than the truth. Sam was tired of complications: Jo Beth turning up out of the blue to remind him of things he thought he'd put behind, a young woman in red boots who had probably never harmed another human being in her life bashed in the back of the head, then refusing to stay relegated to that roped-off compartment of his mind where he kept murder victims.

The Jaws of Life crew finally hauled the body out of the wreckage in the rosebushes and placed it on a gurney.

"Let's see what they've got, Lu."

It didn't take an expert medical examiner to know that John Running Wolf was dead. The thing that would take an expert was deciding cause of death. Were the discolored contusions from the plunge down the mountain in a Ford Lariat or had somebody stopped him on the road, knocked him in the head and nudged the truck over?

Or maybe somebody had tampered with his brakes. Put a sedative in his coffee. There could be any number of reasons a suspect in the Pony Jones murder was found dead on a curving mountain road.

Sam thought about the blunt object that had been found—a post driver—and the way the heavy metal would have sounded as it was brought down on the head of a small rodeo cowgirl, of the way flesh would split and bones would shatter. He imagined his outrage multiplied exponentially, boiling and festering in the heart of a grieving father.

Weaving his way through the forensics team, he leaned down and peered through the shattered window. Nothing there except a Styrofoam cup.

"Bag it and tag it." He walked around the perimeter of the scene, found a cell phone smashed against a rock.

Sam motioned to one of the team, Charlie, a young guy with a cute curly-headed wife at home, twin five-year-olds, a boy and a girl. The perfect family. You'd envy him if you didn't think too much about one of them getting snatched on the way to school, shot while they waited for a hamburger at McDonald's, felled at the rodeo with a post driver.

Charlie scooped the pieces of phone into a plastic bag.

"I want every inch of this vehicle and the terrain around it gone over with a fine-tooth comb."

Charlie nodded, still new enough not to call Sam a pain in the ass behind his back.

"Sam?" It was Luther, standing by the gurney, staring down at the body.

"Yo."

"Nothing else we can do here. The dead don't talk."

They did, though, if you knew how to listen. But Sam didn't get into that. Luther had already headed back up the mountain.

That was the thing. Climbing back up was always harder than going down.

Maybe Sam would quit the force, head to California, live on oranges and almonds, write one of those wise little books that would catch on and make him rich. Shoot, the things he'd seen, he could tell you more about living than any ten of the current self-help gurus put together.

And dying. Don't forget that part.

He twisted his ankle on a rock and nearly went down.

Some days were just shitty.

Jo Beth and Morning Star were hanging onto a kite, their combined weight the only thing that kept them grounded. They laughed as the wind whipped them over the top of a mountain. "Don't let go," Morning Star told her, but Jo Beth couldn't hold on. The string slipped from her fingers, and she watched as her sister was swept away and dropped off the edge of the world.

Jo Beth sat up in bed, her heart racing the way it does when you wake up with the emotions of your nightmare still intact. Her dream was still vivid, the voice of her half sister calling out *Don't let go,* as if Morning Star were in the tattered trailer sitting at the Formica-top pull-down table eating a blueberry muffin.

Stumbling toward her small kitchen, she switched on the TV and opened the refrigerator door, then just stood there reeling, drunk but not for the usual reasons. Jo Beth was unbalanced in the way of a woman who had spent years picking her way through a minefield, only to find she'd just stepped off a cliff.

The diary called to her from the bedside table, a Pandora's box filled with dark secrets and black shadows. Once you let them out, they refused to go back in. They hung from the ceiling and the doorways, clung to your skin and hair, even hid behind the nearly empty milk carton and moldy cheese in the refrigerator.

Jo Beth slammed the refrigerator door then reached into the cabinet and poured herself a shot. She took a sip and waited for the expelled breath, the familiar loosening that signaled the beginning of oblivion.

But the comfort she sought eluded her. With the glass already halfway to her lips, she saw her future as an endless quest for one more drink, one more town, one more hole to hide in.

Flinging the liquor down the sink took all her willpower. Watching it wash down the drain should have left her triumphant, but it didn't. Her battle had just begun. The downhill ride to destruction had been easy. Coming back up was hell.

Whether it was Pony's indomitable spirit pushing Jo Beth toward the coffeepot or her own fierce will, she didn't know. She was merely grateful.

As she put the coffee on to brew, Sonja Livingstone filled the TV screen, reporting an accident that had claimed the life of the prime suspect in the Pony Jones case. Identity withheld pending notification of the family.

In a rare moment of déjà vu, Jo Beth felt the adrenaline high she used to experience every time she and Sam chased down a fresh clue. Cradling her coffee cup, she sat at her small table to listen.

As the camera panned downward, Sonja said, "The vehicle the suspect was driving went down this ravine."

Jo Beth's sharp breath whistled between her teeth. Though they had been hacked away to remove the vehicle, roses festooned the entire hillside.

With all her instincts kicked into high gear, Jo Beth punched in Sam's number.

"Change your mind about that coffee, Jo Beth?"

The sound of his voice brought her crashing back to reality. Any involvement in the case through Sam would be a huge mistake. Anything she did, she had to do alone.

"No, Sam. Actually, I made a mistake. I meant to dial Maggie."

"No, you didn't."

Jo Beth should have known she couldn't fool him. They'd worked together too long. If she didn't want him digging around in her business, she'd better come up with something fast.

"I was watching the TV report on the accident. You know that's the Cherokee rose in the ravine where your suspect died?"

"Yep. Is there something about this case you want to tell me?"

"No. Just that. I know you're checking all the Native American angles."

For a while there was no sound except Sonja wrapping up her TV report and Sam breathing into the phone. Jo Beth had the feeling of teetering on a crumbling bridge above a precipice. Somewhere above her was a safety rope. She just wasn't certain she could reach it.

"Jo?"

"Yeah?"

"For what it's worth, you were a damned good detective."

"For what it's worth, thank you."

She hung up and anchored herself to her cup. Her coffee had gone cold, but she had lost her taste for java. What she wanted was answers, not only about Pony's death but about her own past.

And yet the plain facts couldn't begin to tell the story of a person's life. They couldn't delve into the mysteries of the mind, the heart, the soul. How would she ever know the whole truth?

Jo Beth's ringing phone brought her out of her reverie.

"Jo?" It was Maggie, sounding excited. "I found something at the Native American Cultural Center. They keep records of the births and deaths of all the Southeastern tribes. Morning Star died in childbirth, and her mother, Rose Wolf, drowned in the Tennessee River on June 13, 1980."

The floor dropped from under Jo Beth. "That's the same day Uncle Mark told us Daddy had died. Drowned. In the same river."

"Oh my God."

"Keep digging, Mags. As long as you don't get into trouble with James."

"James can kiss my foot."

Shaken, Jo Beth retrieved the diary and sat down at the table.

Wind ruffled the pages and the smell of roses permeated the trailer, though the door and windows were shut tight and not a single fan stirred the air.

Jo Beth scanned the diary entries.

September 15, 1955. RD was married today, a society wedding that made national news. Still, I believe he will tire of her and come for me . . .

March 15, 1956. Morning Star was born. I sent a letter to RD. He will come . . .

June 13, 1956. The anniversary of our meeting. I put on my belled skirt and danced under the willows that grow beside the creek, waiting for RD. Running Wolf must never know. He's enraged and secretive. Sometimes I don't know my brother anymore.

The diary entries for 1956 abruptly stopped. Why would his sister call Running Wolf secretive? Did Jo Beth's father go to Cherokee Rose on their anniversary? The diary yielded no clues, and the people who might have told her were either dead or not talking.

All the entries between 1957 and 1959 were essentially a baby book cataloging Morning Star's progress. The next entry that caught Jo Beth's attention read, "RD's child was born today, a legitimate daughter. How can I hate her? She is bone of his bone, flesh of his flesh, this man I love from a distance." The date was February 8, 1960. Jo Beth's birthday.

How had Cherokee Rose known? Had Jo Beth's birth made national news? No one had ever told her, but considering Clint Dawson's fame, it was a possibility.

Or had Cherokee Rose learned about Jo Beth from Rafe Dawson?

Entries became spotty again and references to RD, scarce. The next one was September, 1962.

Morning Star started school today, a milestone. Running Wolf told me I'm foolish to think RD cares about my daughter or what she does. Though I've never told Morning Star anything about her father except that he was a handsome man who loved her and her mother very much, Running Wolf has forbidden me to speak his name in this house. I don't have to speak his name. My heart does the talking.

By the time Jo Beth closed the diary, Cherokee Rose had ceased being a voice from the past and had become real, a link to the father Jo Beth had barely known, an aching glimpse into her own past.

Now she understood her mother's tears, understood why a watery grave at Witch Dance had been preferable for Cynthia Wainwright Dawson to life in a world that contained a beautiful, headstrong Cherokee rival who danced in a belled skirt and waited for Cynthia's husband beside the willows.

Jo Beth needed air. She burst out the door into a world she hadn't noticed in a long time, a gold and green summer morning seen through sober eyes. Without the noise of highway traffic and a populated suburb, the air of the campground was a perfect stillness for the songs of birds, the skitter of crickets, the slithering of lizards in the grass.

She thought of all those people, dead, who would never know another summer morning. And Pony Jones, herself.

Especially Pony. Her niece.

Jo Beth wrapped her arms around herself, feeling every inch of her flesh, every heartbeat that sent blood pulsing through her veins, feeling her aliveness, her connectedness.

How had they died, Rose and Rafe, then thirty years later, Pony? All of them on June 13?

Taking a deep breath, Jo Beth walked back inside, put on jeans and a T-shirt, strapped on her gun. Next she put on a loose vest. You couldn't even see her holster.

But if you looked closely, if you were an Arctic wolf hiding in the deep woods, a sacred totem with yellow eyes that could see beyond bushes and trees, beyond flesh and bone, you would see her intent.

If you were a killer, you'd run.

While Jo Beth straps on her gun, I applaud. I can see the light in her now, breaking through all them patches that was so dark she couldn't hardly find her way across town, let alone through her life.

Truth makes some folks stronger and other folks it just tears all to pieces. Till I read my grandmother's diary over Jo Beth's shoulder, I'd of swore I was the kind that could stand in the eye of a hurricane and walk out on the other side with nary a scratch, nary a nick in my tough hide to show the hell I'd been through.

I'm learning different. I'm learning there's some things in life that turns you upside down and crossways, and afterwards you can't hardly remember who you was before everything changed.

Why now? That's what I'm going to ask God the minute I get where I'm going and can have a face-to-face meeting with Him. How come He just now wants me to find out I had all them relatives, some of them rich and famous?

When Jo Beth pulls into the Waffle House I forget about family secrets. If the smell of fried food ain't enough to stir up the dead, I don't know what is. I want to start gobblin' bacon and eggs like somebody three times my size. I try to snatch a piece from Jo Beth's plate, but my hand passes right through. I try seven more times before I finally give up. I ain't happy about it neither.

Arms that don't work and hunger you can't satisfy ain't no way to be. I reckon I'm gonna have to spend the first two weeks in Heaven workin' off my resentment shovelin' shit outta the barn. If I ever get there. At the rate I'm going, it don't look like it.

I get my temper settled down, then I try to ignore the smell of bacon by remembering what was in my grandmother's diary.

The entry on June 12, 1980, said "Running Wolf does not want us to go to the rodeo. He says I'm too old to dance—as if forty-two is my dotage. I'm just getting started! John also said it's not right for a girl with Morning Star's education to throw herself away on a bunch of dusty cowboys; she ought to be preparing for medical school. I know my daughter better than he. Morning Star's conflicted. She wants to please her uncle, but her heart is not in medicine. She wants to teach. And she wants to dance at the rodeo. It's in her blood. Considering her heritage, how could it not be?"

And the last entry my grandmother ever wrote was on June 13, 1980 . . .

"Morning Star talks of nothing except a rangy Tennessee bull rider she met today, a man named Titus Jones. He's not charming, he's not sophisticated, he's not even good-looking. And he murders the King's English. Everybody thinks Morning Star's crazy; everybody except me. He's so quiet, at first you don't even notice him. Then you look again and see it's the quiet of a mountain that can endure a thousand storms and provide shelter to others, too. There's something indestructible about him. Like he's not even part of the human race, but something more, something made of rock, perhaps something even spiritual. The word that comes to mind when I look at this man (he's older than Morning Star by a good ten years) is SAFE. I pray this is so."

My mother married my daddy two months later. (Up until now, their wedding date was the only thing I knew about their history.)

My grandmother was a wise woman. She had my daddy pegged to a tee. I wish I'd a known her. If she'd been living when I was born would I have had a different life that didn't include getting knocked in the head?

My throat gets clogged up, but it ain't in my nature to cry and feel sorry for myself, and I ain't fixin' to start now.

"Pony." I hear my mother's voice and feel her arms around me. "It's time."

"Time for what?"

"To let your grandmother tell you the rest of the story, the parts she didn't record in her diary."

I step out of the restaurant alongside Jo Beth and spot my totem standing beside her truck, his yellow eyes shining like spotlights. The circle of light glows so bright I shade my eyes.

"Where is she? Where's my grandmother?"

"In the light, Pony. Be patient. Watch. Listen."

The circle of light expands, blocking out everything except my history. When my grandmother starts speaking, the vistas of the past unfold and her story falls around me like warm spring rain.

ROOTS
of the HEART

≽≼

Cherokee Rose's Story

Will you give your daughter to me that the roots
of her heart may entangle with mine, so the strongest
wind that blows will never separate us?

—*Anonymous Canadian*

Seventeen

The day my future walked into my life, I was seventeen. I was wearing bells on my skirt, and he was wearing an eagle feather on his Stetson.

In Cherokee legend, only medicine men and great warriors wear feathers. Since it was 1955 and there was no longer a call for either, the only conclusion I could draw was that the man was a warrior in other ways.

Turning to Laura Johnson, the woman who was in charge of coordinating the Cherokee dancers at the spring rodeo in Boston, I asked, "Who is he?"

"Your escort for the parade. Rafe Dawson."

"Of the rodeo Dawsons?"

Everybody who had anything to do with rodeo knew the name of its founder, Clint Dawson—even a young, starstruck Cherokee girl, descendant of the remnants who'd hidden in the hills and caves of northwest Alabama to avoid forced deportation from tribal lands, a deadly march that would later become known as the Trail of Tears. I had never imagined anything more for myself than a life defined by the red clay hills and the iron rules of John Running Wolf. Although my brother was only twenty-six, he seemed years older because of the ten years he'd had to bear the responsibility of being man of the Wolf household.

"Rafe is Clint's son," Laura told me that day. "And the man every other bull rider at the rodeo will have to beat if they're to take this year's championship title."

I must have sighed or swooned or made some sound that alerted Laura to my dangerous condition.

"Be careful, Rose. He's a rodeo Romeo. He steals hearts, then breaks them."

It was too late. He'd already stolen mine.

Rafe Dawson saw me then and smiled. And he kept coming, a storm that swept me into its center and wouldn't let go. An Indian blanket that covered me completely. A riptide that tore me from my moorings and carried me in its swift currents till the day I died.

I was too young and foolish to remain discreet. And Rafe Dawson just didn't give a damn. He was the kind of man who went where he wanted and did what he pleased. Or so it seemed to an awestruck teenaged girl. Looking back, I suppose you could say Rafe was the spoiled, favored son of a wealthy man who had never denied his youngest child anything.

When I asked Rafe what his father thought of his dating a Cherokee dancer, he just kissed me and said, "Is that what we're doing, my Cherokee Rose?" Then he whisked me off to a secluded spot and showed me exactly how wrong I was.

We weren't dating. We were far beyond that. We were forces of nature that collided.

I should have known the storm we created wouldn't go unnoticed, especially by my brother. I was in the dressing tent with six other dancers, getting ready for the big rodeo finale, a dance that would be held in the arena, when Running Wolf stormed in.

"Everybody out."

As the girls scattered, I laid the feathered clips for my braids on the dressing table. "John, if they report you, you're going to be in a lot of trouble."

"Not as much trouble as you."

"I'm sure I don't know what you're talking about." My blush gave me away.

John sat down on the small dressing stool beside me, a tall, gangly man who looked like an eagle perching in a nest of sparrows. The big hand he put on my shoulder was roughened from handling the post drivers to pound in stakes that secured the rodeo tents, from using the pitchforks and shovels to feed hay to the rodeo rough stock and muck out the barns.

"You're still a child, Rose. I don't want to see you hurt."

I knew what he was talking about. I'd seen the censoring looks others gave us as Rafe and I slipped away from the crowds. Once, when Mark Dawson caught sight of us, I felt his brother's hatred like a knife in my back.

In 1955, the caste system was still firmly entrenched. Full-bloods had no business socializing with society's upper crust, even if a thin Red line from the Oglala Sioux ran through the Dawsons' veins. Crossing color lines was an offense that would lead to riots and killings later that year, and so much blood it would take generations to wash away the stain.

I took my brother's hand, turned it over and kissed his callused palm.

"John, I know what I'm doing. Rafe loves me. Tonight you'll see. Everybody will see. He's taking me to the dance."

"He's taking a Boston socialite. Cynthia Wainwright."

"No. That can't be true. That was before . . ." I looked at

my flushed face in the mirror, unable to say the words to my brother. *That was before I gave myself to him, body and soul, and he memorized me like a map leading home.*

My brother caught my shoulders, forcing me to look at him. "You'll go with me. And you'll hold your head high. You will not disgrace the name of Wolf by shedding a tear over a man who is merely using you for his pleasure."

I went to the dance, dressed in white fringed leather, heavily beaded with Cherokee roses. The beaded design proved prophetic. The roses were not only a symbol of the Trail of Tears, but also a symbol of my own grief and humiliation.

With Cynthia Wainwright hanging around his neck like a noose, Rafe never came near me. He tried—or so it seemed to me—but Cynthia or his brother always intervened.

"You will forget him," John told me as we packed and left the rodeo for the long journey home.

How could I? His baby was already growing in my belly.

By August, when I could no longer pass my morning sickness off as something I ate, I wrote to Rafe, telling him about the baby, then waited for him to come to me.

But it wasn't Rafe who drove the hundred and fifty miles from Tupelo to Huntsville; it was Mark Dawson.

"Stay inside the house," John told me, then walked out to Dawson's car and got in. I wanted to run after him, but Mother held me back.

"You've done enough, Rose. Let John handle this."

I did what I was told. I was seventeen, pregnant and scared.

I kept watch by the window, and when I saw the car return, saw my brother descend and Mark Dawson drive off, I ran out the door.

"What did he say? When is Rafe coming to get me?"

"He's never coming, Rose."

"I don't believe you. He wouldn't reject his own child."

"He's a Dawson."

"What does that mean, John? He loves me and I love him."

"He doesn't love you. He doesn't want you. You are never to speak his name again in this house."

I obeyed my brother. I never spoke my lover's name again in that house, but not because I believed Rafe didn't want me. I knew that was not the truth. I just didn't know why John was telling me those things.

And so I became secretive. I wrote letters to my darling in secret, even after John told me Rafe had married Cynthia Wainwright. I sneaked to the post office and mailed them, went home and waited. Day after day.

When Morning Star was born in March and Rafe didn't come, I believed I'd lost him. But after the postpartum blues were over, I knew that was not so.

On a shopping trip into the city with John's wife, Martha, I slipped away and called Rafe. He was easy to find through directory assistance. Though Dawson is a fairly common name, Rafe is not.

The gods were with me. He answered the phone.

When I heard his voice, I started crying.

"Rose?"

"I need you, Rafe."

"I need you, too."

He came on the first anniversary of our meeting. June 13. I waited for him underneath the giant willow, deep in the woods where the waters of the creek sang of our love.

After that, we couldn't stay apart. The roots of our hearts were irrevocably bound.

And yet our lives were hopelessly entangled with others. We had to be careful. Too many people were involved, too many people could be hurt.

We met once a year, every thirteenth of June, at the willow on the blue ridge that overlooks the valley. Our love was a separate, living thing, kept apart from the rest of the world, even from our child, our Morning Star.

She was happy growing up in the Wolf household, secure and well-loved. John and Martha adored her, doted on her. I didn't want her confused by a biological father who came once a year.

Rafe stayed with Cynthia till Jo Beth was four. Whether leaving was an act of cowardice or an act of courage, I can't say. I never judged him. I merely loved him.

He never rodeoed again. Once a year, underneath the willow, cocooned in a world that held only the two of us, he would tell me where his travels had taken him. Peru, Brazil, Paris, Rome. He took up spelunking and mountain climbing and deep sea diving. Anything to get the adrenaline rush he had once known riding the bulls.

I never wondered why he didn't divorce Cynthia and marry me. I knew. Rafe was larger than life. He couldn't be contained by four walls. He wouldn't be constrained by legal documents and the rules of society. He was a Peter Pan, a warrior, an adventurer, a god.

And he always came back to me.

For twenty-five years we kept our yearly tryst under the willow tree. Rain or shine. I don't know if we could have done it without Martha. Four years into the secret meetings she caught me.

I was under the willow, shading my eyes for a glimpse of Rafe as he rounded the bend in the winding path that came up from the road below. He was late that year, and I was worried something had happened to him. An accident on the road. An emergency at home. Even worse, a confrontation, our secret exposed, tempers flying and feelings hurt.

When the twig snapped behind me, I whirled around, overjoyed.

"Rafe, I thought you'd—" Too late, I clapped my hands over my mouth. It was not Rafe who emerged from the dense trees, but Martha.

"I knew you were meeting him here."

"How?"

"I've watched you. Once a year, you come alive. On the thirteenth of June. Last year I followed you here, waited behind the giant cedar while Rafe Dawson joined you."

"Oh, God. I beg of you, don't tell my brother."

Fear and despair turned me to ice. Martha took my hands between hers. "I saw your face, and his. I will never tell. In return, you must do something for me."

"Anything. I'll do anything to keep Rafe in my life."

"John is no fool. He'll find out unless you let me help you keep this secret safe. Confide in me. Let me know what you need and I'll make certain my husband does not tear you apart from the man you love."

"You would defy my brother for me?"

"Yes."

"Why?"

"I have my reasons. Now go. I hear Rafe coming. Hurry down the path to meet him while I make my escape."

Martha helped me set up a post office box in Huntsville so Rafe could send letters without John knowing. And we never spoke of Rafe again.

But once a year, a week before our tryst under the willow, she'd begin making preparations to take Morning Star and John on an outing far away from Cherokee Ridge. They went to the botanical gardens, to the zoo, to comb the gardening centers for the annuals she used to fill the front of her flower beds—petunias and impatiens and the fragrant lavender that should have been easy for a dedicated gardener to grow, but which defied Martha year after year, wilting in the sun and turning brown for no reason she could fathom.

When John sold the ridge to developers, it was Martha who urged him to set aside the densely wooded area where the creek flows year round and the willow stands. John agreed, never knowing he was ensuring a safe place for me to meet the man whose name he'd forbidden me to speak.

On Rafe's fiftieth birthday, he sent a postcard. It was one line.

"Let's get married."

I thought he wasn't serious. I replied in kind.

"Why now? After all these years?"

His answer in return mail was typical of Rafe. "Why not?" He was a man of action, not words.

I drew my own conclusions. His wife had long since thrown herself into the lake at Witch Dance and he had no legal reason to keep our love secret. Too, times had changed, social and color lines were blurring. And Rafe was getting streaks of gray in his hair, a sign that soon his body would refuse to climb mountains and rappel up rock faces and skydive from airplanes.

Maybe, at long last, he needed the comfort of coming home at night to the woman he loved.

And so we laid our plans. The rodeo was coming to the outskirts of Huntsville that summer, the dates perfect, June tenth through the thirteenth.

We would enter the next phase of our lifelong love affair the way we had begun—at the rodeo. We applied for the license on the tenth. Rafe found a justice of the peace who would be willing to leave his office in Decatur and come to the rodeo.

Rafe wanted to be married in the arena. "I want the world to know you're mine."

And he did. I know that. But I also know that he wanted to show Mark that he was not his brother's keeper. Over the years, I'd learned of Mark's many machinations to maintain tight control over the Dawson family.

It rained on the thirteenth. Rafe and I talked about postponing our wedding, but we'd kept that date sacred for twenty-five years. Both of us believed in the mystery of sacred dates, totems and signs. And so in spite of the weather, we climbed into my car and headed across the Keller Memorial Bridge to fetch the JP in Decatur.

We never made it. The roads were slick, the brakes wouldn't hold, whether from the rain or from tampering, I'll never know. Nor do I need to know.

As we sailed over the railing, Rafe turned loose the wheel and gathered me in his arms.

"Hold on, Rose, and don't let go."

The river was waiting for us, arms outstretched.

Rescue workers found us together, locked in a final embrace. And we're together, still.

Rafe is here with me, Pony. The grandfather you never knew. The man whose blood binds us all together. Me, you, Morning Star, Jo Beth.

You're like him, Pony. Indomitable. Fierce. Larger than life.

Of all Rafe's descendants, you're the one he identifies with most.

We're here. All of us. Watching over you. We were the whisper that sent Titus running to catch you when you jumped from the hayloft. We were the invisible arms that held you when you cried, the silent lullaby that rocked you to sleep at night. We were the spirit song that fueled your wildest dreams.

And we are the love that waits for you.

Until then, you have the Cherokee roses.

My grandmother fades, then vanishes, leaving me with memories of her story, questions still unanswered and my Arctic wolf standing by Jo Beth's truck, his yellow eyes staring right at me.

There's waterfalls in his eyes and a whole galaxy of stars, there's trees that reach to the sky and critters that walk on rivers in deep frozen winters, there's the mystery of silence and the comfort of hope. There's a trinity of lessons in the past, and if the good Lord's give me one thing, it's sense enough to learn the things my grandmother told me.

The Universe is a whole lot bigger than just me. In the grand scheme of things, I ain't important enough to be asking God why. It's enough that I can lay my head on the grass and look up at the stars and know that while I was living I was loved.

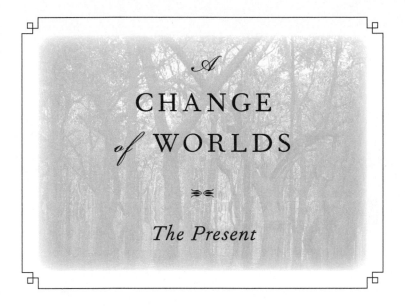

A

CHANGE
of WORLDS

⧓

The Present

There is no death, only a change of worlds.

—*Chief Seattle, 1780–1866*
SI'AHL
SUQWAMISH AND DUWAMISH

Eighteen

It didn't surprise Jo Beth to see the Arctic wolf standing in the parking lot of the Waffle House. She stared into his beaming yellow eyes trying to read his message. Ancient truths were buried there, but his story was not for her.

What she saw was the wolf's courage. What she knew, even before she started her pickup and he loped alongside, was that the power of the wolf would be with her when she confronted her uncle. The power of the wolf and the spirit of Pony.

The resolve in her grew so fierce she didn't even recognize herself in her rearview mirror. Sitting in the parking lot of the Marriott, she was a woman with fangs and claws, a woman who would tear your throat out if you told her a lie.

She wet her lips, nodded at her reflection, then patted the gun in her holster. She was ready.

At the front desk, she asked a bored-looking young woman filing her nails to please put a call though to one of their guests. The woman—Myrtle, her name tag said—laid down the file, picked up the phone and dialed, then handed it over the counter to Jo Beth.

"Uncle Mark. I need to see you."

His shock registered in a palpable silence. Finally, he cleared his throat. "I have rodeo association meetings all day. We'll have dinner this evening. My treat."

Jo Beth wanted to chew through something, starting with the telephone receiver and ending with the legs of the baby grand piano. It was amazing how you could drift through ten years hardly noting whether it was day or night then, suddenly, you couldn't stand to lose one single minute.

"I have to see you now. I'm in the lobby. I'm coming up."

"This is not a good time."

"It's going to be even worse if I have to go to the newspaper with what I know."

Within five minutes Jo Beth was standing in Uncle Mark's third-floor room. The curtains were open to a view of the Saturn V in Tranquility Base. Beside the rocket, Uncle Mark looked shrunken, insignificant, not all the godlike figure of her childhood imaginings.

Although there were two chairs in the room, he didn't invite her to sit down. Her phone call had already set the tone. This meeting was not a friendly social event.

"Why did no one ever tell me I had a sister?"

"That's ridiculous. You don't have a sister."

"Not anymore, I don't. She died giving birth to my niece, Pony Jones."

Did Uncle Mark's face lose color? It was hard to tell. He was old and had already lost the high Dawson color of youth and good health. Besides, the harsh morning light coming through the wide window would turn anybody pale.

"Where did you hear such lies?"

A good detective never reveals her sources. Though Jo Beth was no longer on the force, and it was questionable whether she'd ever been good, she wasn't about to tip her hand.

"Didn't you know, Uncle Mark? The truth has a way of coming out."

"Who have you been talking to?"

"If it's a lie, what does it matter who told me?" And why had he asked her twice to tell him the source?

"It matters, Jo Beth. The Dawsons are an important family. You've never understood that. There will always be somebody who wants to bring us down."

It had been a long time since Jo Beth had called on her instincts to tell whether someone was lying. And Mark Dawson was a skilled statesman, a seasoned spokesman who was as much at home in front of an audience as he was sitting in his own chair watching TV.

If she wanted the truth she'd have to rattle him. For that, she'd need bigger ammunition than a sister who was dead.

"Did my father leave us for Cherokee Rose?"

Uncle Mark turned his back to her, walked to the window and closed the blinds. Was he avoiding her question? Setting the stage? Or both?

In the softer glow of the lamps, his flesh seemed to firm on his bones, his face to settle into the imposing lines of a man who knows how to take command.

"Sit down, Jo Beth." He motioned toward a chair. "I'm going to tell you a story. Something I should have told you a long time ago."

It seemed churlish to stand, and besides, she was exhausted from a sleepless night and an overload of information. She crossed the room and sat in the chair behind the desk. It would serve as barrier and anchor. With her uncle, she needed both.

Ever the gentleman, Mark Dawson waited till she was seated, then took the chair beside the window.

"Your father was too charming and handsome for his own good. Women flocked to claim his attention. Cherokee Rose was no different. But she was nothing to Rafe, just another pretty young girl at the rodeo who liked to fantasize about the man who was so far out of her league, she could never hope to have him."

Uncle Mark leaned back in his chair, relaxed, as if he were telling a bedtime story. He lapsed into a dramatic silence, letting his words sink in.

Jo Beth's mother had kept a picture of Rafe on her bedside table, even after he walked out on them. He had the movie star looks that made her uncle's story credible.

Who was the one spinning fantasies? Cherokee Rose in her diary, or Uncle Mark, facing her across the room?

He folded his hands loosely in his lap, a man completely at ease.

"Nobody believed that Indian dancer, and the rumors died down. If I'd thought you'd ever hear them, I'd have prepared you." He leaned forward, his palms open, his face earnest. "Now you know. Whoever has told you these lies is probably bent on causing embarrassment to our family."

"After all these years? And with everybody involved dead? How could that embarrass us?"

"You'll never understand what it takes to be a Dawson."

"You've never understood what it means to be human."

"You've just proved my point." He stood up. "And now, if you'll excuse me, I have important meetings."

Jo Beth refused to play that game—abandoned, irresponsible niece put in her place by elegant, important uncle. Not today. Not ever again. Needing reassurance, she slid her hand under her vest and felt the solid, deadly weight of her gun.

"Did you see Pony Jones the day she died?"

Two spots of color fanned into his cheeks. "I've had enough of this, Jo Beth. If you wanted to play cop, you should have kept your head out of the bottle." He strode across the room and jerked the door open. "My advice to you is to go back to that shoddy trailer you call a home, uncap a bottle of Jack Daniel's and get drunk. Obviously, that's the only thing you know how to do well."

The part of Jo Beth that longed to follow his advice acknowledged she deserved her uncle's parting shot. But the part of her that was unfolding like a moonflower under a clear summer night wanted to prove him wrong. She stood slowly, holding onto her fragile, newfound dignity.

"Don't send me any more Christmas cards." Jo Beth walked out without looking back.

Her courage nearly deserted her when she passed the restaurant off the lobby. Inside they'd have a padded corner booth, a wine list.

Steeling herself, she pulled out her cell phone and dialed. "Mags, meet me at Dunkin' Donuts."

This was the part of his job Sam hated most: telling the family that someone they loved had been killed. Even worse, that they couldn't have possession of the body because the death had been under suspicious circumstances.

John Running Wolf's house was not what Sam had expected. Located south of Huntsville on the periphery of a ritzy golf course on Cherokee Ridge, it was all sharp angles and glass, the kind of house where you could stand in the foyer and think you were in a fancy hotel atrium, the kind without corners and hallways that made any sense, where you could ask for the bathroom and never find it till you had already peed in your pants.

What sort of money did it take to build a house like that, and where did Running Wolf get that much dough? He hadn't impressed Sam as a man of great means. But he had certainly looked like a man who would do what it took to get what he wanted. People do all sorts of things for money. Even kill.

Making a mental note to check into Running Wolf's financial dealings, Sam rang the doorbell.

If the woman who opened the door was Martha Wolf, she was unexpected, too. While Running Wolf had had the gnarled look of an oak tree bent under many storms, this slight, gray-haired woman had aged well, taken care of herself. She was attractive and fit with lively black eyes and a ready smile.

And she was fully dressed with her face made up, even at this hour. That struck Sam as odd. Lana wouldn't even have been out of bed.

"Mrs. Wolf? Mrs. Martha Wolf?"

"Yes?" Her smile didn't waver as she stood blinking in the sun, facing strangers.

"I'm afraid we have some bad news."

Her hand flew to her chest and the color left her face. "Is it John?"

"It is. I'm sorry, Mrs. Wolf. May we come in?"

She nodded, looking too numb to speak, as if her bones had turned to water. He hoped she didn't faint or go into hysterics. No matter how many times he saw it, Sam always felt helpless in the face of grief.

He went through the door first and took her elbow, but wasn't surprised when she stepped back. Martha Wolf struck him as the kind of woman too proud to let herself be supported by strangers.

She led them into a room with so many windows and skylights it was like being seated outside. Martha Wolf sat upright in a wing-back chair with her ankles crossed and her hands folded in her lap, her grief showing only in the slight tremble of her lips.

As gently as he could, Sam told her everything he wanted her to know, which didn't amount to much more than where the accident had occurred and the fact that she couldn't claim the body until their investigation into cause was finished.

She gripped the arms of her chair the entire time.

"John didn't come home last night. I expected he'd be late, but around one this morning I called the police. They said . . ." She pressed her hands to her lips and squeezed her eyes shut. When she opened them, she was calm, steady, dignified in the way Sam had always admired.

Lana had never been dignified. She wore every feeling like a new red dress with the price tags showing. The bigger her anger, the bigger the price tag for fixing it. Which was always his job.

He was grateful he didn't have to fix Martha Wolf.

"The police told me John had not been gone long enough to be a missing person."

"I'm sorry, ma'am." Sam glanced at Luther. What was he doing hulking over there by the door? Why didn't he help Sam out?

He knew the answer, of course. Luther hated this kind of call more than he did. When he was stressed out, he ate. He'd gone through a whole box of doughnuts on the drive over, then made Sam swear not to tell his wife.

Sam wanted a piece of Juicy Fruit, but Martha Wolf didn't strike him as the kind of woman you'd chew gum in front of.

"Can you tell us who your husband was with yesterday? Who he saw or talked to?"

"I don't know. John had gone to the rodeo. It could have been just about anybody."

"Do you know why he went to the rodeo?"

"He loved it."

"So he went often?"

"Well, not so much anymore. John and I are getting up in years."

Martha Wolf was disarming, the way she referred to her age. But there was something hidden about her, too, some part of herself she was shutting away from Sam. Was it merely her grief or was she hiding something else?

"Was there a particular reason he decided to go to this rodeo?"

"What do you mean?"

"Did he mention any names? Anybody he particularly wanted see, like Pony Jones?"

All the color drained out of Martha's face. "The girl who was murdered."

"Yes, ma'am. Did your husband mention her?"

"No. Not that I recall." She twisted her hands together in her lap and shifted in her chair.

It was the little things Sam noticed, the telltale signs that a person was not telling the truth. Why was Martha Wolf lying? Was she covering for her husband, or did she, herself, have something to hide?

Sam caught Luther's eye, and his partner finally strolled into the room. Luther took the chair closest to Martha, a ploy he always used when he wanted to make a witness feel uncomfortable. Get in his face. Make him sweat. Make him think you know something he's not telling and you intend to sit there until you get it out of him.

Sam felt a sudden and unexpected pity for Martha Wolf. He was getting too soft. Maybe he ought to pack up his things and head north. Some godforsaken place in Alaska where he wouldn't be able to see anything for miles around except snow and ice. No unsafe streets. No brutal murders. No messy emotions.

"Let's go over this again, Mrs. Wolf." Luther made a steeple of his fingers, bit back the burp from too many doughnuts. "Maybe there's something you missed, something that seems unimportant but might be just the key to help us find out why your husband's pickup truck went off the road."

"I've told you everything I know."

"Now, Mrs. Wolf, could you tell us again who your husband knew at the rodeo?"

Martha leveled a look at Luther that made him squirm, much like a third grader caught cheating on his test.

"If you're implying that either my husband or I had anything to do with the murder of Pony Jones, then you're no longer welcome in my house." Martha Wolf stood up. "I'll show you out, Detectives."

She all but slammed the door in their faces.

"Nice going, Detective," Sam said.

"Yeah? I didn't notice her getting all warm and fuzzy with you."

Sam climbed behind the wheel and headed back to the station. "She was lying to us, Luther. What's she hiding?"

"Damned if I know. The Pony Jones case has more twists and turns than this mountain road. Stop up ahead."

"Where?"

"Dunkin' Donuts."

"Sarah's going to kill you."

"She'll never know unless you go blabbing your big mouth."

"Tell you what. Get me a cream-filled doughnut while you're in there and I won't say a word."

"Are you blackmailing me, Sam?"

"Yeah, but I'm cheap."

Nineteen

When Jo Beth saw Maggie enter the coffee shop, she waved, then watched as her friend made her way toward the corner booth.

People smiled when Maggie walked by. Her sundress was the color of sunshine. If you looked closely, you could see optimism floating along in her wake.

"Hey, Jo." Maggie flung her yellow lizard-skin bag onto the table and slid into the booth. "You look ready to throttle somebody. What's up?"

Jo Beth related everything she'd learned from Cherokee Rose's diary, as well as her latest visit with Uncle Mark. "One of them is lying, Mags. I don't know whether the diary is filled with fantasies of a lovesick woman or whether my uncle is covering up the truth."

"I found out something that might help you, Jo. One of mother's friends, a retired English professor, taught Morning Star at the University of North Alabama. And get this. She was there as the first recipient of an academic scholarship set up by the estate of Clint Dawson."

Jo Beth felt as if she'd opened a box of shadows, every one of them capable of covering you with so much darkness you could disappear and never find your way back.

"My grandfather was benefactor to universities all over the South, even after his death. Uncle Mark administered his estate."

"I don't believe in coincidence, and neither do you. I'm going drive to Florence and track down the truth. Dinner's at my house tonight at seven. If you're not there, I'm going to hunt you down."

As Maggie headed toward the parking lot, Jo Beth sat with her hands anchored to a cup of coffee going cold, staring at the empty spot where her friend had been.

Ain't no use feelin' sorry for yourself.

When she heard the female voice again, it came as no surprise to Jo Beth. If the Wisdom Keepers could speak through wolves and roses, a rodeo cowgirl could speak from the grave.

It also didn't surprise her when Pony Jones began to materialize—long black braid hanging down her back, red cowgirl shirt fitting loosely on her slight figure, a Stetson that made her face look like a child's drawing of a small, perfect valentine, blue eyes that looked right through you.

Sometimes your own longing gets so strong it can call up a miracle.

Mark Dawson's a lyin' snake. Now, git up, dust off your britches and git to work.

The ghost of Pony Jones was every bit as sassy as reporters portrayed her in the newspaper features and TV specials that dominated the media. What the media didn't show was the compassion shining from the girl's eyes. They couldn't know how it was possible for a dead girl to reach across the table and put her hand over Jo Beth's heart. They couldn't begin to imagine the emotions stirred by Pony Jones's gesture.

The crater Jo Beth had dynamited inside herself filled with

longing and regret, determination, resolve and a love so big Dunkin' Donuts couldn't contain it. It escaped through the windows, spiraled down the street and curved toward the river.

Sitting there in a public place, Jo Beth cried without sound. It was remarkable how many losses you could bear and how many ways you could think of to shove them aside, cover them up, pretend they never happened.

Telling herself she was done with pretending, Jo Beth watched as the image across from her grew dim. Bit by bit Pony vanished until there was nothing left except a patch of dust motes shimmering in the sunlight that filtered through the window.

"Jo Beth?"

Sam Donovan's voice carried all the way across the small restaurant. He was at the door and he was heading her way.

When you're talking to a ghost, scrambling to find firm footing in a quicksand of lies, and barely hanging onto newfound sobriety, the last person you want to see is the man who reminds you of events that tumbled you into a ten-year alcoholic oblivion.

"I saw your truck outside." Sam smiled at her. She didn't offer him a seat, but he slid into her booth anyway then signaled a waitress who brought him a cup of coffee.

"If I had a penny for every time we grabbed doughnuts and coffee, I'd be rich," he said.

"Are you here to stroll down memory lane or are you tailing me?"

"Neither. Just got a doughnut hankering and happened by."

"Yeah, and pigs can fly."

Sam was still a good-looking man, not much changed until

you looked closer. His eyes held stories you wouldn't want to hear unless all the lights were on and somebody you trusted was nearby.

They sat there staring at each other, separated by an ocean of memories that could suck you under and drown you if you didn't know how to swim.

Thanks to Pony Jones, she was keeping her feet firmly planted on the shore.

"You caught me. I saw your truck. My gut tells me you're tracking Pony's killer."

"I thought your gut told you to get a doughnut, Sam."

"Obfuscation won't work with me."

"Are you still working crossword puzzles at stakeouts?" The other cops used to tease Sam about his vocabulary.

"Quit the song and dance, Jo. Where's Titus Jones?"

"I don't know."

"I think you do."

"I've been called worse than a liar."

Wadding two sticks of Juicy Fruit into his mouth, Sam had the good grace to look embarrassed.

"Listen, Jo, I don't mean to be a hard-ass."

"Since when?"

"What's with women and word games? You ought to be born with instruction books."

"Are you talking about Lana?"

"I'm talking about all of you. Lana included." He jerked a napkin out of the holder and wadded his gum inside. "I'm warning you, Jo. If you've got information pertinent to this case, you'd damned well better share it. Don't go playing the Lone Ranger on my turf."

"Wrong gender, Sam." She stood and left the restaurant without another word.

Anybody watching Jo Beth walk off—and that included Sam Donovan—would see a woman who carried herself with dignity and purpose, a woman who'd had the last word. Even if she had to hide her shaking hands in her pants pocket, she would show no more weakness in front of the man she'd once called partner.

On the way back to the campground, Jo Beth tried to think of all the reasons she had for holing up in her trailer and forgetting her quest. For one thing, she was hanging onto sobriety by her fingernails, and had no idea whether it would last or whether she'd wake up and reach for the nearest bottle. For another, she had lost count of all the things she'd done wrong. She could no longer remember how many people would still be alive if she hadn't been the one sent to rescue them.

But there's a mercy in that kind of forgetfulness, a chance to start on a clean page and write your story so the ending will come out right.

Jo Beth parked her truck in the campground that was still empty of any trailers except her own. She was thinking that the only way she'd ever know the truth about her family's connection to Pony was to get it out of Titus Jones.

She didn't relish the idea of facing him again. He was too complex. A fierce, jagged piece of stone that could cut you to pieces one minute, then a clear, cool brook the next, a gently flowing body of water you could step into neck deep and know you'd never drown.

She glanced beyond the fence for any sign of movement,

human or otherwise. Today there was no Arctic wolf in the thicket, there were only the Cherokee roses—a perfect stillness of white sentinels waiting to see what would happen next.

All her instincts told her Titus was not there.

Back inside her Silver Streak, she spotted Cherokee Rose's diary where she'd hidden it underneath a messy stack of magazines and paperback novels. When she opened it, longing and sadness flew from its pages like blue moths. They landed on Jo Beth's shoulder, perched in her hair and covered the center of her chest right over her heart. She was so weighted with Cherokee Rose's emotions she could hardly sit upright.

Still, she climbed back into her truck and headed toward the rodeo. If a man searching for his daughter's killer was to be found, that was the first place to start looking.

Standing in the rodeo stands searching for Titus Jones, Jo Beth was Somebody Else, somebody so unformed and uncertain, she didn't even leave footprints. She was a silhouette traveling without a map, without landmarks. Everything she'd ever known had been rearranged—her history, her beliefs, even her memories.

The only thing that had not changed was rodeo. It didn't matter that your throat was parched and your hands shook and nobody much cared whether you got up the next morning or were found in bed without a beating pulse, the rodeo withstood it all, plaited itself into a rope you could hang onto.

Holding fast to the rope, Jo Beth left the arena and set out for the rough stock pens. Wouldn't the father of an iconic female bull rider naturally gravitate there?

Rodeo bulls saved all their energy to pit against the cowboys who had the hubris to try to ride them. They didn't mill about in the mindless way of cattle headed to the slaughterhouse.

With names such as Diablo, Devil at the Crossroad and Hell on Hooves, they were specially bred for the qualities that made them deceptively docile in the pens and raging furies in the rodeo ring. But these bulls were restless.

Searching for the cause of the turmoil in the bull pen, she quickened her step. Along the edges of the pen there was a flash of something. A sleeve? A man's head? As she got closer she saw it was Titus Jones, walking among the bulls without fear.

Recognition flashed in his eyes at the same time. The Titus Jones she'd come to know, however briefly, was so closely connected to the earth he could read the winds and hear the heartbeat of trees. He could have vanished before her eyes, and she'd never have caught him. But he kept moving toward her.

And then she saw the cause: Buckin' Billy Rakestraw was rounding the corner of the bull pen and heading toward the parking lot. Straight toward Jo Beth.

Titus would take a shortcut through the bull pen for only one reason: he was chasing Pony's killer.

Long-buried instincts took over. Jo Beth bolted to the left, trying to cut Billy off. He turned his shoulder and plowed into her, sending her sprawling onto the pavement while he sprinted off.

Several tons of bull parted like the Red Sea as Titus emerged to scale the fence, a Moses on a mission of Biblical proportions. With Jo Beth on the ground and his quarry getting away, Titus knelt beside her, never even glancing up as Billy vanished between the parked vehicles.

"Go on. Get him. I'm all right."

"I ain't leavin' no woman hurt in the dirt."

"Dammit, I'm not hurt."

"I don't cotton to cussing women."

"You stubborn old coot, I don't want you to *cotton* to me. Or coddle me, either."

"I gotta see if you're hurt."

His big hands moved along her arms, his callused thumbs rough against her skin. She tried to read his eyes, but it was like staring into a deep pond, trying to see the movement of water beneath the ice.

Except for Maggie, nobody had ever cared whether Jo Beth had a broken arm. An unexpected tenderness rose in her. Hard on its heels came the feeling that she'd stepped into quicksand. If she weren't careful, she'd sink.

"I can take care of myself. Let go of me."

"I aim to see about you. I can fix the wings of crippled birds and set the bones of rabbits caught in a trap."

"I'm not a crippled bird."

"Ain't you?"

Without effort or embarrassment, he lifted her onto his lap and carefully felt along every inch of her legs.

Drunk, she would have punched him in the face. Stone cold sober, she had no protection from the onslaught of feelings— embarrassment, outrage, and a sudden, shocking awareness that she was still a woman. Passion and disaster were the same; they could descend on you with the force of tornadic winds, and there was nothing you could do but stand by while they swept you along in their path.

If Titus saw or felt anything at all except how scrawny she was beneath her denim, his face didn't show it. In case there was a god, Jo Beth thanked Her for minor miracles.

"I reckon you'll live."

"Glory be."

"Ain't no cause to be sacrilegious."

"Then you ought to quit acting like God Almighty."

Abruptly, he released her. She wobbled upright and dusted off the seat of her pants. For a moment they stood side by side, the last two people on earth you'd expect to have any reason at all to be in each other's company.

Reminding herself of why she'd sought him out in the first place, Jo Beth said, "I came to ask you if Morning Star was really my half sister. Or was that merely the fantasy of a starstruck Cherokee dancer?"

"The past is done with. Let it alone."

"You're the one who gave me the diary."

"I wisht I could take it back. Go on home."

Jo Beth felt an insane urge to stamp her foot. "Stop treating me like a dimwit and answer my question."

"I got better things to do than stand here jawing with you."

Defying him was like trying to argue with a rodeo bull. As Jo Beth cast about for a way to get through to Titus, she wondered if her life might have turned out differently if she'd found a way to communicate with Sam so many years ago.

"Titus, I'm not trying to interfere. Please. This truth is as important to me as finding Pony's killer is to you."

A flicker of something came into his eyes. Contempt? Hatred? Compassion? With this rocklike man, how could you know?

"I just seen Rose once. She didn't say nothin' about your daddy."

"Then how did you know about him?"

"I learnt about him when Running Wolf come up my mountain to take Pony."

- Anna Michaels -

"Rose's brother?"

Titus nodded. "Running Wolf was many things, but he wasn't no liar. Morning Star was your sister."

The way Titus stated the simple facts removed all doubts in Jo Beth's mind. Her uncle had lied. Even worse, he'd perpetuated a horrible, lifelong hoax on Jo Beth.

If it was me, I'd skin him alive.

"Titus, I have to know something else. If Pony found out somebody had betrayed someone she knew, would she say, 'If it was me, I'd skin him alive'?"

Suddenly everything he felt for his daughter showed in Titus's face. In that moment, it was easy to see how a woman would be attracted to a man like that, a man filled to the brim with love and admiration and joy so great you could catch hold and it would fly you to the moon.

"How come you asked?"

Jo Beth never considered not telling him. No matter how low she'd sunk in the past, she'd never stooped to unkindness. Besides, she trusted him.

What did it mean when you could trust a man who was almost a stranger more than you could trust your own flesh and blood?

Why had Uncle Mark told her those lies for so many years? And why keep it up now that everybody concerned was dead?

Sometimes the search for the truth takes you down roads you'd rather not travel. But Jo Beth was determined to travel them, anyway.

"I ain't got all day."

"Sometimes I hear her voice."

In spite of her shocking revelation, Titus remained as locked down as a prison under siege.

"Pony ain't talkin' to you. Stay outta my business."

When he walked off, Jo Beth felt like grabbing his shoulders and shaking him. Couldn't he see that she might be the only friend he had in Huntsville?

"Stubborn old goat."

He might have heard her or he might not. It didn't matter. Jo Beth had the last word, and that was what counted to a woman struggling to regain control of her life.

As she sprinted toward her truck, the voice Titus said she couldn't hear shouted at her.

Stop!

This time she didn't question who was speaking or why. Jo Beth stood still, quieting her mind so she could hear the energy pulsing around her. It came to her first as a whisper of intuition, then a tug of urgency.

Following her instincts, she backtracked toward the barn that lay behind the bull pen. It was relatively cool and dark inside the cavernous structure. She blinked till her eyes could make the adjustment.

The air around her pulsed with a red energy so strong her heart raced. Telling herself to slow down, take her time, Jo Beth stood in the center of the barn, drained herself of all thought. In order to connect with the energy of a departed spirit she had to be an empty vessel, open to all possibilities.

She knelt on the hay-littered ground and closed her eyes, waiting. The sweet smell of hay lulled her, while a mosquito lazily buzzed her head. Pigeons in the hayloft called to each other with soft, mournful cries.

Jo Beth knew better than to be fooled into complacency. She could sense the red haze gaining fury. With the suddenness of a lightbulb exploding in your hands, the red haze swirled around her with such force she toppled sideways.

Righting herself, Jo Beth crawled on all fours, following the trail left by rage—dark energy and the faint scent of blackened embers. At the back corner of the barn she raised her right hand and inched it along the wall.

Jo Beth jerked her hand back. Loss howled from the wall as chilling as the cries of a white wolf. The spatter pattern, so faint you had to lean in close to see, had dried black.

"I'm going to hunt you down like the mad dog you are."

Jo Beth made the promise to the one person who would hold her accountable, the person who would measure her by strict standards and would make no allowances for backsliding: she made the promise to herself.

Twenty

A week ago, if you'd told Titus he'd be sitting in the parking lot of a motel in Decatur, Alabama, planning on killing a man in cold blood, he'd have run you off his mountain with a load of buckshot in your britches. But a week ago, he hadn't seen his daughter laid out cold in the morgue.

After Jo Beth had made him lose Billy's trail at the rodeo, he'd picked it up again out in the parking lot. Buckin' Billy had been a fool growing up at the base of Titus's mountain. Time hadn't taught him a thing.

He hadn't even looked behind him when Titus caught up with him at the Raceway service station on I-565, then followed him across the bridge. The sawed-off, bowlegged bully didn't even check his back when he swaggered into room 116.

The girl with Billy had a long dark ponytail that reminded Titus of Pony at sixteen racing across the pasture on her Appaloosa, Pony coming into the house in the evening with her cheeks rosy from sun and wind, bending over to kiss Titus and laugh about the prickly beard he hadn't shaved in two days.

Even Pony with her face scrunched up in rage.

Longing and memories washed over Titus. The door of the motel wavered then vanished altogether, and Titus was sitting at the rodeo watching Pony spin into the ring. It was her first ride against the men, and they'd put her on the meanest bull in the circuit.

Though the crowd was cheering, he could tell they didn't hold out much hope for her, a little bit of a thing hanging onto a two-ton bull with one hand and a plaited rope.

But they didn't know his Pony. She and defeat had parted company the day she was born, motherless, red-faced and defiant.

She covered her bull the full eight seconds, then strode out of the ring grinning and waving. Brand-new bull-riding champ of the Professional Rodeo Cowboys Association.

Titus walked taller that day. Forget what folks said about pride being a sin. Some days, pride was the only thing that kept him putting one foot in front of the other. Pride and Pony.

He was making his way through the rodeo crowd when he saw Buckin' Billy. Saw and heard.

"That bitch won't steal another championship from me. I'm gonna take her out of the ring, one way or the other."

Three bull riders covered with dust and humiliation let out a cheer. One of them said, "What you plan to do, Billy?"

"Woo her, screw her and keep her barefoot and pregnant in the kitchen. Where she belongs."

Billy spotted Titus then, and his face turned red.

"Them's some big plans, Billy."

Billy balled up his fists. "You planning to stop me, old man?"

"You ain't worth my time."

"Don't think I'm gonna let a sorry excuse for a cowboy like you get in my way."

Beyond Billy, his daughter came laughing through the crowd.

"Now's your chance, Billy. Pony's headin' your way."

It didn't take Pony long to get the lay of the land. If Billy had the sense God gave a billy goat, he'd have turned tail and run. Instead, he swaggered up to Pony and asked her to go with him to dinner.

She scrunched her face up the way she used to when she'd tell Titus about Billy's latest slur against her and how she'd beat the tar out of him.

"I ain't goin' to dinner with you now nor no time in the future, Billy Rakestraw. I'd as soon eat dead possum settin' on a skunk."

Pony's rages, through rare, were as explosive as her smiles. Titus had lived in the sunshine and shadow that was his daughter. She was the air he breathed. His life had been bigger because of her, brighter.

Now, hiding in his truck in a motel parking lot in this godforsaken town, he was somebody he didn't even know. Somebody he didn't much care to know.

Titus wiped the sweat out of his eyes and waited on Billy to get inside, get comfortable with the idea that he was safe from the reach of the law and the lawless. Titus didn't second-guess himself about Billy's guilt. If he wasn't guilty, why had he run? That and his history of hatred toward Pony sealed his fate. As far as Titus was concerned, he had his daughter's killer.

Trying to catch his breath, Titus rolled down his window. There was no sound, no movement. Nothing rose on the still air except the stench of hot asphalt and his own grief. Finally, Titus got out of his truck and reached for his gun.

He didn't care who saw him. If Billy was the one, Titus was fixing to kill him. And after it was done, he didn't care what happened to him.

It didn't take much effort to get through the door. Living

alone on a mountain you learned all sorts of things. No locksmith was going to drive up a road that petered out to help you open up a padlocked shed after your daughter lost the key down by the creek playing treasure hunt.

Billy didn't even hear him come in. He was too busy trying to get out of his britches.

But the girl did. Sprawled on the bed in tight jeans Pony would have scorned as an *advertisement*, the girl stared at Titus, openmouthed, bug-eyed and pale.

Titus motioned her out the door, then poked the barrel of his gun into Billy's back.

"I'd get them britches back on if I was you."

"Jesus!"

"He ain't here."

Billy scrambled on the floor like a barn rat.

Daddy, don't.

Was it Titus's conscience telling him not to pull the trigger, or was his own despair conjuring up his daughter's ghost?

When the report was delivered, Sam was sifting through evidence on the Pony Jones case and trying to get Jo Beth out of his mind. She'd been lying at Dunkin' Donuts. And he intended to find out why.

He ripped into the envelope, pulled out the report then stood there disbelieving.

"Bad news?" Luther, who had had both feet propped on his desk, jumped up.

"We've got the murder weapon, Luther. The blood on the post driver was a match to Pony's."

"What about fingerprints?"

"No matches yet." Sam was already strapping on his gun.

"Somebody at that rodeo knows something and we're going to find out."

He was headed out the door when Barb prissed toward him. Every step she took was calculated to show off her shapely legs.

"Yo, Barb. Looking good, kid."

"So are you, hot stuff."

"What you got?"

"A woman on the phone asking for you. I think you'd better take it."

The hysterical woman identified herself as Buckin' Billy's girlfriend. According to her story, a tall, rangy man with a mountaineer twang had burst in on them, told her to get out and was now holding Buckin' Billy hostage.

Sprinting toward his unmarked car with Luther right behind him, Sam explained the call. Then he slapped the siren on top and tore off toward the west side of town and the Tennessee River.

"You think Titus Jones was the man who broke up Buckin' Billy's tête-à-tête?"

"Tête-à-tête? Are you going highbrow, Luther?"

"Naw. Sarah's listening to French tapes. Wants me to take her to Paris next year."

"Shit."

"That's what I told her." Luther popped a Tums into his mouth. "You think Titus is our man?"

"Give me one of those." Sam stuck out his right hand. "Who else would hold a gun on Buckin' Billy? Let's just hope he didn't flush our bird from the cage."

When Sam and Luther stepped into room 116, the reason the bird hadn't flown was immediately evident. His jeans and shorts were drying on the wall-hung air-conditioning unit while Buckin' Billy, wearing nothing but a T-shirt, lounged on the bed watching a violent TV show.

"What happened here, Billy?" Sam strolled around the room checking it out, while Luther guarded the door in case Billy decided to bolt. "Titus Jones scare the shit out of you?"

"Kiss my ass."

"You're not my type. I just want to ask you a few questions."

"Not without my lawyer."

There were days when Sam wanted to herd all the three-piece suits in a room, back a tractor-trailer up to the door, load them in then ship them off somewhere. Anywhere but his jurisdiction.

Before Prohibition, cops weren't hogtied by the law, and bad guys got what they deserved. You could ask the tough questions in a tough way and nobody whined about criminals' rights. Nobody went on a talk show and became an instant pop hero telling his sordid story. Criminals didn't make more selling TV rights than cops made in ten years.

"Luther, let's get this piece of shit out of here."

When Jo Beth arrived on Devon Street it was that peculiar time of evening when the shadows had chased the last bit of light from the sky and lurked underneath trees waiting to pounce. Sometimes you could skirt around them but if you weren't careful, they'd reach out to pull you in, and suddenly you'd feel as if you'd been swallowed by sorrow.

The shadow from the Natchez crape myrtle in Maggie's front yard took hold of Jo Beth and filled her with a need to weep. She would have gone back to her truck if Maggie hadn't appeared in the doorway.

In bare feet with the light pouring over her from the front

porch fixture, she looked as if she wore a halo. By comparison, Jo Beth felt dingy. With Pony's spilled blood still crying out to her from the barn wall, she was not fit company for a woman who served tea in real china cups and kissed her children every night before they went upstairs to bed.

"I was getting worried about you."

"I'm sorry, Mags. I lost track of time." Jo Beth didn't mention what she'd found. Telling the story would bring blood into the house on Devon Street, and everybody knew that once blood stained a house, nothing inside would ever be the same.

"That's okay. I didn't cook, so nothing's getting cold. Oh, but I can't wait to tell you what I found out in Florence." Maggie linked arms with Jo Beth, then led her into the house, calling in her best cheerleader voice, "James, look who's here."

He held out his hand, but his stiff face and body language made it perfectly clear he'd rather have anyone in his house except the woman who was the cause of his wife's afternoon wild-goose chase and the bucket of Kentucky Fried Chicken sitting on his table.

Their boys came downstairs for dinner, so Jo Beth didn't have to worry about making small talk. With teenagers conversation became a whirlwind, spinning around the table so there was no room for anything except youthful energy.

After dinner James excused himself to his study to work, while the boys scattered like spilled BBs. Before they left, they both kissed Jo Beth on the cheek and stood blush-faced while she rumpled their hair.

After they left, Maggie motioned her to the den. "Why don't you get comfortable while I get coffee?"

Jo Beth sank into a chair with the same relief you'd feel in the quiet after a storm. While she waited, she tried to imagine Pony's last few minutes in the barn. She might have been sitting on a bale of hay thinking about her rodeo ride, planning how she would stay atop a snorting, kicking, bucking bull long enough to retain her championship title. Or even how, if she got very unlucky, she might lose to one of the cowboys itching to hand her a defeat, a woman with the audacity to match skills with the men on their turf.

Jo Beth imagined how someone came inside and started talking, the talk turning to an argument so fierce the killer grabbed the first weapon handy and hit her over the head as Pony turned to walk away.

Or had the murder been premeditated? Was the killer such a coward he'd waited until Pony's back was turned so she couldn't fight back?

When Maggie came into the den carrying two cups of coffee, Jo Beth was glad for the respite. In the house on Devon Street you could slip into another role as easily as you could change coats. You could become the kind of woman who had coffee and bridge with girlfriends on Tuesdays and sold raffle tickets for the church fund-raiser on Fridays.

Over coffee Maggie told how she'd driven to Florence to visit her mother's friend, how she'd stayed later than she'd meant to so she could walk in the flower gardens.

"Did you learn anything about more Morning Star?"

"Brace yourself."

"For what?"

"Your father came to Morning Star's graduation."

Jo Beth used to wonder if she'd dreamed her father, if she'd ever had him at all. Maybe Cynthia had found Jo Beth on her doorstep and made up Rafe Dawson to give her child a history and a sense of connection.

Under the guise of sipping her coffee, Jo Beth tried to breathe. "Did your mother's friend speak to him? How did she know it was him?"

"She was having a flaming affair with the history teacher, who was a rodeo buff and recognized Rafe Dawson from his pictures." Maggie reached for her hand. "I'm sorry, Jo."

"Don't be. It's another piece of the puzzle, Mags."

When Jo Beth left the house on Devon Street, the moon was half hidden behind clouds that held the threat of rain, and only a part of the Little Dipper was visible. It was the kind of gloomy night where thoughts turn dark and memories become the stuff of nightmares.

After her father had left, Jo Beth used to stand outside and pick out the brightest star in the sky, then close her eyes and make a wish. It was always the same, that when she woke up the next morning her daddy would be there.

Even after she was grown and far too disillusioned to believe that wishes on stars came true, she still hoped she might look up someday and see him on Christmas morning or her sixteenth birthday. Or her graduation.

Had Rafe Dawson appeared at Jo Beth's graduation, too? Had he been sitting in the back of the auditorium, hiding in the shadows so nobody would see him, hoping for a glimpse of the daughter he'd left behind?

Or had he hated the woman and the child who had taken him away from Cherokee Rose? Had the Native American dancer with bells on her skirt been the love of his life, his soul mate, the woman he couldn't live without?

Once Jo Beth had believed in such things as wishes on stars, love everlasting and dreams that came true. Sometimes she wished she still did.

By the time she arrived at Sleepy Pines Campground, it had started to rain again. Before she'd found Pony under the roses, Jo Beth would have taken that as a bad omen, a sign she should shut herself up in her trailer and fend off the dampness with a bottle or two.

Anybody seeing her in the trailer would have seen a small, disheveled woman staring at her kitchen cabinets. What they wouldn't see was the battle raging inside her, the fierce need for alcohol met by an equally fierce spirit. When Jo Beth finally emerged from the battlefield, the only evidence of her triumph was the spark in her eyes.

After wrapping a scarf around her hair, she grabbed a flashlight and plunged through the thorny vines into the deep woods.

She was tired of being the woman you abandoned, lied to, avoided. If Titus Jones was still hiding in the woods, she'd find him. Forget that she had a lousy sense of direction and the last time she'd searched she'd become hopelessly lost.

Jo Beth didn't need a map to tell her where she was going. She had willpower and determination and a flashlight. And if necessary, she'd scream until he came to her just to keep her quiet.

Twenty-one

Titus sat in his pickup in the deep woods beside the campground, his forehead resting on the steering wheel. The sudden scent of roses filled the cab, but he didn't lift his head. He was so weary he didn't even make a fist.

Buckin' Billy had not killed Pony. Titus had known that the minute he heard Pony's voice: *Daddy, don't.*

Or had he known it before?

Titus didn't like to think of himself as a hotheaded man who'd gone wild-goose-chasing after a cowboy just because he'd mouthed off about Pony many years ago.

But there it was, staring him in the face. His own weakness. He could live side by side with God's critters in perfect harmony, but he'd been holed up on his mountain so long he didn't know the first thing about people.

A prime example was Jo Beth, a falling-down drunk one minute and a wounded wolf the next, circling around you looking for your weak side. There was no figuring her out. The best you could do was keep your distance and hope she didn't chew off your leg.

Titus was no longer sure he even knew his own daughter. All those years she was gone riding the bulls. All those secrets locked away in her diary.

The fragrance of roses became so strong Titus had to lower the window. Still, the scent pulled at him, drew him toward the glove compartment where Pony's diary lay.

Titus had never ignored the signs, and he didn't aim to start. Besides, what was the use of secrets now?

When he reached into the glove compartment, the book fell open as if it had been expecting him, as if Pony herself had pointed out the page.

As Titus began to read, his daughter's childhood dreams spilled over him, a flood of longing for a feminine touch in her life. Titus split open like a butchered hog.

His lips moved. He might have whispered her name or he might not. Slaughtered animals didn't do much talking.

He felt her coming, then, striding toward him the way she always did when she aimed to have a serious talk, the sound of her boots resounding through the woods, their rhythm crying out to him—*why?*

If he could see her one more time, if he could hold his child in his arms, he'd tell her that he'd only wanted to protect her. He'd never meant to deprive her of her family.

Pony would have loved having an aunt. He understood that now.

As the sound of her boots came closer, he recalled a moment he'd almost forgotten, something he'd paid scant attention to at the time: Pony, in the fields, weaving a garland of black-eyed Susans for her hair, playing make-believe with girls who were nothing more than figments of her imagination.

Pony had been a tomboy. He'd believed she was content in overalls, her hair braided without a ribbon. Now he understood that's all Pony knew. Because of him. Because he'd kept secrets from her. Because he'd kept her away from any Wolf and any

Dawson who might have claimed her. Because he'd kept her away from Jo Beth.

It was not easy to see himself true and clear, the flaws and fissures in his character exposed, his motives trotted out and studied under the beam of complete honesty. If you let it, self-examination could crack your heart in two and you'd have to spend the rest of your life numb, every emotion you tried to feel draining through the hole.

But there was also a mercy in the truth. After he found Pony's killer, Titus would start over, do better, live open.

He put her diary back in the glove compartment, got out of his truck and fell on his knees. Then he waited for Pony to appear and pour her grace on his bowed head.

When her footsteps halted, he looked up to see her standing in the mist underneath the canopy of a dripping oak tree, her hair covered by a scarf, her face as fragile as a porcelain teacup.

"Pony?"

"No. It's me."

When Jo Beth walked into the clearing, Titus felt cheated. Confused. He'd felt his daughter coming, heard her voice. He'd even smelled the sweet scent of hay and rich earth she always carried with her.

He remained in a kneeling position, still unbelieving. "I thought Pony was here."

"She is." Jo Beth pressed her hand over her heart. "In here. No thanks to you and Uncle Mark and the rest of you who were involved in keeping my niece out of my life."

Titus rose from the ground without haste or embarrassment. That was not his way.

"You've had your say. Now you can go."

"I'm not finished yet."

She had spunk. He had to give her credit.

The rain had stopped. Jo Beth took off her scarf and shook the moisture from her hair, hair as dark as Morning Star's, black hair that could make a man forget everything except the scent of a woman's skin.

It was the first time Titus had felt his animal nature stir since Morning Star died. He knew God had a sense of humor. Till now, he'd never figured it was warped.

"Aren't you going to invite me to sit in the truck?"

"I ain't in no mood for socializing."

Jo Beth's chin went up a notch, then she started searching around till she spotted a tree root pushing through the earth like a pair of arms you could fall into. She plopped down like somebody you couldn't budge till Judgment Day.

"Ain't no use gittin' comfortable. You ain't stayin'."

"You have to be the most stubborn man I've ever met. I'd call you an old coot, but I don't think you're all that much older than I am."

Titus hadn't ever expected to laugh again. But there it was. Hanging in the air between them like a reveler who'd crashed a funeral thinking it was a party.

"I thought you might be human," she said.

"Are you?"

"Barely. More lately than I've ever been."

"Why?"

"Because of Pony. She makes me ashamed of my own weakness." Jo Beth picked up a stick and snapped it in two. "I found where he killed her."

"I did, too."

"I thought you might have seen it."

He'd not only seen it; he'd never forget it. Titus didn't think he could ever look at another barn wall and not see a river of blood gushing from his daughter's head—so much the killer would've had to clean the floor and tote out the hay from the runoff. In his haste, he'd forgotten the walls.

"How'd you find me tonight? You ain't got no more sense about finding a trail than a sucklin' pig."

"A yearling would be more flattering."

Jo Beth Dawson was right pretty when she smiled. Titus didn't respond. He didn't aim to flatter her. He didn't even plan on having a conversation with her.

"Have the rest of your say and get it over with. I ain't got time to fool with you."

"Did you find Buckin' Billy?"

"How come you want to know?"

"Well, did you?"

"I found 'em."

A raindrop inched down her cheek and dropped off the end of her chin. If you looked close enough, you could see Jo Beth Dawson pulling patience around herself like it was a scratchy robe she'd rather not wear.

"You are the most ornery man."

She tossed the two pieces of stick into the woods, but she didn't budge. If you could judge folks by their bullheadedness, they'd be a perfect match. Titus nearly cracked another smile. Instead, he sat there and waited her out. He had all night.

"Obviously you wouldn't still be here if Billy killed Pony," she said. "Who do you think did it?"

"It ain't none of your business."

"You brought me into this when you told me Pony was my niece. I *have* to know."

He'd always believed Pony's stubborn streak came from him. Now he could see how the Dawson blood put a steel rod in her backbone and a don't-mess-with-me look in her eyes.

Titus was not the kind of man to strike up bargains. But his daughter filled him so full, he couldn't tell whether it was his heart or hers beating in his chest. Sometimes love made you do the unthinkable.

"On one condition," he said.

"Name it."

"You won't interfere. The killer's mine."

Her thoughts flew into his mind like magpies. She was trained to follow the rules, bring criminals to justice. But was justice always served? What would she do if Pony was hers?

Titus knew her answer even before she delivered it. He lowered himself to the tree root beside her and waited.

"I'm no longer a detective, Titus."

"You toting a gun."

She patted her vest. "How did you know?"

"I ain't blind."

For a long while, there was no sound except the rain dripping off trees and the combined sounds of their breathing. The surprise of it was that Titus was glad to have somebody besides Dog to sit with. Even more surprising, he was glad it was her.

Finally, Jo Beth pushed herself up from the tree root. "I'll bet you haven't had a decent night's sleep since you got to Huntsville."

Titus sat very still. The waiting felt like a held breath.

"Listen, there's no use in staying out here cramped up in your pickup when you can stay in my trailer."

Her small kindness meant more to him than it ought. Still, he was beholden to no one.

"Much obliged but no, thank you."

"That's just plain mule-headed. June in Alabama is hotter than hell. Even at night."

"I don't pay the weather no mind."

"Good grief. Who in their right mind would want to sleep in this heat when they could be on a pull-down bed under an air conditioner?"

"You might as well save your breath."

"Why? So you can get the best of me one more time? Listen, you old curmudgeon, you'll be safe in my trailer. If anybody tries to bother us, I'll shoot them."

"You the damnedest woman I ever met."

"I thought you didn't cuss."

"You'd make a mule cuss."

Titus reckoned the sky was fixing to fall, the trees were fixing to jerk up their roots and start running for safer ground, the world was fixing to come to a screeching halt. He was going to say *yes*.

Maybe it was because he was too old to keep sleeping cramped up in a pickup. Maybe it was because she'd worn him out with her stubbornness. Or maybe it was because he needed to hear the sound of somebody breathing nearby.

As they walked back through the woods, Titus led the way, otherwise they'd have spent the rest of the night thrashing around, lost.

The trailer was smaller inside than he'd imagined. He felt

too big. Afraid he was going to bump into something, knock something over, he crammed his hands deep into his pockets, which was not his way. He liked to hold himself loose and tight at the same time, a man ready to spring into action.

Now that Pony was dead, he thought he'd seen everything the world had to throw at him. He'd thought he was ready for anything. Except this. A dark-eyed woman standing so close he could smell the soap she used to bathe.

The scent put him in mind of the mountain wildflowers he collected in a Mason jar. Trying to shut his mind to the smell, he stood there and waited for whatever came next.

With Titus Jones looming over her, Jo Beth felt the way you would if a giant redwood tree walked into your tiny trailer and took up residence. Overcrowded and overwhelmed.

"Sit down," she said. "I'll make us some coffee. It's going to be a long night."

"Amen."

She was relieved to see he had a sense of humor. If you knew where to look, you could find small mercies in everything.

He tried to cram his long legs under the table but they stuck out at odd angles and his big feet took up all the space underneath. He looked as uncomfortable as she felt. Though Titus had the weather-toughened look of a man who could uproot small trees with his bare hands, he also gave off the air of a remarkably humble man, a man who preferred shadows to limelight, cool mountain streams to the raging river of city streets gone bad.

She turned on the TV to fill the silence that was spreading through the trailer like smoke. Then she retrieved Cherokee

Rose's diary and placed it on the table in front of him along with a cup of coffee.

"How much of this story do you know?"

"Not much, I reckon. Only what Running Wolf told me."

"I need to know what you know. I think if we pool our knowledge, it will help both of us. It might even help you find whoever murdered Pony."

The only sign Titus gave that the words pierced him was the way his eyes turned to blizzards. If you looked into their center too long, you might get sucked in, you might lose your soul. You might start thinking you wouldn't turn Pony's killer over to Titus, that you wanted to avenge her yourself.

"What is it you want to know?"

Her father, that's what she wanted to know.

"Did my father ever see Cherokee Rose again after he married my mother?"

"I can't say."

"Can't or won't."

"I can't say because I don't know."

Titus sat on her bench like a knife, the bladed edges of him so sharp he could cut a man to pieces and not think about it twice. That he didn't scare Jo Beth was testament to the man. Underneath his lethal exterior ran a wide river, its waters flowing with good and solid pieces of character you could climb onto like a raft and float.

But Jo Beth had no intention of hanging onto his raft or any other. She was on fire to discover the truth, and she intended to find it even if she had to stay up all night picking the pieces out of him bit by bit.

It wouldn't be her first all-night vigil. The only difference was, she'd had her liquor then. Suddenly a need for alcohol gripped her. She set the coffee cup down to avoid telltale spills, then took a deep breath while she fought to get the upper hand.

"What do you know about Running Wolf?" If Titus noticed her epic struggle, he didn't acknowledge it.

"He opposed my marriage."

"Why?"

"Running Wolf said no good ever come to his family from rodeo cowboys."

"You were a rodeo cowboy?"

"A bull rider. I taught Pony."

"You taught her well."

"I killed 'er."

She didn't attempt to offer sympathy. Everything about his rigid posture and his frozen eyes said he wouldn't have accepted it.

"What else did Running Wolf tell you?"

"After Morning Star died, he come up Doe Mountain and told me he could keep Pony safe."

"Good grief. From what I've seen, you'd take on a grizzly bear for Pony. I don't understand why Running Wolf was worried about her safety."

"He said if I didn't let him take her, somebody else might find out about her and try to take her away."

"Who?"

"You ain't gonna let it go, are you?"

"No."

"The Dawsons. Your people."

"That doesn't make any sense. My grandfather was one of

the most wonderful men I know. Did Running Wolf say why my family would want to take Pony?"

"No."

Jo Beth wasn't even close to getting a full picture. There were too many missing pieces.

"When I was growing up, I didn't know about Morning Star, let alone Pony. As far as I know, none of the Dawsons knew about your daughter."

Except that whisper behind closed doors about Morning Star. So very long ago it might have been a dream. Or a nightmare.

"Your family's powerful. A lot of years had passed before Pony was born. He said if they found out they might want to turn a third-generation child into a Dawson."

"And so you kept her on that mountain."

"Like a prisoner, you mean?"

"No. Safe."

"Ain't nobody safe."

For a moment Jo Beth wanted to tell him that *she knew*. She wanted to spill her story onto him and watch it run off again, water over rock, changed and somehow cleansed. The urge passed and she stood beside him, but deeply separate, each of them encased in their own reserve and their own versions of their common history.

"Tomorrow I'll go to Cherokee Ridge and talk to Running Wolf," she said.

"It won't do you no good. He won't tell you nothing."

"I can try."

She could no longer live with herself if she didn't. A few days ago she'd begun her journey to Huntsville as a woman who cared about nothing and attempted even less. And now her heart was laid open and her future hinged on uncovering the past.

Suddenly the tiny space was filled with images of Pony. From the wall-hung TV, Sonja Livingstone was narrating a special on the life of the iconic rodeo cowgirl.

And standing beside the TV was the ghost-girl, her eyes daring you to look away, her mouth moving.

I'm glad I got to see how a whole family feels, even if I had to die before it happened.

Titus's face looked like a two-by-four that had been ripped by a buzz saw, then left raw and splintered. Jo Beth didn't have to ask if he'd heard Pony: she knew.

She reached up to turn off the TV.

"Leave it be."

As her niece's life unfolded through a few old photographs and the eyes of those who had known her, Jo Beth saw herself. She saw the layers of hurts and fears, wonder and laughter, dreams and disappointments arranged into a shape that made her who she was today.

Could she rearrange the layers and become something different, something better?

Sonja Livingstone wrapped up her special on Pony Jones, and Jo Beth turned from rare and painful introspection to the matter at hand.

"There's a bed in the back. You can take that. I'll sleep here. The bench converts to a bed."

"I ain't takin' your bed and I ain't puttin' you to no trouble. The floor's fine. It beats being wadded up in my pickup."

"It's no trouble. Besides, you're too tall to fit on the pull-down."

He didn't argue further. She pulled down her bed then lay there listening to his quiet movements behind the curtains.

Pony's spirit hovered just to the right of her. Though she was blessedly silent for once, Jo Beth could hear the echo of her niece yelling, *Cowboy up.*

When Jo Beth had been a detective, she'd sacrificed sleep, meals and even herself in pursuit of lawbreakers. What would she sacrifice to find out the whole truth about her family?

She closed her eyes, aware of every breath Titus took—but somehow soothed by the sound. It was like being watched over by God.

Twenty-two

Sam arrived at the department sweaty from his morning run. The autopsy report for John Running Wolf was waiting on his desk. Heart attack. Death from natural causes.

Sam picked it up and plopped it on Luther's desk. "Take a look."

Luther read with his lips moving and his fingers running down the lines. Usually this didn't bother Sam, but with the case dragging on and Jo Beth's presence pricking like a splinter under a fingernail, he felt his temper rising.

"Well?" Sam's voice was sharper than he'd meant. He moderated it. "What do you think?"

If he kept on letting the ragged edges of his temper show, he was going to have somebody in the department on his back saying he needed a leave to get his act together. Or even worse. Some kind of professional anger management.

"We release the body and have Sonja all over it telling the folks who pay our salaries that we let Pony's murderer get away and now he's dead and won't have to pay for the crime."

The idea wasn't as far-fetched as Luther made it sound.

"The heck of it is," Sam said, "she could be right. If Billy was telling the truth, he didn't do it."

With his lawyer present, Billy had told them he knew he was the prime suspect because he couldn't keep his mouth shut. Everybody who had ears knew he hated Pony. He'd run because he was scared somebody would try to pin the murder on him. Sam's gut said he wasn't lying.

"And if somebody else didn't kill Wolf because of what the Indian knew, then Wolf could be our murderer." Luther was good at that, picking up Sam's logic and carrying it to the next step.

"Won't that be just dandy? Trying to get a confession from a dead man. Come on, Lu."

"Where're we headed?"

"Crime lab. You're going to lay on the whip about getting fingerprints off that post driver."

"It's your turn. I did it last time."

The chances were slim that whoever had killed Pony and methodically ditched the weapon and moved the body would have forgotten to wipe off his prints.

Their options were running out. If they couldn't dig up fingerprints, that left a confrontation with Martha Running Wolf as the only alternative. Sam didn't have the stomach to drag a newly bereaved widow down to the station and grill her on the chance she would know whether her husband was a murderer.

There was another factor at play, too, one Sam didn't like to think about, much less plan for. Seeing Martha Wolf in her house hearing the news that her husband wouldn't be coming home anymore, Sam had pictured her living the rest of her life alone, rattling around in a big house still sometimes listening for her husband's footsteps three years after he'd been gone.

Then he'd applied her situation to himself, imagined what it would be like in ten years living in his apartment alone, facing retirement or already retired, time on his hands, his accumulated aches and pains worse every year, maybe even doctor bills piling up. No big bankroll for his old age. No wife. No kids. Sam didn't even have a dog.

Maybe he ought to get a dog. A big old golden retriever. At least he'd have somebody waiting for him every night, somebody to talk to, even if the only response was a wagging tail.

Sam was getting too soft for his job. He was getting to the point where he couldn't view events for what they were. He kept seeing the undercurrents, the riptides, the "no man is an island" ripple effects.

Forget the golden retriever. What he ought to do was get some huskies, go up to Canada and run the Yukon Quest. That would toughen him up.

When Titus woke up, he was instantly aware of Jo Beth sleeping beyond the curtain and Pony hovering over him. He didn't question why his daughter was hanging around in Jo Beth Dawson's trailer. He just lay in bed, grateful.

If you didn't look closely you'd think Pony was a trick of the light pouring through the blinds. But Titus made a practice of close observation. He saw the gathering of light with a father's heart, and what he saw made him weep.

Pony shimmered there, whole and perfect, her hand outstretched, calling to him. One word. *Daddy.*

The vision was both curse and blessing. His lost daughter offering grace.

In the quiet of dawn, Titus saw his front porch materialize, watched as Pony sat on the front steps beside Dog, listened as she spoke to the old hound.

I miss Mother the way you'd miss ice cream if you never had it. You'd wonder about its sweetness and the way it would taste on your tongue, the way it would make you feel special.

Titus wasn't a man to dwell on the past. It was over and done with, and no amount of regret would change one whipstitch.

But the vision drew him gently backward, its tender mercy Pony, herself—the outstretched hand she placed on his heart, the smile that said *I forgive you.*

He hung onto his daughter's smile the way you would dive into a cool river on a blistering summer day. Straining his eyes, he watched until the collection of light scattered and Pony was gone.

Titus got up then and put the bed back to rights. He'd slept in his clothes. He didn't subscribe to the loose morals of today's society. In his book, it wasn't proper to undress in the same dwelling as a woman unless she was your wife or you were in separate rooms. That thin curtain between him and Jo Beth didn't qualify as a wall.

He parted the curtain and there she was in a nightshirt that swallowed her whole, tousle-haired and vulnerable as a newborn kitten.

Though there wasn't an ounce of flesh showing except her frail arms and a glimpse of coltlike legs under the long shirt, she gathered the neck of her shirt in one hand and wadded it into a fist. Titus wanted to wrap a blanket around her and lead her to a rocking chair.

She watched him with doe eyes while he stood there without the least idea what to say. When she finally released her fist and turned to start the coffee, he was so grateful he would have danced a jig if he knew how.

She looked at him over her shoulder. "You're not leaving, are you?"

"It's time to go."

"Have coffee first. It beats stopping at the Seven-Eleven."

"Might as well."

While the coffee perked, she asked him how he'd slept and he said "fine." He never was much for small talk, and suddenly he was right in the middle of it. It was amazing how change could sneak up on you when you least expected it.

Jo Beth poured two cups and sat at the small table, but Titus wasn't fixing to sit down with her. First thing you knew he'd be getting comfortable with the idea of somebody to talk to and he'd lose track of what he came to do.

"Tell me more about Pony. The news special said she'd always known she was destined to make history. I find that remarkable."

"Some things you just know. God always sends you signs. But you got to get quiet and listen hard."

"When I was four, Daddy told me the legend of the Wisdom Keepers. I wonder if he got it from Cherokee Rose."

"Morning Star taught me. You got to pay attention to something besides yourself."

"And you taught Pony."

"It was the mountain. If I didn't learn nothing else, I learned that them mountains is going to be setting there till Judgment Day."

As he sipped his coffee, the remembered feel of mountain breezes soothed him, turned him generous and expansive. "We ain't no more enduring than a dandelion blowing in the wind. Our time on this earth is brief, and if we want to make something of it, we'd better set up and pay attention."

"Maybe Pony learned from the mountain, but it was you who put a voice to it, Titus."

Sometimes, suddenly, there is grace, wrapped in a package so small you'd hardly notice unless you were paying attention.

Slightly embarrassed, Titus stood up. "I gotta go."

"How will I find you?"

"You won't. I'll find you."

Outside the sky was still streaked with pink, a child's finger painting of dawn. Titus headed toward the woods, his thoughts following him like owls crying in the night. He was thinking about Jo Beth and Pony and the rodeo and a killer who might get by with murder. He was thinking about revenge and damnation and wondering if there would ever be any redemption for what he was aiming to do.

Anybody looking at him wouldn't see a single thing on his face except determination.

It was just after eight a.m. when Jo Beth left the campground, late enough to call Maggie without waking the entire household to find the address of John Running Wolf in the phone directory.

It took Jo Beth twenty minutes to get into the city and another twenty to get to the address on Cherokee Ridge. Forty minutes to think about what she was going to say.

Instead she thought about living in a movable house with no place to call home. She thought about loneliness and fear and Social Security and Christmases without children. She thought about the color red that could eat you alive if you let it. Rage and blood and even passion.

By the time she arrived at the huge house with the postage stamp yard sitting right on the ninth green, Jo Beth was wishing she'd taken up Maggie's offer to come with her. She was wondering why she hadn't put on a dress to meet a woman she wanted to impress enough to gain entry into her home. She was wondering why she had put on her fringed vest to cover a shoulder holster and why she was packing a gun.

She sat in her truck on a concrete apron facing a three-car garage, gripping the steering wheel, torn by indecision and wracked by need. The need for alcohol, but most of all the need to find out about the ghosts that could both haunt and heal. She sat so deeply buried in herself she didn't see the woman coming toward her.

The tap on her window made Jo Beth jump. Her hand flew to her holster.

Tearstained and tragic, the older woman standing beside her truck was carelessly put together—baggy pants and white tee showing underneath a man's blue-striped, button-down shirt, straggles of gray hair falling from underneath a wide-brimmed Panama hat, old garden gloves stained from repeated usage, clipping shears in one hand, a flat basket of roses in the other.

Cherokee roses.

"Do you need some help?"

It wasn't until the woman called out the question that Jo Beth realized the scent of roses had seeped through the cracks, deprived her of oxygen and made her want to weep. Jo Beth had to roll down the window to get some relief. The woman was standing so close she couldn't open the door without knocking her down.

"I'm looking for John Running Wolf."

Horror crossed the woman's face. Jo Beth wouldn't have been surprised if she'd run her garden shears through the truck door.

"Who are you?"

"Jo Beth Dawson."

"Did you say Dawson?"

"I did. Is this where John Running Wolf lives?"

"Young woman, are you not aware my husband is dead?"

If there were such a thing as a hole to China, Jo Beth would have leaped into it and disappeared. When she was a child she used to shut her eyes and pretend she had jumped down the hole to China and found her father.

One of the great tragedies of growing up was losing magic.

At least, Jo Beth hadn't lost her manners.

"I'm sorry. I didn't know." When had it happened? How?

"It was on the news this morning."

"I am so sorry. I didn't see the news. I would never have disturbed you." Jo Beth turned the key in the ignition.

"Don't leave. Please. I'm Martha Wolf, and I need to talk to you."

Martha Wolf led her past a stylish, modern living room and straight into the kitchen, the room usually reserved for intimate chats with family and close friends. Jo Beth was neither. Had Martha led her there because she felt more comfortable surrounded by her well-used pots and pans, or did she somehow feel more comfortable with Jo Beth than with other perfect strangers? And if so, why?

"How do you like your coffee?" In spite of her recent tears, Martha Wolf was very much in charge of her emotions.

"Just cream."

Martha got half-and-half from the refrigerator, poured the

cream into a tiny crystal pitcher, and brought it to the table along with a platter of chocolate chip cookies that looked homemade. There was only one cup of coffee on the platter.

"I can't stand to sit. I hope you don't mind." Martha walked back to the granite-topped island and started arranging roses. "These sprang up everywhere last night. After John . . . died. His sister was Cherokee Rose." Martha's hands stilled and she stared at Jo Beth. "But you would know that, wouldn't you?"

"I do now. But I didn't until after Pony Jones was murdered."

"My husband didn't do it. That's why I invited you in. Because you are a Dawson."

Jo Beth didn't follow the logic. Had grief unhinged Martha Wolf? Sometimes the only way to learn was not by asking questions but by being still. Her grandfather had taught her that.

Jo Beth sipped coffee and selected a cookie while Martha's hands moved among the roses. She placed them in the pottery vase with Native designs on the side while Jo Beth waited.

"There were things John kept from me. Rose tried to, as well, when she was alive." Jo Beth nodded, and Martha continued her story. "Did they think I wouldn't know? Did they think their secrets wouldn't leak like acid and burn everything in its path? Including me?"

Martha Wolf looked directly at Jo Beth in a way that demanded an answer. This woman was a stranger to her, but if she held back now, she might never find what she was looking for.

"I felt the same way when I learned that Morning Star was my half sister."

Martha Wolf left her roses and sat at the table beside Jo Beth.

"It's no accident that you came here this morning. 'You must speak straight so that your words may go as sunlight into our hearts.'"

"Cochise. Chiricahua chief."

"How did you know?"

"I have a small strain of Native blood. And my grandfather was fond of quoting Native wisdom."

Martha reached out, then sat very still looking down at their hands, linked not only by touch but by the tapestry of their interwoven history.

"You remind me of Morning Star. The same cheekbones and finely defined mouth."

"What was she like?"

"Smart and funny. Taller than you, her brow a little wider. It nearly killed me when my niece died. And now Pony."

"Did you know Pony?"

"Only what I read in the papers after she became famous. After Morning Star died, John and I had wanted her to live here with us. To keep her safe."

"Safe from what? Titus appears to be a man who deeply loved his daughter."

"I don't question his love or his judgment. Neither did John. But John knew things Titus didn't."

"What things?"

Martha picked up a cookie and broke it in half, nibbled the chips off the side, lost in a place Jo Beth couldn't go. Finally she sighed, put the cookie down and folded her hands in her lap. Apparently Martha Wolf was no stranger to tragedy. She knew a lot about composing herself, presenting a dignified front.

"Rafe's family bitterly opposed his involvement with Rose. She always believed he left her because his family put pressure on him." As Martha talked tears rained silently down her face, but if she was aware, she gave no indication. Even when they leaked into the corners of her mouth and dribbled down her chin, she didn't stop to brush them away.

"She believed the Dawsons were the reason Rafe didn't come back, even when he found out she was pregnant."

Jo Beth's chest hurt the way it would if she'd eaten too much spicy food then gone straight to bed. Clint Dawson had not only been a loving grandfather to her, he'd been a god, a man grown so huge in her mind he could straddle two rivers. He'd loved children, always been kind to them, magnanimous in his support of the orphaned, the sick, the neglected.

She couldn't imagine her grandfather in the role Martha Wolf had cast him.

"Then my father never came back?"

"Follow me. There's something I have to show you."

Martha led her beyond the golf greens to a well-worn footpath that wound through dense underbrush and trees so thick you couldn't see around the next bend. Jo Beth heard the brook before she saw it—swiftly moving water so clear you could see fish swimming along its rocky bottom.

Beside it was an ancient weeping willow.

"This place is beautiful." And haunting. Jo Beth wrapped her arms around herself, suddenly chilled. Though there were no roses visible, the scent was everywhere, clinging to the branches of the willow, floating on the air, rising up from the earth. "Do you come here often?"

"I come here every day. As a reminder." Martha gazed across the water. "This is where they met. Once a year, every year till the day they died."

"My father?"

"Yes. And Rose."

The past sang through the water, whispered through the willow, and in that moment, Jo Beth understood love. What we have, we can't keep. Life—and death—will sweep it away. We hold love while we can, the bits and pieces burning through us like a streaking comet. Afterward, we are left breathless and branded.

"He loved you and often spoke of you to Rose." Martha might have been reading Jo Beth's mind. "Though he was never a part of Morning Star's life, he also loved her. In his own way, I think he even loved your mother. Rose used to say Rafe's love was too big to be contained in one place."

Martha sat down suddenly under the willow, as if telling the story had sapped her strength. "We do strange things in the name of love. When John tried to keep Rafe and Rose apart, then Morning Star and Titus, he said he was acting out of love."

Jo Beth sat beside Martha and reached for her hand. The bond that held them together was formed of the bones and blood of the people they'd loved and lost.

"I've often wondered if things would have turned out differently if I hadn't kept John's secret. I've wondered if all of them would still be alive."

"What secret?"

"They made a deal. Money in exchange for silence. Once I heard them talking on the phone. On Morning Star's birthday. What irony."

Instinct told her this was where the answers lay. Not at the rodeo, not on the streets, but under this willow where the scent of Cherokee roses floated in honeyed clouds then wound around Jo Beth's chest and squeezed her heart.

"You see, John hated the union of his sister and Rafe as much as the Dawsons did. Native pride, I think. He struck the deal, took the money and gave his word that no claim would ever be made on the Dawson name or the Dawson fortune."

As if she had gathered force from her confession, Martha lifted her chin and looked into Jo Beth's eyes.

"My husband never spent the money, not a penny of it. Morning Star's daughter might still be alive if Titus had let John take her when she was a baby. John would have kept her safe."

"Nobody can keep you safe from murder. Trust me, I know."

"You were a police detective."

Knowledge of Jo Beth's sordid history showed on Martha's face. But so did compassion.

"Even with a gun and badge, I couldn't keep the victims safe."

"I can't help but wonder if Pony would still be alive if John hadn't sent the money back."

"When?"

"Two weeks before the rodeo."

Some words can bury you in grief and regret. Jo Beth sat dumbfounded while Martha Wolf continued to spill the story. She wished she'd never come back to Huntsville, never found a body, never started digging in the past.

Ignorance was so much easier to live with than truth, it was a wonder anybody ever bothered to sort facts from lies.

⇒ Twenty-three ⇐

After Martha ended her story, Jo Beth sat beside the older woman, hanging onto her hand. Sometimes a comforting touch was all it took to keep you from falling off the edge of the earth.

For a while there were no sounds except the singing of the winding waters and the sighing of the wind. It was Jo Beth who broke the silence.

"I can see Rose and my father. I can see everything, right here under this tree."

"You're all I have left of Morning Star. Come back anytime. I won't always be here, but the willow tree will."

Leaving Martha under the tree, Jo Beth reeled toward her truck. She felt as if she were on the worst bender of her life and she hadn't had a drop to drink. She put her key in the ignition, then sat there with the engine idling while she tried not to drown in pain. The only thing that kept her upright was the scent of roses.

She was barely aware of leaving the ridge, of navigating the curving roads to Sleepy Pines Campground. Every piece of her history had been smashed, rearranged. She didn't know if she'd ever find herself in the rubble.

"What am I going to do?"

You know what to do.

It didn't surprise Jo Beth that Pony had risen up from the dead to answer her question. What surprised her was the feeling that Pony was touching her hair—a light touch, a brush of angel wings.

Hush now. Don't cry. God give me and you enough grit to ride a bull. I done tamed mine. Git out there and find yours.

Jo Beth didn't plan on going to that extreme, but her newly acquired spirit guide was right. She had to find out if Martha's story was true.

Parking her truck on the campgrounds, she sat there deep-breathing till she collected herself enough to enter the Silver Streak. Sweat beaded her upper lip as she stood in the middle of her trailer, pulled her gun from her holster and checked the magazine to see if it was fully loaded.

"You won't be needin' that." Titus filled her doorway. "You ain't gonna shoot nobody."

Until he walked into her trailer, Jo Beth would never have imagined that he was the person she most wanted to see. She would never have imagined the tenderness of feelings that can take root and grow in plain sight of yellow crime tape.

He towered there like a redwood tree that had suddenly sprung up from the floor.

"I don't think I've ever been as glad to see anybody in my life." His only reaction was a nod, but Jo Beth refused to regret her confession. When you had as much to regret as she, you learned the difference between what should and should not be on the list.

"I think I know who killed her, Titus."

He was so still she could almost see branches growing from his torso, green leaves sprouting and swaying. A woman who has just been to hell and back on Cherokee Ridge might want to

sit under his shade and rest. She might want to simply breathe—
if she were brave enough to trust her feelings to someone else's
care.

"Don't you want to know his name?"

"I done figured it out."

The world tilted and Jo Beth almost fell over the edge.

What had been complex before Titus came into the trailer
was now complicated beyond Jo Beth's ability to make sense of
it. Her search for the truth had irrevocably bound her to Titus
Jones, and he was bound to a killing certainty that would bring
down vengeance on her doorstep.

"You have to let me talk to him first. Please."

"I ain't stoppin' you."

"What will you do?"

"An eye for an eye."

When the call came, Sam was standing at his stove in his boxer
shorts, frying bacon. It was his day off and he was looking
forward to doing nothing more strenuous than the crossword
puzzles in the *Huntsville Daily News*.

Leaving his bacon sizzling, Sam searched for his phone
under the newspaper and a clutter of plastic Walmart bags
piled on the kitchen table. He finally found it on the bathroom
counter, where he'd put it after a vague notion had struck that
something important might occur while he took a leak.

When he saw Jo Beth's name on the caller ID, Sam got the
feeling of ghosts walking on his grave.

"Yo? What's up?"

"Sam, have you checked out the barn at the rodeo?"

"Luther's got a team there now." Jo Beth used to have such
uncanny hunches he'd once accused her of being a voodoo

priestess. He didn't have to ask if she'd been in the barn. "What'd you see?"

"He killed her there."

"He?" Sam jerked open the medicine cabinet, pulled out his stash of Juicy Fruit, crammed a wad into his mouth and waited her out. Direct questions turned Jo Beth evasive. Always had, still did.

"I've got to go, Sam."

"Jo . . . wait." Miraculously, she did. But how could you clear ten years of misunderstanding in ten seconds? "If you think I should have done something more for you, tell me. I'm too old for guessing games and too ornery for regret."

"You were the only one I trusted."

"You think your fall from grace was my fault? That's not fair, Jo."

"I'm not saying you were at fault, Sam." There was silence on her end, then a long, hitching breath. "I'm saying I wish you could have saved me."

She said good-bye without giving him a chance to reply. Sam stood by the toilet staring at the phone. When he smelled burning bacon, he bolted to the kitchen, jerked the skillet off the burner, then grabbed a dish towel and started fanning.

Great God Almighty. He was going to burn his house down. And all because of Jo Beth Dawson.

Sam cleaned the frying pan and started all over. Funny thing how easy it was to start all over with the things that didn't much matter.

While the bacon sizzled, he wondered how things would have turned out if he'd tried to get help for Jo Beth instead of enabling her. Sometimes it was the things you didn't say, the things you didn't do, that you regretted most.

Sam was turning the bacon in the skillet when his phone rang again. He turned the heat off this time.

It was Luther, calling with a report from the team who had been combing the rodeo grounds for days looking for evidence that Pony had been killed there and then moved. They'd found two sets of patent prints from the barn near the bull pen. If the murder was done in the heat of passion, the post driver would have been lying around, a handy murder weapon.

"Pony's blood is on the prints, Sam."

The stride length and step width would tell them something about the size and weight of the owner. If they got lucky, there'd be tread patterns, a designer imprint.

"I'll be right there, Lu."

Forget bacon, forget crossword puzzles, forget Jo Beth.

Today was going to be a bad day for somebody who thought he'd gotten away with murder.

Sitting in her truck in the parking lot of the Marriott, Jo Beth pocketed her cell phone. The call had assured her that she was two steps ahead of Sam on the investigation.

Still, dread paralyzed her. She didn't know what scared her most, that Martha would be right and she'd have to accuse her uncle, or that she'd be wrong and Jo Beth would have failed her niece.

She could turn around and leave. She could drive off and let Titus and the law handle it, whoever got there first. What did it matter to her? What was one less Christmas card a year?

Where was Pony when she needed her? What would she say? "Stand tall"? "Don't let the bull throw you"?

Through the tunnel of years Jo Beth heard echoes of Clint Dawson. *You've got winning in your blood, Jo Beth.*

She had to come face-to-face with her uncle, pull aside the mask and see what lay underneath, even if the sight left her sleepless the rest of her life.

When Jo Beth bailed out of her truck, Pony's fierce spirit and her grandfather's strong character screamed through her blood. Inside the posh hotel, she didn't bother with manners. She didn't call up to his room and announce her presence. She knew his room number. She wanted to catch Mark Dawson unaware.

She took the elevator, marched down the hall and pounded on his door. There was a deep silence, the kind where you know someone is waiting on the other side, conflicted and uncertain. She rattled the door handle and pounded some more.

"Go away. I don't need room service." Mark Dawson sounded old and tired.

Jo Beth searched inside herself but couldn't find a smidge of sympathy. She couldn't find much of anything except a gaping hole where the past as she'd known it had been ripped out by the roots.

"Open the door or I'll shoot the lock off." When he didn't answer, Jo Beth drew her gun then banged the door again. "I mean it. Stand clear or get shot. I'm coming in."

Mark Dawson jerked the door open so fast she almost fell through.

"For God's sake. Get in here and shut up that infernal racket. Are you drunk?" He slammed the door shut then saw her gun. "Are you crazy?"

"I wish I were both."

The curtains were drawn and the room was dark except for one lamp beside the bed. His suitcase lay open on the bed, his clothes spilling over in an untidy pile.

She pointed her gun toward a chair by the window. "Sit down. I want to talk."

"Stop waving that thing around and get out of here. We've said all we need to say." He sat in the chair anyway, a paper lion whose seams were already tearing apart.

"John Running Wolf's wife told me her husband made a devil's bargain with my family."

"I won't dignify her lies with an answer. Jealous, ignorant people will always try to bring down the rich and famous."

"Did you make the bargain or did my grandfather?"

The grandfather Jo Beth remembered would never have made such a bargain. If he had known he had another granddaughter, he'd have been in touch with her. He'd have made sure Morning Star knew she was loved by her father's family. He'd have given her anything she needed, including his name.

While Mark Dawson sat without speaking, Jo Beth couldn't catch her breath. All she wanted was one shred of evidence that the remnants of her family would hold strong and noble, that she could take the remaining threads and weave a future for herself.

Though Mark had the room's air conditioner turned on high, Jo Beth was sweating. Her gun wavered and she steadied it with her other hand.

"Tell me the truth, or I will shoot you. So help me God." Her fierce whisper turned her uncle pale. "It was *you*. You made the bargain."

His guilty silence turned her into a battering ram.

"When Running Wolf sent the money back, you thought he'd finally told his niece the truth, didn't you? You had to make sure a famous young bull rider with a mountaineer twang and not much polish didn't tell all those reporters surrounding her that she was a Dawson."

"Thank God Daddy never knew."

All the air left the room, and Jo Beth was forced to breathe regret. But also relief. Her granddaddy was still the hero of her childhood.

"You killed her?"

"It was an accident. I just wanted to make sure she kept her mouth shut."

Jo Beth's history unraveled and streamed behind her like a tattered ribbon. After today, it could never again be used to tie up a pretty package. When the rodeo parades passed by, the banner of Clint Dawson would not be carried high by his son Mark. If justice was served, Mark Dawson would be sitting in a prison cell paying for the crime of murdering rodeo's brightest star.

In his chair, Mark Dawson was talking and talking. Now that she needed some time to think, he wouldn't shut up.

"I only wanted to pay her off. Keep her quiet. The girl wouldn't listen to reason. She fought like a wildcat. All that kicking and screaming, calling me a coward and a rat's ass. The post driver was there. In the barn." He started wringing his hands. "I thought I'd never get her blood washed off."

Jo Beth waited for her uncle to express remorse, to beg God for mercy, to fall on his knees and pray for forgiveness. She waited for any little sign that Mark Dawson was filled with regret and was going to turn himself over to the police.

Instead, he stood up, walked to the bed and closed his suitcase. While her heart cried for justice for her niece, her body was frozen in the knowledge that she would not lift her gun against her own kin.

He walked past Jo Beth, a red necktie and a shirtsleeve trailing from his suitcase, walked past the closet that still held his tailor-made suits and hand-tooled, designer cowboy boots.

When the door closed behind him, the last thing she saw was the triumph on his face. He'd gambled on the bonds of blood and won.

Jo Beth sank into the chair and her gun slid to the floor. Sometimes the past could press so hard you might never be able to rise.

Aint no use cryin' over a horse's ass.

Pony's voice was a good, stiff breeze. But it was not the wind coming off a breezy spirit that catapulted Jo Beth to her feet. It was love. Her heart swelled like tides to the pull of the moon. It grew so big it could cradle a lost rodeo cowgirl and her grieving father. It could even include a former partner whose only crime was misguided love.

She grabbed her gun and hit the door running, only minutes behind her uncle. When she got to her pickup, Mark Dawson was driving out of the parking lot. She grabbed her cell phone and dialed, then cranked her car and backed out while she waited for Sam Donovan to come on the line.

"Yo?"

She told Sam everything, including the direction Mark Dawson was headed.

"Stay put, Jo Beth." By the time Sam added "I mean it," she was already out of the parking lot, following Uncle Mark west toward Decatur.

As Jo Beth barreled toward catastrophe, she had no illusions she could stop it. She wasn't even going to try. Her family had unleashed a deadly virus of deceit and betrayal that had spread through three generations. And she was the last one standing.

For the first time in ten years, she would *stand*. Because of Pony. Because of Maggie. Because of Titus. Even because of Sam.

And because of you.

There was mercy in Pony's whisper, a grace that finally allowed Jo Beth Dawson to forgive herself.

Twenty-four

Sitting in the parking lot at the Marriott, waiting, Titus felt Pony's death like a slit throat. He was remembering what it was like when Pony had been alive, what it was like to be standing in the middle of his tobacco patch and hear her laughing from one of the trees she'd climbed on the ridge beyond the fence.

Pony's laughter was like migrating yellow birds. It swooped and soared in a cloud of bright wings that broke apart, then fanned across your head, brushed over your skin, tickled your own funny bone till you found yourself standing in the freshly turned earth hanging onto a hoe and chuckling for no good reason you could think of. Except one. Your daughter was alive.

When Mark Dawson ran out of the hotel, climbed into his Lincoln and gunned the motor, Titus pulled out behind him. The Lincoln picked up speed.

What did it matter? As far as Titus was concerned, Dawson could run all the way to hell and he'd follow.

In the rearview mirror, Jo Beth's truck came into view. Titus should have known that after she found out the truth, she wouldn't stay out of it. She had strength you didn't notice when you first met her, qualities that made pity impossible.

Titus couldn't let himself think beyond that. He was planning on killing her next of kin.

Though it was so hot outside you could see heat waves rising from the road, Titus suddenly felt a chill. Old folks would say it was ghosts walking on his grave. Sirens squalling in the distance told Titus it wasn't ghosts walking: it was Sam Donovan, coming to stop him.

Anybody on Doe Mountain would think that was right funny. When Titus Jones set his mind to something, there was no stopping him.

Pony had been just like him. His Pony. Lying in the morgue, cold and alone. And he couldn't even take her to the mountain.

The Lincoln hit the bridge at such a speed the car swerved into the railing. Dawson ricocheted off the bridge and corrected his course, while Titus swerved to keep from rear-ending him.

In his rearview mirror, he could see Jo Beth's truck closing in while sirens screamed closer.

Titus hoped Mark Dawson felt the breath of hellfire and damnation at his back. He hoped the man felt fear a million times greater than his daughter would have felt when she realized she was facing her own murder.

He wanted Dawson to tremble at what was coming. He wanted the monster to know he'd tasted his last rib eye steak, swigged his last martini, slept on his last set of clean sheets in a fancy hotel room that cost as much per night as Titus's best mule.

Hatred like that could eat you alive. Titus didn't care. Life without Pony would be just passing time till he died.

Up ahead, Dawson's Lincoln wobbled as he fought for control and lost. The next impact shot the front of his car through the railing.

Titus braked to keep from sending the Lincoln into the river. Behind him, Jo Beth's tires squealed. Both of them came to a halt mere inches from the Lincoln.

Titus barreled out, with Jo Beth a split second behind him.

"Stay put. He's mine." Titus pulled a knife from his boot then sprinted toward the Lincoln seesawing on the bridge.

Jo Beth kicked the door of her truck shut and trotted after Titus. Seems like all his life he'd only known headstrong women set on doing exactly as they pleased. Let her come. Her presence wouldn't change a thing.

One nudge would tip the Lincoln into the river. And with it, the man who didn't deserve to go that way. Drowning was too easy. A reprieve. A mercy Titus didn't aim to grant.

Dawson slumped over the wheel, blood running down the side of his face.

"Is he dead?" Jo Beth was right at Titus's shoulder.

"He'd better not be." That's all Titus asked. At this late date, he didn't aim to be robbed of revenge. "Dawson? Can you hear me?"

The man roused slowly and turned toward the window. When he saw Titus, his face clenched in terror.

"The car's fixin' to go into the river. Climb to the backseat. I'll try to put weight on it till you get out."

Dawson shook his head, while Jo Beth leaned around Titus and yelled at her uncle. "Do as he says. You can trust him."

Titus's intent wavered. Morning Star had trusted him beyond and above all men. So had Pony.

"I'm your only chance, Dawson."

Patrol cars roared into view, then cops swarmed the bridge, blue lights flashing.

"Titus Jones! Stand down. Back off." It was Donovan. Screaming through a bullhorn.

Titus paid him no more attention than to a cloud of mosquitoes swarming around his head.

"Dawson, if you don't get out, I'm coming in there to get you." If Dawson went into the river, Titus aimed to be right behind him. "And I ain't countin' to three."

Jo Beth put her hand on his arm. "Titus." That's all she said, one word that sounded like a prayer.

He was aware of the net tightening, the guns being cocked and aimed, the barked orders the way you'd notice a cop show on TV but go on fixing your bologna sandwich anyhow.

But most of all, he was aware of Jo Beth watching him with a perfect stillness that reminded him of a newborn fawn on a mountain—uncertain, curious and yet irresistibly drawn toward a brook where anything could be waiting.

Titus relegated the noise from the bullhorns to so much static, then eased open the back door. The big Lincoln wobbled. Dawson's scream was thin and reedy for such a big man.

Leaning into the backseat, Titus tried to hold the car on the bridge with upper body strength, muscles honed by clearing boulders from tobacco fields strained till his veins felt as if they would burst open.

Mark Dawson's screams died to a whimper.

"Did my daughter scream when you killed her?"

"I didn't mean to. I swear to God."

"There ain't nobody but me and you on this bridge."

"And me." Jo Beth moved closer to the car. If it went over, Titus would barely have room to maneuver.

"You in my way, Jo Beth. Get back."

In the same way you know a mountain lion is going to stand

and fight even though you're the one holding the gun, Titus knew she was going to say no.

She dug her heels in, and her next question screamed past him like a bullet. "Did you kill my father, too?"

The railings creaked and the car teetered closer to the river.

"For the love of God! Get me out of here."

Titus could smell sweat and fear, hear the railings groan as they gave way, feel the back end of the car come loose from his grip. Around him, the cacophony grew.

"Stand down, Titus, or we shoot."

"Sam! No!"

As Jo Beth stepped between Titus and Sam Donovan, the noise on the bridge increased but Titus was listening to another sound. His daughter's voice, calling to him from the air, the river, the center of his heart.

Daddy.

Daddy.

Catastrophe raged all around her, but Jo Beth was still upright. She didn't know if she was standing on her own two feet or if Pony Jones was propping her up.

As the Lincoln took a nosedive, Mark Dawson flew out of his car and dangled over the river, both hands locked onto a broken section of railing. Then everything turned red—the water, the bridge, the man. Even the air. It was the Wisdom Keepers, telling the bloody story, a story that had changed them all.

As Jo Beth's past collided with her future, she fought for breath. She thought she might die on the bridge. Then through the swirling clouds, she saw Pony. And she *did* die. But there was no corpse and there would be no burial.

The fog lifted as quickly as it had come, and Jo Beth watched pieces of herself being carried off in red clouds. She emerged lighter. Almost free.

Titus was hovering on the bridge, looking down into the face of his daughter's murderer. The knife blade glinted in his hand.

She could almost hear Titus's thought merging with hers. Kill or forgive? Avenge or grant mercy? Titus didn't have long to decide. Sam was closing in, yelling at Jo Beth to get out of the way.

She planted her feet wide, called up the wisdom of ancestors. " 'May the Great Spirit shed light on your path. There is no death, only a change of worlds.' "

Jo Beth felt Titus's intent before he did. She felt his goodness. When he stretched over the railing and caught her uncle by the wrist, she knew that nothing, not even his beloved daughter's murder, could turn him into a killer.

Sam's worst nightmare unfolded on the bridge—the cops helpless to stop a vigilante killing while Jo Beth Dawson stood right in the middle of it. Nobody on the entire SWAT team could get a clean shot. Sam lifted the bullhorn.

"Move, Jo Beth! You're in the line of fire." She didn't pay him any more attention than if he were a fart in church. He turned to the SWAT team. "Stand down, I'm going in."

When Sam got closer he saw Titus drop his knife, lean over the railing, offer Dawson a hand. For a while it looked as if Titus would haul his daughter's killer over the railing. Then, inexplicably, Dawson let go.

What happened next, Sam would remember till the day he died. The river rose out of its bed and swallowed him up.

Dawson's head bobbed awhile, then he was sucked under. The river had him now, and it didn't mean to let go. The water churned and boiled and then turned red, a river of blood.

Suddenly there was no such thing as order on the bridge. Folks were hanging over the railing, some of them screaming, some praying.

Sam wasn't doing either. He was smelling the scent of Cherokee roses as the river lay back in its bed, then turned smooth and blue and calm again. He was feeling something creeping over him that he hadn't felt since Pony Jones was murdered.

A sense of peace.

⋑ Twenty-five ⋑

Maggie was kneeling in her flower beds, pulling weeds, when she was overcome with a need to weep. Sitting back on her heels, she gave in to the urge, though she could think of no single reason why. Just the small ones—the daily wounds of living that collect because you're too busy or too tired or just plain too scared of what you'll do if you give over to sorrow.

She'd pulled off her gloves and was wiping her face when she spotted the Cherokee roses. In full bloom. Covering her entire front fence.

Maggie got off her knees and approached the fence the way you would a pretty package somebody had left on your front porch and you didn't know whether it was a birthday surprise or a bomb. She hadn't planted roses. Especially not Cherokee roses. Granted, they were glorious, but they were also willful and wild. They'd take over your property if you'd didn't keep them pruned back.

The scent of roses was so strong it filled the yard. It soared into the air and swirled down Devon Street. It formed great clouds and hovered over the entire city.

Up and down Maggie's street, the scent pulled women from their houses and drew them toward their fences, newly festooned. Women who hadn't spoken to each other in ten years leaned over their fences to chat. Women who never laughed could be heard giving way to full-throated mirth. Women who hadn't cried since they were children were openly weeping.

Nobody questioned why. Especially not Maggie. How many times in your life do you get to be part of a miracle?

The river claimed Jo Beth's uncle while the scent of roses nearly brought her to her knees. Or was it grief? Outrage? Guilt? Any combination of emotions so raw she splintered into fragments of flesh and bone held together by blue jeans and a T-shirt.

"Titus?" She touched his shoulder, but he seemed not to have heard her. As he walked off, she thought of robots without emotions. She thought of dark hills and forbidding mountains. She thought of a rock tumbling downhill, gathering force till it became an avalanche that buried everything in its path.

When Sam headed after Titus, Jo Beth planted herself in front of him.

"Leave him alone. You don't need his statement today. I saw it all and so did you."

Facing her former partner, Jo Beth knew her request could go either way. But she was counting on the Sam Donovan she'd once served with and admired, the man tough enough to shoot you if he had to, but wise enough to understand that the best men didn't have to use force and guns. The best men had other weapons—honor and true courage and decency.

"I'm sorry about your uncle, Jo." Sam put his hand on her shoulder. That he chose decency over the chance to grandstand in front of half of Huntsville's police force made Jo Beth cry.

She hated tears. Avoided them at all costs. Especially in public.

Sam knew that. He stepped between her and the crowd, shielding her while she got herself under control.

"If I hadn't called you, none of this would have happened."

"Don't go down that road again, Jo."

She pulled herself together. Today she was immovable, invincible. Tomorrow, maybe not. Death inspired easy confessions. Life-changing events brought out hasty resolutions.

"Because of who your uncle was, we'll try to handle this as quietly as possible."

"No."

"Why not?"

"Because Pony was who she was. A young woman who didn't deserve to die."

As Jo Beth walked toward Titus's old blue truck, she realized she might never know whether Mark Dawson had anything to do with the so-called accidental deaths of Cherokee Rose and her father. It seemed too coincidental that Rafe's brakes would fail on the very day he set out to marry the woman Mark Dawson hated. Still, she was struck with a lightness she hadn't felt in a very long time. Some secrets were best left in the past.

Titus sat in his truck staring at the swirl of activity. Climbing in beside him, she sank into a cocoonlike silence that made talk idle and questions useless.

On the bridge, the HPD herded spectators back to their cars. Emergency road crews set up orange cones around the broken railing. A TV crew arrived.

On the riverbanks, rescue swimmers pushed boats onto the water and called to each other in voices high with dread and excitement.

Jo Beth might as well have been back in Hot Coffee eating a blueberry muffin. The frenetic activity seemed unconnected to her. The only connection she felt was to the quiet man who had survived death and temptation and his own misguided intentions.

Jo Beth put her hand over his. "It's over, Titus." His only answer was a nod. "I'm going up Cherokee Ridge to tell Martha Wolf. She loved them too."

He looked at her then, the ice in his blue eyes thawed and breaking apart. "I aim to take Pony back to the mountain."

She understood that was his way of saying good-bye. Jo Beth climbed down, then watched as he cranked up the old truck and headed back toward Huntsville where their incredible journey had begun.

Sam was packing to leave. Probably not permanently, but who could tell? Everybody who had been on the bridge the day Pony's killer drowned in the Tennessee River had changed. Even Luther, who hadn't altered one hair on his head in the twenty-five years Sam had known him.

Luther had stopped eating doughnuts.

It was a small thing, insignificant compared to the tsunami of transformation taking place in Sam. The bridge and the red river were part of it, even the day he'd first seen the body under a blanket of roses. But if Sam had to pick one moment when he knew he would never be the same, it was the day he'd stood beside Titus Jones in the morgue and pulled back the sheet from Pony's face. You couldn't witness the power and fierceness of such love without having something inside you forever altered.

Sam wasn't good with words and had always steered as far away as he could from self-examination. But if he had to put a name to what was slowly unfolding inside him, he'd say tenderness. But he wouldn't say it out loud. He wasn't ready to put on long robes and go to the top of a remote mountain.

All he wanted to do was drive to the Alabama Gulf Coast and catch a few fish. And while he was at it, catch his breath.

Maybe even talk to Lana. But first, there was another woman he had to see—Jo Beth Dawson.

He snapped his suitcase shut then walked through his apartment turning off lights and electrical appliances. On the TV, Sonja Livingstone was standing in front of a bin of yellow squash at Sav-A-Lot. Her suit matched the squash.

She smiled into the camera, showing off her perfect teeth and her red lipstick. "I'm here in the grocery store, where people are standing in the produce section or the cereal aisle or the butcher shop talking to each other. At first they talked only about the day the river ran red and roses sprang up all over Huntsville. Now they're merely talking, asking about each other's aunts and grandmothers and cousins and uncles. I call it the Phenomenon of Pony Jones, the famous female bull rider who . . ."

Sam turned off his TV, then unplugged it. Mark Dawson and the press conference Jo Beth granted after his death had been at the forefront of the news for one day, then the miracles had knocked them right off the headlines.

For Jo Beth's sake, he was glad. He made one more check of his apartment and grabbed his suitcase. For a man traveling nearly three hundred miles for an unspecified length of time, he was traveling light.

Sam opened his front door, whistling. You couldn't do that with a mouthful of Juicy Fruit gum.

"Going somewhere, Sam?"

His first shock was that Jo Beth was on his front porch. His second was what she wore.

"I see you've put your red boots back on, Jo."

"It's high time, wouldn't you say?"

"Not loud enough for you to hear."

Her laughter was so much like the old Jo, he thought that someday there'd come a time when they would drive over to Decatur, sit on the banks of the river that had turned red, and reminisce. Just friends, talking.

"I didn't want to leave without telling you I don't blame you anymore, Sam. I'm putting the past to rest."

"I hope this doesn't mean *gone and forgotten.*"

"You never know, Sam. One of these days I'm liable to turn up on your doorstep."

"I'll keep a light in the window and the coffee hot, Jo."

Watching her walk away this time shouldn't be hard, but after he told her good-bye, Sam went inside anyhow and puttered around till he knew Jo Beth would be gone.

When he came back out, the dog was sitting on the sidewalk by his Mustang. It wasn't much of a dog. Its hair was coming loose in patches and it looked like it got by scrounging from garbage cans, but it had the kind of eyes that spoke of loyalty and character. Here was a dog who would eat hot dogs every day without complaining, one who would sit by your chair and never gripe that you watched too much baseball or drank too much beer, one who would sleep at the foot of your bed with a wadded-up pair of your dirty gym socks.

Sam squatted and scratched the animal's head. The best he could tell, it was a golden retriever mix.

"What's your name, old boy?" The dog wagged his tail and licked Sam's hand. "You look like a Ben to me."

Sam opened the back door and the dog hopped in. It might as well go fishing, too. Every mutt deserved a second chance.

After she left Sam's place, Jo Beth said good-bye to Maggie, who cried, and Martha, who promised to stay in touch. Then she went up the ridge to say good-bye to the willow.

If you closed your eyes, you could hear your history repeated on the wind until its edges became blurred, bearable. If you listened long enough, the world might right itself on its axis and you might discover you could walk without falling.

Jo Beth wrapped her arms around herself, listening. What she heard was not the stories in the wind, but a footstep.

Suddenly, Titus loomed between her and the sun, then stood beside the willow with his hat in his hand. Was he waiting for her invitation to sit down? It was hard to tell. He was a man who said little and his face revealed even less.

The only time she'd been able to read him was the day they'd sat in his pickup truck on the bridge. All he'd said was *I aim to take Pony back to the mountain,* but the rest had been carved in his face, a gratitude so wide and deep he couldn't even speak of it.

"Won't you sit down?"

"I ain't got time. I'm headed back to the mountain. With Pony." He smoothed the brim of his hat with one callused thumb. "I'm askin' you to come with me."

"For the . . . funeral?"

"Ain't gonna be no funeral. Just me and Pony." He twisted his hat. "You the only fam'ly I got now."

Her Silver Streak was parked at Martha Wolf's house waiting to take her wherever she wanted to go. The last place she'd have guessed was Doe Mountain.

"Yes." She said it just like that. One word. A destination. She couldn't remember the last time she'd hit the road with a map, a plan and a destination in mind.

Twenty-six

The mountain was waiting for her. A green place where she could rest.

Jo Beth had followed Titus across north Alabama and the Cumberland Valley, and now she was at this jumping-off place in the northeast tip of Tennessee. Titus stopped his truck at the base of the mountain and got out.

"That trailer ain't going to make it all the way up."

Jo Beth didn't ask why. She left her Silver Streak at the bottom of the mountain, a turtle home she no longer needed. As she followed Titus on the buckling, neglected road in her truck, vistas opened beyond the trees, wide open spaces where she could run if she wanted to.

When she saw Titus's cabin, saw the Cherokee roses waiting beside the door, Jo Beth thought it might be possible that in this place you could even learn to fly.

She parked her truck beside his, hopped out and stood in the front yard, trying to take it all in, the modest cabin where Pony had been born, the old bull snorting in the pasture, the straight rows of tobacco, the split-rail fence with woods behind it so deep she could walk for miles without running into another soul.

"We're home."

As Titus led her inside and pointed out her room, Jo Beth marveled at the possibility that his simple statement might prove true.

It was time.

Titus knocked on Pony's bedroom door, where he knew Jo Beth would be standing at the window in bare feet, just as she had every morning since they'd arrived, soaking up the peace of the mountain.

Nobody had to tell him that. He'd be in his bedroom putting on his overalls or in the kitchen making coffee and he could judge by the sound and direction of her footsteps where she was going and what she was wearing on her feet.

He could read the rest in her eyes.

Though it wasn't yet daybreak, she came to the door dressed in a loose shirt and baggy jeans. Behind her, Pony's bed was already as tidy as if his daughter had been in the house that morning and done it herself.

"I'm taking 'er up the mountain."

"Do you want me to come?"

"Me and Pony started this journey together and I reckon we gotta end it the same way."

"I understand. For what it's worth, I love her too."

He believed she did. That was the thing he'd seen in her all along, flowing through her like a river—a deep capacity for love. Where it was taking them, he didn't know. All he knew is that he wanted to ride its currents.

He got Pony's ashes from the window seat that overlooked the east side of the mountain. It had been his daughter's favorite spot. He used to find her there watching the sunrise, sprawled out with her chin propped on the ledge, her forehead pressing against the cool glass.

"Ain't it the most awesome sight you ever seen?" she'd say. "If I had to be anything else, I'd want to be the sunrise."

When Titus stepped out of his cabin, he wasn't surprised to see that the hollows and ridges had turned white overnight. The Cherokee roses that flanked his front porch had grown three times their size, while those along the pasture fence had spread their branches like arms to embrace the entire mountain. Roses rambled along the roof of his barn, sprouted from the top of his woodshed and climbed oaks and pines and cedars, where they cascaded in scented waterfalls.

In the still morning air, the sweetness was so overpowering it stopped cars at the foot of the mountain. People on their way to work turned around and drove back home to hug their wives and children.

Titus crossed the fence and headed up the rocky terrain. The Arctic wolf appeared suddenly in his path. They stared at each other till they came to an understanding, then Pony's totem turned into the woods and Titus followed. Brambles and overhanging branches parted to make way for him.

When Titus and the wolf came to the top of the ridge, the sun was waiting for them, its pink and gold arms spread wide. He hugged his daughter's ashes close to his chest, letting his love and prayers flow to her from his beating heart.

Then he lifted the urn high and watched while the wind caught Pony and lifted her toward the sunrise. Soon he would turn back to his cabin, where Jo Beth waited. But for now, he stood on the mountaintop, his daughter's love and the fragrance of roses pouring over him in tender mercy.

I'm as graceful as a red-winged hawk, and I'm headin' straight up toward the most beautiful light I ever seen. Beyond the light my mother and my grandmother stand with their arms open wide, and I know my job here on earth is done.

Below me, my daddy's standing on the ridge, shading his eyes. I tell him I love 'em, I tell him good-bye. But it ain't no hard good-bye. It's like I ain't even leaving him. It's like I'm setting right there in the center of his heart, that I'll always be there, every piece of me whole and complete.

Ain't that a sight? Me, Pony Jones, learning how to leave yet at the same time stay. There ain't no telling what all I'm fixing to learn. Before you know it, I'm liable to be rearranging stars. I always did want to look up in the middle of the day and see a bunch of them shining over my head.

"Look out, God!" I yell. "Here comes Pony Jones."

Sitting on the window ledge facing eastward, Jo Beth knew the precise moment Titus let go of Pony's ashes. The colors of the rising sun glowed with such intensity she had to shade her eyes. The room vibrated with sound, wind sighing over harp strings, the sound of a soul rising. Outside, rose petals swirled upward like the beating wings of white doves.

"Good-bye, Pony."

There would be no answer, only the certainty that love had replaced the heavy souls of the dead, and that Pony's father would soon come down the mountain.

Jo Beth walked through the cabin, opening every window while warmth and hope rose up through the worn wooden floors, soaked through the soles of her bare feet and took up residence under her breastbone. Light ricocheted through the cabin, and for a moment, she stood in its center simply breathing.

Then she went into the kitchen to make coffee and afterward carried two cups onto the front porch, where she waited for Titus. Whatever happened next was up to the roses.